"I just wanted to ~~~~~~~~~~~~~~~~~~~~~~~~
Alex offered Maria a dozen red roses.

She froze for half a second. "How dare you show up here? I don't want your apologies or your flowers."

"There's no need to make a scene. Just give me five minutes to explain. That's all I'm asking for."

He moved toward her. Maria's breathing became shallow. She couldn't be this close to him; she turned to walk away. Alex reached out to her, his touch searing her skin. Somehow his lips found hers. He wrapped his long arms around her body and let his large hands stroke her back as he took her in, kissing Maria to her very soul.

When he finally let her go, she reached back to slap him. He smiled and caught her hand in a single, swift motion. Passion ignited his eyes, making them appear sexier, sultrier. He gently kissed the palm of the hand that sought to strike him.

"Your one chance to do that happened last night. You are going to stroke me with these hands from now on."

His words were softly spoken, meant for her ears only. Maria flushed, a deep red coloring her almond skin.

He brought his face close to hers again, but this time he whispered in her ear. "We need to go to your room. I have my orders."

Maria's lips quivered in anticipation, but there was no kiss. She was jolted back to reality. They were standing in the middle of the hotel lobby. The bouquet was on the floor.

"Follow me," she managed after a few calming breaths.

Worth the Wait

Katherine D. Jones

BET Publications, LLC
http://www.bet.com
http://www.arabesquebooks.com

ARABESQUE BOOKS are published by

BET Publications, LLC
c/o BET BOOKS
One BET Plaza
1900 W Place NE
Washington, DC 20018-1211

All Kensington Titles, Imprints, and Distributed Lines are available at special quantity discounts for bulk purchases for sales promotions, premiums, fund-raising, and educational or institutional use. Special book excerpts or customized printings can also be created to fit specific needs. For details, write or phone the office of the Kensington special sales manager: Kensington Publishing Corp., 850 Third Avenue, New York, NY 10022, attn: Special Sales Department, Phone: 1-800-221-2647.

First printing: July 2004
10 9 8 7 6 5 4 3 2

Printed in the United States of America

This book is dedicated to all those behind the scenes, behind the lines, and behind our freedom, especially the men and women who work for the departments and organizations with initials: NSA, FBI, CIA, DEA, ATF, SS, and the individual armed forces.
Thank you for all that you do.

ACKNOWLEDGMENTS

I'd like to thank the wonderful people in my life who have helped to make this possible. To my husband, children, and family, I thank you for your support and love while I figure out just what the heck I am doing. Whew! Sometimes it seems like it would be easier to work nine to five. The writing life is no joke, but it is worth it in the end. I thank and appreciate each and every one of you.

I would also like to thank my extended family, the aunts, uncles and cousins who have expressed their joy over this accomplishment. You honor me with your support.

To my friends, old and new, thank you for being there, listening and caring—as always, Kim and Vivian, and now my new friend Clara, to name a few.

I have to thank the folks at BET books, and mention Linda, Kicheko, and especially Demetria, for continued support. Or should I say, continuous patience!

A big thank you as well to my agent, Cheryl Ferguson, for her amazing tolerance, persistence, and patience.

To the readers and aspiring writers, thank you for your support. Keep reading and writing. God bless and keep you.

All thanks to my Lord for strength, courage, and wisdom. I've learned there was a reason for those three particular attributes in Ms. Arie's song. Without them, this project would never have been completed!

Prologue

Chile, 1994

Who knew the girl he was seeing was the favorite niece of the infamous Cali Cartel family? It would have been funny if it hadn't been so deadly serious. He had no idea when he joined the basketball team that he had actually joined a den of drug dealers, thieves, and worse. He was just a naive boy from D.C. who wanted to play ball overseas. The world of drugs, crime, and murder had never been part of the bargain.

Kevin suspected that the Rojas family tolerated his presence because he was Valenca's latest toy, not because they approved of the couple. Kevin knew her family dared not say anything publicly for fear of making their strong-willed daughter rebel right into his arms. He assumed they thought she would tire of him soon enough. Neither was looking for anything serious. They could enjoy basketball and spend time sightseeing and practicing Spanish. Her family was never rude or unfriendly, which suited Kevin just fine.

Most of his rare visits to her home were uneventful. That is, until his search for a restroom netted him more than he bargained for. Valenca's aunt, Valencia Rios, was in town. After a few months in Chile, Kevin was fluent in the family's dialect of Spanish. What he overheard made him stop in his tracks. Aunt Valencia was scheduling the drops and stops for all the teams in the Chilean league.

Kevin listened spellbound as Carlos Guzman, his team's equipment manager, detailed the next few drug drop points and how the money was to be picked up. Kevin felt his blood run cold. He realized every game— every win, every loss—was orchestrated by Valencia Rios.

Kevin hurried off to find Valencia before he was found listening behind closed doors. He could not be sure how much she was involved in the family business. When he found her, he came up with some weak excuse to go back to his quarters. Kevin needed to think.

Why was he in Chile? His teammates seemed to be in on the scheme. Why hadn't he been asked to join the party? What did they want from him? Or was he being used and he didn't even know it? Kevin felt a massive tension headache coming on. He took a couple of aspirin and sat down to think of a plan.

He didn't know who was friend or foe. Kevin kept to himself in the locker room and any time off the court. He felt like the walls were coming in around him. He wasn't sure which way to turn.

But soon his options became crystal clear. On their way back from an exhibition game in Barcelona, one of his teammates became deathly ill. He was choking to death, and he couldn't be helped. The team's doctor, who had to be rushed from one of the other buses, seemed to be slow in coming. Kevin couldn't believe the lackadaisical attitude the doctor had toward the man. The teammate died before they were able to reach the nearest hospital.

The coaches and trainers were strangely nonchalant, as if they had expected it. A chill ran through Kevin's body as they removed Sanchez from the back of the bus. Had Sanchez changed his mind about being a part of the network? Kevin was scared now. He was an American living in a foreign country—the only place he could think of to go was the American Embassy. Kevin decided then that he needed to seek refuge.

When Kevin went to the embassy, he met with a man introduced to him as Agent Carmichael. Agent Carmichael listened to Kevin and said, "Thank you sir, we will be in touch as soon as we have had time to process this information. In the meantime, try to act as casual and normal as you can. The worst thing you could ever do is act like you are suspicious of anyone who is part of the team. You have my personal number. Call anytime, day or night."

Yeah, right, act naturally, Kevin thought. The next two weeks of his life became a living nightmare.

Chapter 1

Kevin was sweating, his pulse racing. Nervousness and trepidation threatened to overwhelm him. The room he was in was probably fifty degrees, or cooler, a typical government building. Irritated, he wondered why they couldn't regulate these things better.

Kevin ran his fingers absently through his hair as he waited. He tried his best to remain cool and collected, but the past eighteen months had proven to be more than he could handle. He'd lost a lot—the woman he cared about, his job, basically his entire life. He looked around the room. It was cold, sterile, just like his life.

He turned his head toward a noise at the back of the room. The door opened slowly. A well-built man of medium height walked in. He wore a dark blue pinstriped suit. His close-cropped hair was gray at the temples. Agent Michael Spates entered the room, coffee in one hand, large manila envelope in the other.

Kevin watched him but didn't say anything. He steeled himself for what he was about to face. The agent didn't pay attention to the icy reception he'd received. He'd done this enough times to understand the stress that was involved.

Agent Spates regarded him with intelligent brown eyes.

"Would you like a cup of coffee? I can have one sent in for you."

Kevin made eye contact with him and just shook his head no.

Agent Spates sat down directly across from him at the small steel gray table. He spread out a large quantity of papers.

Kevin continued, maybe out of nervousness, maybe not to seem like a jerk. "No thanks, I prefer to just get on with this. I don't mean to sound ungrateful. I'm just a little anxious, know what I mean?" This wasn't where he'd thought he'd be at thirty-nine. Starting over should have been a choice, not a demand.

Spates nodded. "I understand. I've got a lot to go over with you. We don't have a lot of time, and I need you to be sure you've got it all down."

He pointed to the papers from the envelope that he'd placed on the table. "Your new life is in here. Everything that we've been working on to get you on track." Agent Spates paused then took a good look at Kevin. He noticed how the past year and a half seemed to have aged him. "There'll be a team in Memphis to assist you in the transition we discussed, but only for about two weeks. After that you are on your own."

Through the years Kevin had adopted a relaxed, easy sense of style. He wore a mixed blend olive green sweater and black microfiber slacks. As a pro ballplayer, he'd always had to have his clothes tailored. Few could boast his kind of build. He was tall, 6'5, with a powerful chest and chiseled arms and legs. Kevin kept in shape by using weights regularly and running thirty miles a week. He was still a handsome man, but there was a maturity about him—his black, wavy hair had a touch of gray peppered in it, and his gold-flecked dark brown eyes appeared wise.

Spates handed Kevin documents for him to study. Kevin had already received a verbal briefing and had an opportunity to give the team feedback, but today was more official. This was on paper, virtually set in stone.

Kevin looked at Spates long and hard. "I'm ready, let's begin," he said.

Two rooms over in another small briefing area, Agent Maria Thomas watched the video of last week's newscast. She had already watched the tape five times. Each time she had the same reaction. A lump the size of a golf ball formed in her throat, threatening to choke her. "I know this is a tough one, Maria, but we need you," Agent Chapman said. "These guys are right up your alley. You know you're the best weapons person we've got in this region."

Agent Maria Thomas pushed her sable brown bangs out of her eyes. Her shoulder-length hair hung loosely, grazing the top portion of her blouse. She looked more like a glamour queen than an agent quite capable of deadly acts.

She leaned up against the table, where she was positioned in front of the small screen. She held the television remote tightly in her hands. Maria was silent, deep in her own thoughts. She didn't trust herself to talk yet; the emotion was still too raw. Brian Williams was a good friend of hers, a member of her former unit, and she knew that this had to be killing him.

She swore to herself, ignoring the others that were in the room with her. She hit rewind on the remote, then play. Her attention was riveted to the television. The other three agents looked at her and then to each other. No one dared to make a sound. They knew she was taking the case, which almost made them feel sorry for the perpetrators.

The newscaster said, "Tragedy struck a Baltimore city

playground this afternoon when two teens were mercilessly gunned down by unknown assailants riding in a large black SUV. According to witnesses, the two were playing basketball when the vehicle drove up slowly and fired several shots in the teens' direction. The young men are identified as sixteen-year-old Davonte Smith and seventeen-year-old Keith Williams. Smith died on the scene. However, Williams is reported to be in grave condition at Sinai Hospital."

She stared at the screen, black now because the tape had run out again.

"Keith may never walk again," Maria said to no one in particular.

She turned to face her colleagues. Two were her peers, and one a senior agent. There was no emotion in her voice as she spoke. "When do you want me ready to leave?"

Executive Assistant Director Bee McCoy looked at the young agent skeptically. "Agent Thomas, we are still developing the case. We need more prep time. This thing goes deeper than we'd ever imagined. Preliminary information indicates some pretty heavy international heavy hitters are involved. We've discovered a network that will have to be infiltrated. We already know one agent has been killed. Preparation is critical. The Bureau is dedicating office space for you here in the Baltimore field office. Quantico is too far to do this effectively.

"I'm here to advise, to work your budget, etc. However, this is your case. You pick the team, you help develop the mission profile, and you're in charge. Just let us do our jobs, too. Remember Brian is one of us. We all feel the same."

Maria regarded her stoically. "Yeah, but Brian saved my ass a time or two. I owe him," she stated emphatically.

It was the closest she had come to emotion since entering the room. Agent McCoy looked at her woman to woman. She knew what it was like to lose a child, but emotion was dangerous in this kind of game. She'd lost her own son and daughter to a terrorist bombing while they were traveling overseas. McCoy had overcome the pain by becoming an expert on terrorism and organized crime and making sure her agents were safe.

She hoped Agent Thomas wasn't in for more than she could handle. She would just have to make sure that she had every asset in place. Top brass wouldn't constrict her budget for this case—too much was riding on it. One of their own might lose his son.

Agent McCoy looked at her protégée. "If you think that you can handle it, then get those bastards."

"Consider it done, " Thomas said.

There was a lot to put in place now that the mission leader had been selected. "Agent Thomas, I've got to meet with the assistant director later this afternoon. I want to reconvene with you tomorrow. Bring your preliminary list of team selectees so that I can contact them and organize a meeting. We need to get a jump on this thing. We'll meet at 0800 hrs. Go home and pack some things. Tomorrow will be a long day."

"Yes, ma'am, I understand. I'll see you in the morning. There's one call that I'd like to make myself, though."

Agent McCoy gave her a knowing look. "Helene?"

"Yes, ma'am. She's the only one other than you I really trust to watch my back."

"I know you two have been almost inseparable since the Academy. Make the call. I'm sure that she'll relish the chance to get out of Quantico for a few months."

"Thanks, I'll see you in the morning."

Maria opted to stay in town. After a day like today, she

didn't feel up to the two-plus-hour trek back to Quantico. She called a local Baltimore hotel and arranged to stay in town for a couple of days. As soon as she was settled into her hotel room, she placed the call she had wanted to make all day.

"Helene. *Hola chica*, it's me. I wanted to call you as soon as it became official. I'm gonna be working on something big, and I need your help."

"Hey girl, how ya doing? I heard about Brian. Have you talked to him yet? I got a heads-up from McCoy this afternoon. You know you can count on me. Besides, we can do some shopping and eat in B-more while we get ready."

Helene paused, then said, "Maria, anything you need, you got it, and I mean that."

"Helene, thanks. I don't know if I can really pull this off." Maria let out a sigh, her breathing uneven and forced. She had been holding on to her emotions so tightly, her chest felt like it was going to burst. "I feel so bad for Brian and those kids." Maria paused before saying, "Did you hear the news tonight? There were three more shootings in this area near Druid Hill Park. Helle, we've got to get these guns off the streets."

"Hon, you know my computer and I are here for you. As soon as McCoy gets the paperwork done, I'll be there."

"Thanks, babe, that's what I needed to hear. We can catch up when you get here. I'm at a hotel right across from the Inner Harbor, and I'm checked in for a few days. I'll come back to Virginia to get my clothes this weekend. Right now I am just too beat. Call me tomorrow, okay?"

"Sure, Maria, you get some rest. You know the motto: The Special Corruption Unit always gets their man. You just hang in there, lady. It will all work out, you'll see."

* * *

The next morning McCoy began the briefing. She introduced several other agents who could serve as part of the team. The case had taken on a life of its own. It had become less about revenge for a fellow agent, and more about stopping a horrible gun-dealing network from taking over the U.S.

Maria listened as McCoy spoke. "Our preliminary information shows a link between the guns that were used in the Smith and Williams case and seventeen others. The guns are of Russian make. We've discovered the locals are using them on streets in gang wars, but we need more information. We have intelligence in the area providing us with bits and pieces, but we are just now starting to get a real feel for what's going on. We have enough to get started, but we have to make sure that we get this one right. This is no ordinary case, and you know I've worked on some doozies."

"The folders on the table contain the latest information we have on the Russian Mafia. We believe one of their cells is providing the guns. Our sources have come up with a few names, but they have to be checked and double-checked. If you look on page twelve, you'll see a grid we are developing."

McCoy stopped to wait for everyone to catch up to her. "I'm going to let Agent Chapman review that information with you."

Agent Chapman stood, pointing to a map on the projection screen. "We got lucky and caught a break with some handguns. By matching serial numbers that our resources in the area identified, we have been able to trace a shipment of weapons from Odessa to points in the south and southwest. Two weeks ago, we traced a small shipment of guns from Russia to a Tennessee gun show. What we are working on now is who, how, and where. Basically we are

following the money. We should have more in a few days."
Agent Chapman turned off the projector and took her
seat.

Agent McCoy added, "Thank you, Chapman. The
most recent estimates indicate that the Russian mob
controls about 40 percent of private industry in Russia,
and 60 percent of state-owned companies. Those numbers are significant—that means, whoever is in power is
in their pocket. So we don't expect cooperation from
the government. They are part of the problem, too.

"What is most important to remember is that the Russian Mafia is well organized, intelligent, brutal, and
almost impossible to penetrate. Almost."

Agent McCoy paused for effect. She wanted her
agents to understand the gravity of the situation, especially the younger ones.

"Agent Maria Thomas, who probably needs no introduction, will be on point for this case. We've put together
a preliminary cover for her. She is Maria Manez, a gun-
runner from the East Coast. She's a high roller, forceful
and efficient. We are spreading her name all around the
United States, and pretty soon everyone in the business
will have heard about her. This is going to be one of our
big-budget cases, but the stakes are high and I need to
know from everyone in this room right now if you think
you can handle it."

Agent McCoy looked at each agent directly. No one
wanted to publicly back out, but she knew they would
come to her individually if there was a problem. McCoy
had selected each agent already present. Agent Thomas
would do the same for her direct team.

"You've had a lot to digest and look over. Let's break
for thirty minutes, then come back to this. The next item

on the agenda will be team composition, unless there are any questions."

Before getting up to leave the conference room, she looked in Maria's direction. "Thomas, walk with me."

The Baltimore field office was a large building, typical of most government facilities. The hallways were long, and most offices and cubicles were configured in a maze. Agents McCoy and Thomas walked along the corridors, meandering through the maze, speaking when spoken to. McCoy was trying to feel Maria out in a nonthreatening way, and she knew it.

When they stopped to look out the window into the courtyard, Maria took the opportunity to speak candidly. "Ma'am, I'm not going to lie to you and tell you that I'm not scared. I am. But I know that I'm doing the right thing. We may be going up against a giant, but I'm more than willing to put things on the line. Not just for Brian, Davonte, and Keith, but also for every other parent and every other kid who doesn't deserve this kind of crap. Every gangbanger, two-bit hood, hustler, and child can get their hands on one of these guns. We have to do this. *I* have to do this."

Maria was breathing heavily. Her hands were shaking from a sudden increase in adrenaline. "Yeah, I'm scared. . . . But I'll be more afraid if I don't work on this case. I can do it, ma'am. Trust me on this one."

Agent McCoy spoke softly. "When I look at you I see me before I lost the kids. I was ready to take on the world; I had everything going for me. . . . Now, I have this. You do a great job, Agent Thomas, and you give it your all. But learn when to say no. There comes a time when your passion for justice shouldn't outweigh your passion for life. Seek that balance, because when you lose that opportunity, you don't get it back."

Maria looked in her mentor's eyes and saw her pain.

"Ma'am, what I see in your eyes is something I don't want to see in Brian's and any other parents' out there. This case is mine, and I don't intend to fail."

McCoy smiled inwardly. "If I had any doubt of that, I wouldn't have chosen you. I just need you to know for yourself, and you've convinced me of that. Come on, let's get out of here. I need some coffee."

Agent McCoy moved away from the window quickly, but not quick enough for Maria. She watched McCoy wipe a single tear from her eye. The lump was back in Thomas's throat, but she felt confident about her purpose. A relationship, children—they could wait. She wasn't ready for that kind of commitment yet. Besides, how would she explain being more willing to clean her gun than her bathroom to a man?

They picked up coffee from the break room before returning to the meeting. They walked back to the conference room in virtual silence. Not much more needed to be said. Each entered the room putting their conversation out of mind. It was time to get back to business.

Maria took the lead this time. She sat at the head of the large table, next to Agent McCoy. She took a deep breath and rolled a marble between her fingers before beginning. It was her totem, and she never went anywhere without it. Very few knew her secret.

"My specialty, as most of you know, is weapons. I also have a certain expertise in languages, mostly romance language, but some Slavic dialects as well. I'm not going to bore you with my resume, but you need to know that I am ready for this case. My record speaks for itself. I've worked under some of the best agents in the Special Corruption Unit. I came up under the tutelage of Eric

Duvernay. We didn't always play by everyone's rules, but we always played by our own—get the job done."

Maria clasped her hands together before continuing. She didn't want to say this last part, but if she didn't address it, human nature would cause it to be an issue.

"I am sure some of you have heard the rumors. Yes, we were once romantically involved, but that was a long time ago. I don't make it a habit to become involved with other agents, and personally, I wouldn't recommend it. This mission is important to me, it's important to the senior agents, and to the director. But more significantly, if you are going to work on this case, it should be important to you. I hope that we can work this case without backbiting, backstabbing, bickering, and confusion. I don't work well under those conditions and therefore, cannot tolerate it. For the sake of argument, let's assume everything you've heard about me is true. Get over it, and we can get on with it. So that's my speech. I only make it once."

Maria paused to let her words sink in. "Now we need to talk about assignments."

She went back to the briefing booklet that had been prepared for the agents. "There are some jobs that are locked, of course, but there are also some assignments where we have more flexibility. Over the break more material was added for you to study. Looks like we'll have some late nights getting ready for this one. There's some background information that I want to draw your attention to briefly, and then we can move on. Let's turn to page twenty-seven. This information won't be put up on the screen, so please follow along."

She flipped to the section that she had highlighted. "This information explains how entrenched the Russian mob's operatives are and gives you a better understanding of what we are up against. It will also provide you with a framework for how we are going to profile this mission."

Maria paused. She was moving into the role of educator. She had studied Russian politics for previous cases. "In a nutshell, the Russian Mafia grew out of progress. The West pushed for democracy but didn't pay attention to how the infrastructure would be impacted. The Mafia filled the void created by the vacuum. They provided jobs in a failed economy; structure during destabilization; and food, clothing, and shelter. They also created a thriving drug culture, and increased the murders, rapes, torture, and kidnapping of those who opposed them. We asked for Democracy—what we got was Mafiocracy. What that means, from what we have been able to determine so far, is that tight-knit groups of people like the mob decide the fate of the nation. These people are without a moral compass, without compassion, and without care and concern for the people. Is that our problem, you might ask. Not really, that was, not until the guns they produce and sell began to kill our kids. We estimate, in the last six months, Russian guns have killed over three hundred kids and young adults around the nation. Anyone who thinks they want a gun can get one. Irresponsible people, psychotic people—anyone. There is no such thing as a registry or a waiting period. Have fifty dollars—have gun."

Agent McCoy stood up now. "This is where you come in. We are not foolish enough to think that we can destroy their whole network, but we are smart, and bold enough to think that we are going to destroy those who are selling guns in this country."

Chapter 2

Kevin hadn't realized how much his Spanish had changed while he lived in Chile. And since the Bureau wanted to exploit his Hispanic heritage, now he had to relearn how to speak.

The safe house was located someplace in the hills of western Maryland. He didn't know exactly where they were, and he really didn't care. He had been spending time with agents who would help him make the transition, so his days were filled with immersion in Puerto Rican culture. In his classes, he was relearning the dialect he'd grown up with to help him blend in when he reached his new home.

Agent Spates had decided, given past experiences, there would be a more concerted effort to change his life. The Bureau's first thought was to place him in a nice neighborhood with a large Hispanic population, but the final details would be worked out before he left for Memphis. Kevin found the trickiest part was maintaining the accent. The last thing he wanted to do was draw unnecessary attention to himself. His adventures with Valencia's henchmen—being kidnapped, shot at, and almost killed—were enough to motivate him. Kevin had the Special Corruption Unit, specifically Agent Maria Thomas, to thank for his life. She ran into the room just in time to prevent Valencia from killing him. He often wondered what had become of the sable-haired beauty with the perfect marksmanship. He was forever in the agent's debt, and she would always hold a special place in his heart. Kevin was going crazy in the safe house, but after his harrowing experience before, he appreciated the Bureau looking out for his safety.

He would be leaving in one week to make his final transition. His new identity would move him from the metropolitan Washington, D.C., area to Memphis, TN. He would have a large condo, a new sporty car, and a successful business. In terms of changes, he couldn't complain. The Bureau had done their best to provide him with a comfortable life, and that was much more than most got in protection. Kevin turned off the tape before it finished. "I've had enough for one day," he said to no one in particular. He needed a distraction. He walked into the kitchen to find Marisela, deck of cards in hand. "Marisela, how about another game?"

Agents Marisela and Juan were assigned to help him during the last few weeks of his training. She looked at him crossly. "Alexandro, how many times do I have to tell you, no! My job is to keep you safe—not baby-sit you. Now, go do your lesson and let me get back to work." She was making his favorite dish, white rice, beans, and chicken.

Kevin was not in the least put off by her manner. They both knew he had her wrapped around his little finger. She was a five-foot-four-inch firecracker, and Kevin loved her. She was much like his own *abuela*. He inhaled the wonderful aroma of her cooking. Marisela allowed him to watch, but touching her pots and pans was strictly forbidden. Fortunately, Kevin memorized all of her recipes.

He smiled at her devilishly. "I love it when you call me Alexandro. Say it again." His laughter was infectious.

Marisela crossed her arms over her ample chest and gave him a cold look before erupting into ripples of her own laugher. "Just one more week of you, one more week. You know you almost got me fired?"

Marisela leaned toward Kevin conspiratorially, pointing toward a back room. "You know Don Juan over there puts everything in his report. Poker playing is not a part of my job duties. For this case anyway." Chuckling, she continued. "Besides, you are a sore loser. There'll be no rematch for you. Now get back to work. I have to test you later this afternoon." Dramatically throwing her hands up in the air, she said to him in jest, "Just one more week, *hijo.*" Marisela was delighted. Now this young man she would miss. She prayed nightly for his safety and happiness. Alexandro Milbon (whom she knew as Kevin) was a good man and he deserved it. Incorrigible, but a worthy young man.

In Spanish, he called over his shoulder, "Let me know when dinner is ready. I'll set the table."

Kevin walked back into the living room where he had been studying. The rooms of the safe house were brightly decorated. He guessed the soothing yellow was the Bureau's attempt to keep depression at bay for the inhabitants. Becoming an entirely new person could be a little discombobulating.

Despite his best efforts the words sounded strained even to his ears. "Hello, my name is Alexandro. Pleasure to meet you." He took one more disdainful look at his work, then sat down again. He couldn't wait to get to Tennessee. All the preparation had set his nerves on edge, though he knew the studying was worth it. He had learned a lot about the history of Memphis, and looked forward to settling there. His basketball career had taken him all over the world, especially in the countries of South America, but he had never lived farther south than northern Virginia.

The Bureau had done an excellent job of putting together a new life for him. No one would be able to detect him by credit card or bank withdrawals. His assets had been frozen and moved into government custody. Unlike most people in the witness protection program, he would not lose everything. Kevin had worked out a deal that would allow him to be as comfortable as before, maybe more. Never a spendthrift, he had always used his money wisely. His new life would be more than satisfying. It seemed the biggest stumbling block in his transition was his identification with one culture over another. Kevin had always identified with being a black man, but now he needed to become more comfortable with his Puerto Rican identity.

Kevin looked out the window at the oak trees that dominated much of the region. *How long had they been here? How many of his lifetimes?* The forest was constant, nothing like his life had been. There was a time when his life was just about basketball; it was his passion. Then there was the debacle of playing in Chile, only to discover that the team was a cover for a Chilean drug cartel. After he helped to destroy the organization, its matriarch, Valencia Rios, hunted him down.

Well, maybe, Memphis would be the place where happiness dwelled. *Better to be optimistic.* He would be moving soon and nothing was going to change that. *Now what?* He was almost afraid to imagine that this would be it, that he would have stability.

He longed to be like one of the oak trees he stood watching. Rooted, unmoving, and strong. These past several months had turned his life upside down. When he walked out these doors he would be someone he didn't even recognize. For right now, though, he needed to concentrate on the business at hand.

He needed to go back to his material. He walked slowly toward his study area to turn the tape on again. He stretched his long arms and legs before beginning.

Looking down at the photographs of his condo, sports car, and the nightclub all of which Alexandro Milbon was the proud new owner, he wondered if Memphis would be a place he could finally call home.

Chapter 3

The room was dark and musty; the smells were mixing with the pungent aroma of foreign cigarettes. The two men embraced warmly, ignoring the dank atmosphere. This was the first meeting between the two in several months.

The older man, Nikola, led the younger, Mikha, to his makeshift office.

"Nikola Mudiuranov, thank you for seeing me. I know that you are a very busy man. My associates and I see this as a profitable opportunity for all of us."

"Mikha, there is plenty of time for business. What of your father? I was sorry to hear about his illness. But I see and hear that he has trained you well."

Mikha cringed inwardly. Thoughts of his family were always disturbing. "Thank you for asking. It has been hard on my mother, but she is strong."

"But where are my manners? Come, let us drink."

Mikha watched as Nikola pulled an expensive bottle of vodka and two crystal glasses etched with gold out of a drawer from beneath his desk. Mikha took the opportunity to really look at his surroundings. He noticed that the makeshift office housed all the latest technological equipment. It was equipped with every device from A to Z, with special emphasis on equipment that detected surveillance systems. The dampeners hampered even the twelve-hour radar sweep. Mikha was impressed.

"Na vasha storovyeh u." Nikola made a toast to health and wealth.

Mikha breathed a silent sigh of relief. The toast was a good sign. No code words were used to indicate a problem. In his line of work, every day was dicey. He understood that he could be killed if he displeased the old man. Their families had known each other for generations, but in this business blood wasn't thicker than water, and money meant everything. Allegiance could be changed if the price was right. Mikha respected Nikola, but he knew that respect didn't mean trust. And trust didn't mean that you would live another day. Their system was much like the gangland system of Chicago's roaring twenties.

During Gorbachev's attempt to reform the Soviet Union, he was blind to how exactly changes were implemented. Where the government failed, the Russian Mafia succeeded. The United States heralded perestroika as a way to spread democracy and freedom. The reality is that U.S. aid only succeeded in providing the seed money for the rich to get richer, and the poor to get poorer.

Mikha watched his own grandfather go from being a comfortable business owner to a beggar on the street when his "boss" no longer needed his services. Mikha and his childhood friends learned to steal and scrape, managing to stay out of trouble and survive long enough to reach adulthood. He had learned to do ugly things. But in Odessa, Moscow, and anywhere else in the former Soviet Union, it was all about survival. Death was so commonplace he had no more tears—only ambition and the drive to escape his lot in life.

Mikha had joined the Mafia as a drug runner in his hometown of Odessa, eventually settling in Moscow after two years as a soldier. The mountains of Afghanistan proved to be a good training ground to gain weapons experience and perfect his killing skills. Perhaps most important to him were honed intuitive skills. He had the instincts of a cat, which had saved him from several life-threatening situations.

Mikha regarded Nikola coolly. Mikha itched for the chance to expand his small-time business. This was an opportunity of a lifetime. The guns were inexpensive, easy to transport, and one of their best sellers. But Mikha didn't have the network to meet the demand. He wanted to expand his business and move from Texas. It was too damned hot, and he wanted to push toward the East Coast, where the real money was to be made.

He wanted to move to Memphis, become a part of Nikola's inner circle. The women knew how to treat a man here. The food was decent, not spicy like in Texas, and the weather was manageable. His frequent trips to Atlanta, New York, Washington, D.C., and Philadelphia were paying off, but he was starting to feel like Memphis was home.

Viktor and Gregor were a part of his operation and were helping him to expand the base, but they were of Russian descent and had never lived in the Republics. They knew nothing of current protocol. He was teaching them how to survive in the Mafia culture.

Their plan was that Nikola would provide the infrastructure, and Mikha and his people, the local connections.

Nikola poured himself another drink. It was his fourth, Mikha noticed. "Misha, what can Nikola Mudiuranov do for you?" Nikola leaned forward in his chair.

He would listen to the proposal before deciding if Mikha would live or die today. He didn't need problems, and as long as the young man didn't present any . . .

Nikola had heard good things about the Texas operation. They moved a decent quantity of guns and made an adequate profit. He knew Mikha to be an ambitious young man. He had known many like him—some made it, some didn't. The key to longevity was protection. With the right protection, a man could do all right in the organization. The key was to trust no one, not business partners, family or friends. No one.

Mikha noted that Nikola had used the familiar nickname for his name. He hoped that was a positive sign.

"I have a small, successful operation in Texas, but I am ready to move on. Ievik Gogolanov is content to stay there and protect our interests. He is a capable man; he does what must be done."

Mikha shifted. He had to contain his enthusiasm; lack of emotion was a much safer tactic. He didn't want to appear too confident; after all, he was asking for assistance. Arrogance had no place in the Russian system.

"There is a growing demand in this area as well as points more along the East Coast. We've been checking into a few deals and have identified some potential buyers. You would, of course, receive a proper percentage.

"We ask your indulgence as we put things in place. We would need you to secure police protection and guarantee the safe passage of the guns from the dock workers and others who might think to interfere." *No need for those pesky American initials—FBI, ATF, CIA, and DEA.*

"How much are we talking about?"

Oohspech—Success. "Based on what we've been doing in Texas and the increase in demand we've seen so far, we are talking two to three million a month, plus our expenses, of course."

"And your buyers?"

"We've been doing business with a connection out of Baltimore. Just small numbers to see if they can handle the volume. We've been impressed with their ability to move the product and they are asking for more. We are looking at developing a more lucrative long-term relationship. So far, they've been mostly ghetto buys, and we're looking to expand."

The old man nodded with approval. He stubbed out the butt of his cigarette before lighting another. "Mikha, I like what I hear. Set something up in a few months. I would like to meet with them."

Mikha noticed that living in America did nothing to improve Nikola's teeth. They were short and yellowed, the dental work distinctly eastern European.

"Yes, Nikola Mudiuranov." He hid his disappointment. He had no intention of waiting a few months before making a deal. He had worked too hard to sit on his hands now. Nikola was powerful, but he was an old man. Mikha possessed the impatience of youth. He wouldn't wait long to make his move.

Da dna. They toasted again to their new venture.

With business complete, they made arrangements for pleasure. Mikha liked them tall and exotic looking. He loved the private clubs in Memphis. They weren't the small, dirty places he had known in Moscow. He couldn't afford the nice places of the rich and famous. At home he'd had to settle for dumps and dives. It was not the best of situations, and he was much happier being in America. In Memphis, they were clean and beautiful. They came in all shapes, sizes, and did anything for the right price. Mikha could take out all of his frustrations.

Chapter 4

Three months later

Agent Maria Thomas, now Maria Manez, was putting her clothes away in the Peabody Hotel, one of the swankiest hotels in Memphis. She'd arrived with a collection of designer clothing and shoes that would make Imelda Marcos jealous. The Bureau had spent a fortune on her new identity providing clothing, accommodations, and business tools. However, the expense had served its purpose, and her cover as one of the country's top gun dealers was firmly in place. She had selected five members for her team, and everyone was in position.

Maria looked over her supplies. She had an assortment of identification, guns, an agency-generated list of buyers, and a portfolio complete with a list of numbers for her offshore accounts. She packed everything neatly in two small suitcases to get ready for her meeting at an Agency safe house on the outskirts of the city.

For the case, the safe house doubled as the command center as well. Assistant Director Spates had insisted on it. Security was extra tight for this mission. Agent cover stories had been checked and rechecked, but knowing how concerned he was didn't make Maria feel any safer. She was glad she had Rod. Agent Roderick Radford posed as her bodyguard. She had selected him for several reasons and she wasn't ashamed of any of them.

Maria knocked on the connecting door to her suite. "You ready yet, slowpoke?" she called. Roderick opened the door immediately, his 6'3 frame towering over her. Her breath caught in her chest the way it always did when she saw him. But she forced herself not to lick her lips. Looking up into his hazel eyes sent her libido into overdrive. Would she always have to deal with that? Rod never failed to bring out lustful thoughts. Good thing she was a professional.

Rod was one of those guys that other guys hated. He had great looks, intelligence bordering on genius, and sex appeal that oozed from every café au lait–pore. He'd finished six years of school in four, and could have gone to any private company, but Rod had chosen the Bureau. He came from a long line of servicemen, so it was only natural that he would chose some sort of government job, and that he would be a lifer.

Maria liked working with him. He knew his job, did it extremely well, and he treated her with respect. Respect was something some male agents had a hard time giving the women they worked with. She had come up through the ranks the hard way, earning every accolade, award, bump, bruise, and battle scar. They teased each other mercilessly sometimes, but Rod cared about her and had been there for her since their time at the Academy. The three of them had been like musketeers, she, Rod and her best friend, Helene.

Roderick looked down at Maria's 5'10 frame slightly amused.

"Yes, ma'am, I'm ready. I was just waiting for your signal, or should I say, your bellow? Roderick Radford *a votre service*," he said smiling at her.

She batted her eyelashes in an exaggerated manner. "Oh, Rod, I love it when you talk dirty to me," she said in her best southern belle accent.

Still smiling, Rod looked past her into the room. When he spotted the suitcases, he started walking toward them. *Damn, why did she have to do that thing with her lashes? This assignment is going to be the death of me.* "Is this everything?" he asked.

She noticed his businesslike tone. *Guess fun time is over.* "Yes, that's everything. We should be able to make it in less than thirty minutes. Traffic shouldn't be too bad this time of day."

Radford nodded. "Yeah, you're right. Too bad we don't have time to stop on Beale Street. I could go for some down-home barbecue about now. So exactly how many times has Spates called?"

Thomas smiled wickedly again. "Too many. I told him we would be down there within the hour. He's a great director, but he worries too much." She blew out a restless breath, then continued. "He's going to give himself a coronary one day."

"No, you mean you're going to give him a coronary," Radford teased.

Maria walked toward the elevator. "Yeah, yeah, whatever you say," she called back over her shoulder.

When they reached the SUV parked in the garage, Thomas threw him the keys.

"Other duties as assigned. I'm too keyed up to drive," she quipped.

Rod quickly put down one bag and caught the keys. "A little warning next time. Or was that just a quick reflex test?"

"Sorry, I wasn't thinking, but as usual, you had it under control."

"Yeah, yeah, flattery will get you everywhere," he said suggestively.

Her eyebrows slanted downward in a frown and she gave him a warning look. "Rod, we've had this conversation before. You know how I feel. Once bitten, twice shy. I'm not going down that road again. No matter how tempting."

"That's right, agent. Let'em down easy. You can't blame a guy for trying, especially with the wardrobe you've got."

She had known when she selected Rod for the assignment that he had been carrying around a schoolboy crush on her. However, she didn't allow that to interfere with her wanting him for the mission. She needed him and felt more comfortable with a man of skill beside her; besides, she knew that they were both professionals and they could deal with it. They made a promise to each other not to let hormones get the best of them. Maria hoped it would be so easy as a promise, considering the proximity of their working relationship. He would only be just a door knock away.

When they were seated in the SUV, she smoothed her skirt down. She had to agree she looked good. The red-leather outfit covered her body like a butter-smooth glove. The short skirt showed off her long legs, but it was tasteful. Her two-inch matching designer pumps were divine. Her feet could definitely grow accustomed to $300–$400 shoes. She had on all the proper accessories and looked like she was weighing in at about $1500. *Maybe being Maria Manez wouldn't be so bad after all,* she mused.

She looked over at Roderick, who was just pulling the SUV into traffic. He really was tempting. He had the looks and charm that she found appealing. But if and when she gave her heart away again, she would be sure of the relationship. Besides, she had made a promise to herself. No more office romances and no more impulsiveness when it came to men. She was getting too old for another broken heart.

Maria shrugged, turning her thoughts away from romance and toward the very difficult mission they had ahead of them: to infiltrate the Russian Mafia.

She and Rod continued their journey in amiable silence, each lost in private thoughts of each other and other dangerous cases. Love, lust, and physical attraction had no place in this mission. As time progressed, recognition of that fact would serve them well.

Chapter 5

Alex looked at the purple leather couch that had just arrived. He smiled. Things were finally starting to come together. The club would reopen in a few days, and he was starting to feel like a complete person again. They had shut down for three months during the renovation process, which had helped the Bureau double-check security efforts. But now they were back on schedule and his new club was ready to open.

He had accepted his new identity of Alexandro Milbon. Most times he didn't think he had ever been Kevin Lopez DePalma, former basketball player from Alexandria, Virginia. He had changed so much in the last couple of years he doubted anyone would even recognize him. He was an established nightclub owner now, with connections in San Juan, Miami, and now Beale Street.

The FBI had been very thorough in his cover. His Spanish was unmistakably Puerto Rican, his pedigree perfect for his position. He was never seen with the same woman twice, and as the owner of the club, didn't drink to excess, smoke, or otherwise engage in illicit activity. He ran a clean establishment, one that pleased the locals and tourists alike. *Keep 'em coming back for more,* he thought. Alexandro had taken the opportunity to look around other establishments during his remodelling. He wanted his place to have a more modern, contemporary look. He decided on a style of several groupings of chairs. He used low round tables for patrons to sit their drinks on. The effect was to have conversation pits in strategic locations around the dance floor and some in the rear for a more private, exclusive atmosphere. The club was brightly colored. Very Miami art deco. He loved the vibrant colors of purple, canary yellow, fuchsia, and neon blue. His club, Memphis Nights, was the perfect size to accommodate small, intimate parties or large, gala events. The music was primarily jazz, but after the reopen he would experiment by offering a salsa night.

Alex had fallen in love with salsa dancing while in protective custody. His long legs were particularly suited to executing many of the intricate moves, and he often found himself swaying to a Latin beat in his off time. Marisela had taught him the dance and much more than the Bureau paid her for; she put the younger man to shame in many areas. Her enthusiasm and love of life had helped him overcome the self-pity he felt after his life had changed so drastically. By the time he'd reached Memphis, he was ready to face whatever life had in store.

Alexandro looked at the boxes of promotional and marketing items that had also arrived. Napkins, glasses, T-shirts, and matchbook covers all bearing the logo for Memphis Nights. He was determined to make it the most upscale club this side of the Mississippi. He smiled, looking around. *Not bad,* he thought.

He was more than satisfied with the location on Beale Street; it was on the corner taking up a large portion of the narrow block. His club was in the general area of a couple other places that were tourist attractions, such as the Hard Rock Café and The Pig.

Before arriving, he had learned quite a bit about the street's history. *Guess we share the same checkered past,* he thought wryly. Memphis came into prominence in the 1920s, with the popularity of the city largely due to the goings-on of Beale Street. Gambling, prostitution, murder, and voodoo were just some of its charms. It was even reported that the infamous Machine Gun Kelly peddled whiskey from a clothesbasket along the block. Crime led to the eventual decline of Beale Street, and it wasn't until decades later that things began to improve.

In 1983 the street had begun the transformation that brought tourism and commerce back to the area. Nightclubs, restaurants, and businesses provided Memphis the means to a necessary rebirth. The city bought several blocks and began a very successful redevelopment plan that transformed the area from a site of urban decay to a new urban playground. The street was now the number-one tourist attraction in Tennessee.

He unpacked the supplies, enjoying the quiet of the club. In a couple of more days, he wouldn't be able to hear himself think, and that was a good thing.

"Yo, Alex where are you?"

He was grudgingly pulled out of his thoughts. "Back here unpacking. Come on back, man."

The two men shook hands vigorously. Max spoke first. "Man, I love the new look. I gotta admit, when you told me we were going Deco, I wasn't sure, but you've pulled it together nicely. *Muy caliente* . . . I think the ladies are going to love it."

"As long as the fellas keep buying the drinks," Alex responded.

Max smiled. "I just wanted to stop by to tell you the

new guy will be in tomorrow. I'm going to check on my beloved bar in a few. Did you order those special flavors for me?"

Max loved tending bar almost as much as he loved being an agent. It gave him the opportunity to hone his people-watching skills. He had enjoyed his time in Memphis getting Alex ready for his new life. "Your new bartender's name is Ramon, and don't worry, we've checked him out thoroughly. He's on the up-and-up and should do well for you."

Alex was disappointed, but this change wasn't unexpected. "You moving on, huh? I would ask if you have a new assignment, but I'd rather you not have to shoot me."

Max chuckled. "Yeah, well, it's been real. I know you are going to do fine. I'm going to let you get back to work. I would offer to help, but you know these hands are registered with Lloyd's of London. I can't afford to have anything happen to them."

Alex patted him on the back. "Yeah, right! Go on, get outta here. I am just about done anyway. I'll be leaving in another hour or so. Thanks for letting me know about the change. It's going to be weird without you back there." Alex pointed toward the bar. "You mix a mean Cubano cocktail."

"Thanks, man, I loved every minute of it."

The bar was a chrome-and-glass monstrosity that would suit the needs of the club perfectly. It was designed with all the features necessary to mix the latest designer drinks. Alex himself was fond of the Sour Apple, but made sure he stuck to his limit of one, especially when he wasn't trying to make an impression as a high roller. His life was still a role in many respects. He always had to keep his character in mind.

Max turned serious for a moment. "Alex, man, I know

you have been through a lot, but from what I've seen, you're a pretty squared-away guy with a good head on his shoulders. I know you are going to be fine. Just keep doing what you're doing."

"Thanks, man, your having faith in me means a lot. Your being here has been appreciated too." Alex smiled. "If you ever get tired of the Bureau—my bar awaits."

Alex pulled into the driveway of his condo a little over an hour later. He had been able to obtain the quintessential bachelor pad. Two bedrooms: one that he used as his home office; and a large master bedroom with a custom bed to accommodate his 6'5, 225-pound frame. In contrast to the Art Deco look he adopted for the club, his home was accented with neutral shades throughout. He had a bedroom set made out of solid oak, complete with armoire for his television. He was still an avid basketball fan and enjoyed watching the games in bed. Cream, off-white, sage green, and taupe dominated the color scheme of the room, giving it a soothing feel. There were no bold splashes of color—no neon blue would be found in his personal space. He had a spacious kitchen and separate living and dining areas, for which he was very grateful. He liked having the space to spread out.

He was comfortable in his new community. Aside from a fitness facility, the property boasted a golf course on the lake. His views of the water had been calming to him while he got settled in. He would sit and watch the scenery out of his windows for hours. Looking at the lake helped him to put his life in perspective. As an only child whose parents were deceased, he was all he had to depend on. He was alive, he was being protected, and he had the rest of his life ahead of him.

An added bonus to living in his community was that there was security posted at the entrances and exits. Cars were clearly marked with residence stickers, and no one was allowed on the premises without an invitation.

Alex checked his mail first, then his messages, before heading toward his favorite room. His bathroom had become his sanctuary. He used the space to de-stress, often pulling his long legs into the custom tub he had ordered. Sore from lugging boxes and unpacking what seemed like a gazillion small items, his body hungered for a long, hot shower. He was more than willing to oblige. *Home sweet home.*

Agent Spates waited patiently for Radford and Thomas to arrive. He knew his agents well. There was no sense in getting upset; they would waltz in shortly. They were ten minutes late, but would claim it was traffic. Maybe he shouldn't have paired them together. They seemed to enjoy tormenting him. It was like having two Eric Duvernays. Their only saving grace was that they got such good results when they were together. He suspected having Helene in the mix saved their bacon a time or two as well.

Spates liked the Memphis office, and he was looking at houses in the area. He was giving serious thought to making Tennessee his permanent residence. He loved his house in the Washington area, but the living was definitely easier in this part of the country.

The three agents quickly making their way into the room to sit at the conference table pulled him out of his reverie. They were using a plantation-style house as their base of operation where Spates was positioned as Agent Thomas's paternal uncle.

He looked at the tardy trio with thoughtful, intelligent eyes. *Maybe I'm getting too old for this!*

"Now that you have decided to grace me with your presence, can I presume to start this meeting; albeit fifteen minutes later than the assigned start time." Agent Spates tapped his pen three times before beginning his presentation. When he stopped his agents knew it was time for business. Radford and Thomas were duly chastised and looked apologetically around the room.

Having made his point, Spates continued. "You were given information prior to our coming here, so you know what kind of devil we are up against. Intelligence estimates that there are about 10,000 fatal shootings a year in Moscow. A high percentage of those are suspected contract killings. Those who don't cooperate with the local bosses often find themselves in body bags. Kidnappings are at an all-time high, and over one hundred bankers have been kidnapped and murdered. Extortionists kill anyone who will not launder for them or commit bank fraud."

Spates paused, letting the team catch up with him in the briefing packet. "One of those who butchered and slaughtered his way to the U.S. is our mark. We've been watching Nikola Mudiuranov's organization closely for the past several months, as you all are well aware."

He looked directly at Agent Thomas now. "He met last night with your contact from Texas. Since he didn't exit in a body bag or in pieces, we can only assume that they came to some sort of agreement. We expect contact in the next few days in order to schedule a meet. Make yourself known in town. Go shopping, spend money, and go out to clubs. Let Mudiuranov know that you are already here and that you don't wait for anyone's call. You do what you have to do to make some noise. Just try to keep it down to a dull roar. Let him know that you are a force to be reckoned with, but not irresponsible. That's not the Maria Manez that we've created."

Agent Spates paused. "Just so you know, Agent Williams' son Keith seems to be out of danger. Looks like he will be going home next week. He's using a cane, but thanks to the good Lord he will walk on his own power again. I think we are all in agreement we want these guys and their guns off the streets."

Maria sighed in relief. This was a burden lifted off Brian.

Spates looked around the room. "Now tell me what you've got."

"Rod and I are settled in the hotel. I have appointments around town already. We've made a little noise, but nothing serious. Helene has set up a mobile perimeter. She knows where I am and what I am doing at all times. The last thing I want to do is get caught with my proverbial pants down around these guys. I haven't made face-to-face contact with Mikha yet, but we've been watching his nighttime comings and goings. He prefers them young, exotic looking, and most of all, into pain. His psychological profile shows that he's pretty sick. His stint in Afghanistan succeeded in making him a complete and total sociopath." The agents around the room nodded with understanding.

"Agents Radford and Thomas have been outfitted with the latest surveillance equipment. We've got this *Big Brother* thing going." Helene showed Spates the monitoring equipment she had received just before joining the team in Tennessee.

Rod went to retrieve one of the bags that they'd brought with them. He returned with a selection of guns and ammunition that were suspected of being used in several contract killings in Russia and now in the U.S. "This is the product. We are arranging for a small buy; call it a good-faith measure. This is another test. The Russians are nothing if not cautious."

Agent Spates pulled out his own collection of guns. They were passed around, and all the members of the team took their time inspecting them.

The briefing material in their packets gave a detailed description of the weapons. The gun that they were looking at was similar to the Russian PSM with an eight-round magazine. It was 6.4 inches in length and weighed 16.1 ounces. What had started out as a gun for use by Soviet security forces had quickly become a gun readily available on the black market. The gun's popularity started to rise in Europe before coming to America and being used to kill on U.S. streets. Reports from local authorities indicated that the guns were showing up in almost every major city. The perpetrators of crimes that used this gun were getting younger and younger, and the devastation more incredible.

Spates spoke again. "These guns were actually recovered in a small warehouse in Prairie View, Texas. We only found out about them because one of the neighbors didn't like the way the Russians looked. The local Bureau got a phone tip, which helped recover about five thousand guns. We suspect that they were only being housed there until pick up in one or two more days. They weren't even heavily guarded. The takedown was quick and dirty, with two casualties."

Agent Thomas held the gun in her hand. She couldn't believe all the devastation that had been caused by something that weighed little more than a pound. *You've caused so much pain and trouble. I thought you'd be bigger.*

Chapter 6

"Thomas, can I see you for a minute? I've got some information I am sure you want to hear." Maria looked at her friend Helene. Helene had a mischievous streak a mile wide. It would be interesting to see what her mysterious information was about.

"Yes, agent, right away."

"Don't give me that weary look. You're going to like this." Helene smiled. "I got you an appointment at Personality for tomorrow at 10:00 AM. Yep, you are really moving up in this world."

Maria squealed. "Helene, thank you, thank you! How did you manage to get me in so quickly? I've heard that Antonio is busy for months on out."

"Hey, determination, money, and a talent for getting what I want. Did I mention money? Remember, all this is coming out of your budget!"

Personality was the premier salon in Memphis. Antonio did not take walk-ins or call-ins. Appointments were made strictly by referrals, and he had to interview each prospective client. He was very serious about beauty and maintaining his well-deserved reputation. It was rumored that a shampoo and blow dry started at $80.

"I knew I could count on you, girl. I am so glad that

you and Rod are here with me. I know we are going to do well."

"Okay, it is just a hair appointment. Don't start getting all sentimental on me. Remember 10:00 AM. Now, let me have the pleasure of telling Rod. He will love sitting in the reception area waiting on you. The man has the patience of a newborn. Anyway, you have any ideas on the type of look that you want to achieve?"

Maria smiled wickedly. "You are going to have to wait and see like everybody else. Now let me get out of here. Rod has a hankering for some BBQ. Give us a call later. I've given you my schedule for the rest of the week. Holler at you later, kiddo. I am going to run in and talk with Spates while you give Rod the good news. You know, you two were made for each other."

"That will be the day. He's only got eyes for you, and you know it."

"Yeah, well, after Duvernay, you know my policy. No more mixing business with pleasure. Besides, right now, we've got guns to get off the streets. *Hasta luego!*"

Helene headed toward the conference room where Rod sat reviewing some of the briefing material.

"Agent Radford, I just wanted to review some scheduling issues with you. Do you have a second?"

"Of course, for you, the world. What's up?"

"Well, I just wanted to prepare you for tomorrow. I was able to pull some strings and get Maria a beauty appointment for tomorrow. She'll need you to escort her, of course, and since it might take a little while, I suggest you take some reading material." Helene smiled innocently at the man, galling him to no end.

What did I do to deserve this?, he thought miserably, successfully resisting the urge to wring her pretty little neck.

He had known Helene long enough not to give her the reaction she wanted, so he feigned nonchalance.

"Great, you know this will give me time to catch up on the book I've been trying to finish for months. Then too, I have some crossword puzzles to work on—keep the mind sharp. What are you going to do in the van while we're being entertained?" Rod raised an eyebrow in mock interest. *Gotcha,* he thought.

Nice try. "Oh, I think I will get my legs waxed or something frivolous like that. What do you think, maybe a couple of highlights in my hair? Blonde or red?"

Rod walked away without answering.

Helene buffed her nails on her sweater. *Yep, the girl's got skills,* she thought.

When Maria saw Rod, she swallowed a giggle. Those two were too much. Judging from his expression, Helene had won this round. "Perfect timing, Agent Radford. The AD and I were just finishing. Ready for some barbecue?"

Rod sighed. "I'm ready to go if you are. I'll just clean up my mess and be ready in a second." He nodded toward the director and left the room.

Spates turned toward Thomas. "Am I going to have to referee you three? Please tell me I am not going to regret giving the go-ahead to this team."

"Sir, we would never disappoint you. You can have complete and total faith in us."

"Ummm, get on out of here. I've got work to do, you know."

"Sir, yes, sir. And we'll be here on time for the next meeting. See you later."

"Good-bye, Agent Thomas."

She caught up with Roderick in the conference area. "Okay, Rod, I'm ready."

When they made it to the truck, he finally spoke about what was bothering him. "Okay, tell me why Helene has it in for me. Lately, she seems to get extreme joy from tormenting me. Did I forget her birthday, forget to compliment her on a new hairstyle or new dress? There's this undercurrent of something and I'm not sure I understand it."

Thomas looked at him incredulously. *Why are men so amazingly dense?* "I'm not going to get in the middle of this. I think you guys need to sit down and have a little chat, other than that I don't know what to tell you. You and Helene have been friends a long time. If you think she has issues and is not just messing with your head, call her on it. She's a big girl. Besides, this is a professional operation. We don't need foolishness getting in our way. Mission first!"

Rod answered more testily than intended. "Yes, Team Leader Thomas. Mission first."

"Whoa, why are we having this conversation? Is there something that you want to say to me?"

Maria was right. She wasn't the source of his frustration. "No, I'm sorry. I'm cool. I'll talk with Helle and we'll move on. How about we stop in The Pig for some takeout? Maybe I can't think straight because I am so hungry. You would think Spates would spring for food at these marathon meetings."

The rest of the evening passed by comfortably after they ate their food. There were no more emotional outbursts, and when they retired to their rooms in the hotel, both were able to do so without having to make further apologies. For the moment they were on one wavelength.

Maria sat at her writing desk poring over the information that Assistant Director Spates had given them. There were a total of six members on the team, with Agent Thomas serving as its leader. She felt an awesome responsibility to the rest of the team and to the public. What had started out as a means of revenge was turning into something much bigger. Maria had to quell the uneasy feelings in the pit of her stomach. She pushed self-doubt to the back recesses of her mind and concentrated on the material in front of her. She had to decide her next moves.

Maria studied some fashion magazines and made a decision about the look she wanted. Maria Manez was a mover and shaker. She was in Memphis to make some noise. Agent Thomas would make sure she did everything that she was supposed to do to meet the objectives. She went to bed that night a little more confident about the direction of the case. Mission first. As long as she kept sight of that without distractions, all would be fine.

Rod and Maria entered Personality Salon and Spa at 9:45 A.M. The owner, Antonio, greeted them enthusiastically. Nothing prepared her for the atmosphere that he had created within the space. It was like going from Beale Street to Nirvana. Personality was a two-story structure with redwood floors throughout.

Rod was directed to the waiting area. He was immediately struck by the starkness of the white walls, which played against the see-through fireplace. The result was startling and relaxing at the same time. He was surprised by the amenities that the staff offered, especially when he was provided with a white wine spritzer, fruit, and various imported cheeses on crackers. He made himself comfortable.

Antonio turned his attention to Maria. "Now that's done, let's go to my office, my dear."

Maria glanced at Rod, shrugging her shoulders. "After you."

Antonio pointed to the right as they walked. "This entire lower level is where the spa services are performed. We have two masseurs on staff. We offer manicures, pedicures, massage, and aqua therapy in the whirlpool and Jacuzzi." Maria was duly impressed.

They entered his office, his personal domain. The room was also decorated with stark white walls. Kevin Toney played softly from his Bose speakers, which were placed tastefully on wall mounts. He offered her a seat on one of the deep red leather chairs facing his large desk.

As Antonio's rich bass voice saturated the room, there was no doubting who was in charge in his presence. "Now, let me get a good look at you. Helene didn't exaggerate—you are exquisite. She and I go way back, you know, to when I was simply Tony trying to make it in Dayton, Ohio. We haven't kept in touch over the last several years, so I am surprised she knew where to find me, but then again, that girl was always resourceful." Antonio took Maria's hand in his. "I love your eyes—the color of cognac almost, very deep and very rich."

Maria slowly withdrew her hand, not sure what to make of him. He certainly was an eyeful—tall and well built. He had wavy, textured hair, and a mustache with a sharp jawline. He was ruggedly handsome, not pretty like a lot of the male hairdressers she had come in contact with in her travels.

"Thank you . . . I think."

"Forgive me. I love looking at beautiful women almost as much as I enjoy making them beautiful." Antonio gave a self-deprecating laugh. "Okay, enough about me. Tell me about you. What kind of look are interested in?"

Maria smiled, touching her hair without thinking. "I'm glad you asked. I have a picture of what I want—here it is. I'd also like to have a makeover. I need makeup that is more dramatic than what I wear now."

Antonio took the picture from her hand and arched his left brow. "Hmmm . . . I see." He gave her a lopsided grin. "Let's get started, shall we?" He led her to the shampoo room. The décor was much the same upstairs as it was below with the exception of the color. Here Antonio added a black and white color scheme. The space was functional, warm, and inviting. Maria supposed it was designed to make clients want to spend the entire day there. It was definitely working for her.

After the completion of her services, Antonio personally escorted her to the exit. "Damn!" was all Rod could say when Maria entered the waiting room where he'd taken up residency during her three-hour appointment. Her wallet was two hundred fifty dollars lighter than when she entered, but if Rod's reaction was any indication, it was worth it.

She twirled for him to give him the full effect.

"Girl, what are you trying to do to the male species?"

She smiled. "Ready to go?"

Antonio grasped both her hands. "See you in two weeks." He winked at them before welcoming his next appointment.

Rod continued to eye her appreciatively even after they entered the car. His impatience had ended as soon as he saw her. He was even looking forward to her next appointment. "I've got to tell you, you look fantastic. I would never have imagined your hair cut that way, but the Sigourney Weaver thing you have going is totally working for me."

Maria laughed and shook her head. She was truly the head of a motley crew. "Agent Radford, need I remind you, it is not your attention that I am trying to attract. Talk about melodrama."

"Yeah, well, you got it. I think I am going to have to talk to the director about hazardous duty pay. This might get rough."

She put one hand on a designer-clad hip before asking, "Did you finish your book?"

"Yes, and don't try to change the subject," Rod responded. "I would say the Russians are in for trouble. Maria Manez has just arrived."

Chapter 7

Goran arrived at Mikha's apartment shortly after noon. Mikha looked like he had just gotten up, and the place was a wreck.

"Late night last night? You look like hell!" *Must be the cleaning lady's day off,* he thought.

Mikha ignored him. He needed to figure out what to do. Goran recognized his impatience and sighed in resignation. "Mikha, are you sure you want to do this without the old man's approval?"

"Yes, I'm sure. This is America, not Moscow. We do it my way. I don't have time to dance with Nikola Mudiuranov. This is my deal, and I won't jeopardize it because of his caution. We set things up soon." Mikha toyed with his cigarette. Goran watched him closely. Mikha wasn't so sure of himself. He was nervous, and that made Goran want to tread lightly. He didn't want to end up as one of Nikola's examples, having no desire to die a slow, painful death.

Mikha continued. "There was an incident in Texas. Ievik is handling it, but I don't like the smell of things. We need to relocate and do it quickly. They were sloppy. And they paid for their foolishness. I don't intend to make any mistakes." Mikha's eyes were bright with excitement. He could almost taste success. That meant freedom, which was more precious to Mikha than anything else in the world. He wanted his own niche in the system—his own empire.

Goran continued to watch him intently. Mikha's eyes gave him away. The gleam with which they shone was unmistakable. He was a man driven by power, and that made him very dangerous. Goran resisted the urge to shudder.

"I've been doing a lot of thinking lately. We may be able to do this without the old man. I have a plan," Mikha announced, a determined look in his eye.

Instinctively Goran's gut tightened. He didn't like the sound of this, but he knew Mikha would go through with the plan with or without him. He would hear him out. "Mikha, what do you have in mind?" he asked cautiously.

"We need to know how the U.S. found out about the guns in Texas. We need to know if we are being set up. I need to know if I am being set up. This dealer from Baltimore, we need to know more. I want to set up a meeting in two days. How many guns can we get together in that time?" Mikha moved bottles and dishes off of his table so that they could go over some material.

Goran jumped from his seat. Mikha's apartment had a great view of Beale Street, but Goran saw nothing. His stomach was in turmoil now. "Mikha, you can't be serious—two days?" He saw the expression on Mikha's face and sat down again. He wasn't sure who he should be more wary of—Mikha or Nikola.

Mikha continued shifting through papers until he found the warehouse information that he was searching for. He showed the papers to Goran.

Goran fought the instinct to bolt and responded. "A small shipment, maybe two thousand guns. I can move that many without raising eyebrows and causing suspicion. Also, the payoffs would be minimal."

Mikha was pleased. *This could work,* he thought. "That's good. I have five thousand on hand. Let's see what our Baltimore connections are made of. When they arrive, have Ivan follow them. Matter of fact, I want to know what they have been up to for the past few weeks. Tell Ivan to do some checking. I need to know if they were responsible for that heat in Texas. I am not going to look like a fool to Nikola. This is my chance with the old man."

Goran nodded his head in agreement. At least Mikha would take precautions. Several minutes later, Goran left after concluding his business.

Goran got behind the wheel of his BMW seven series, then looked down at his hands. They were clean. He looked at his feet, which were comfortably ensconced in leather shoes that cost as much as some workers made in a whole year in Odessa. "Why am I mixed up in this?" he asked himself. He was comfortable. His less-than-legal ventures allowed him forays into legal ones. He had a computer company, interest in a mail-order-bride company, a strip club, and a small Russian grocery store. It was his goal to create a Little Russia right in the heart of Memphis. He continued to bring what was left of his family to the United States: Soon all those he cared about would be here in his little utopia.

To that end, Mikhail Stemenovich made him uncomfortable. Mikha had no one to ground him. His parents were alive but would never survive the journey to America, and Mikha had no wife and no kids. He was dangerous. He didn't care about anyone. They were all gone. All Mikha cared about was money and power.

By contrast, Goran enjoyed his life in the United

States. He toasted from Russian goblets etched in gold and ate grade-A beef. He was warm in the winter and cool in the summer, and he had any woman he wanted in his bed at night. Goran was living his version of the American dream.

Goran backed out of the parking space reserved for guests. He liked the exclusive midrise that Mikha lived in, but preferred his plantation-style home in the suburbs. Driving away he listened to Eminem's *8Mile* CD. The words seemed appropriate to his life. "The moment, you own it, you better never let it go. You only get one shot, do not miss your chance to blow."

Mikha got up from the black leather couch where he had been sitting during Goran's visit. He groused his way to the kitchen in search of more vodka.

Fools, they are too small minded to understand. Mikha's thirst for personal power wasn't solely about personal gain. Power was about control, and control was about change. True, he had nothing left in Russia, had no one, but that didn't mean he didn't care. It was so frustrating dealing with those imbeciles who only wanted the trappings of success.

No, Mikha would never be content with what he had. Not here and not now. Russia called to him, and one day he would return. When he did, it would be to take over as the next Prime Minister. Then they would understand. Ironic that he would use American dollars to reclaim the Russia that the Americans had a hand in destroying. It would take a lot of money to reorganize the country, much more than he could generate with his small business. Then there was the matter of decapitating the Mafiocracy. He would need to align himself with true believers. Trust could be bought and sold. That he did not need. He was looking for idealists, those who believed change could and would happen. Believed that Russia could depend solely on Mother Russia. *No more capitalist handouts,* he thought.

He looked around his apartment, trashed from too much partying. He would call a cleaning service later. It was time to start getting things back on track. He took a long, hot shower, and when he was done he was ready for business. *For Russia,* he thought as he dialed Maria Manez's cell phone number.

Chapter 8

Thomas took a deep breath before answering her phone. Mikha was the only one who had this number. They were getting one step closer to the goal. "Maria Manez. Talk to me."

Mikha spoke as if they were long lost best friends. "Maria, it's so good to hear you. Are you up for a little business? I've been talking to my associates—I put in a good word for you, and they are willing to do another small deal. They are cautious, you understand."

"Mikha, I've been waiting for your call. I'm in Memphis just checking things out. Tell your people not to move so slowly. I'd hate to have to take my business elsewhere."

"Maria, Maria, you Americans are so impatient. Our dealings will be very lucrative for both of us. Patience, just a little patience, that's all I ask."

Maria's tone was brisk. "How much product, and when do I get delivery?"

"Six thousand in two days. We meet in the place we discussed before. I didn't realize you were in town already." Mikha adopted the same businesslike tone.

"Don't play games. Of course you did, otherwise you wouldn't be worth your salt."

Mikha laughed. He liked her. She had spice.

"Have you enjoyed your time here? Personally, I love Memphis, and I am looking forward to making it my home."

Maria allowed her tone to warm to him. "It's not Baltimore, but it will do. I plan on checking out some of the nightlife while I'm here, too. Maybe I'll see you around sometime."

Considering his tastes, he found that highly unlikely. "I don't think we frequent the same places, sweetheart, but I'll see you in a couple of days. Have fun."

Mikha pounded his fist on the table. Ivan was slipping. He hadn't reported that she was in town, and that could have been a costly error for him. He needed to be on top of the game at all times. He wouldn't be caught off guard again. Ivan would atone for his mistakes.

Maria turned to Rod. The two agents had been in her room reviewing profiles when the phone rang. "Looks like things are about to heat up. We need to schedule a meeting to make sure everyone's in place. Guess we will be stopping by the bank tomorrow. We meet the Russians in two days. We better let Spates know."

"You got it, I'll give him a call. Helene, too."

Maria looked at him intently. "Are you two cool? We all need to be on the same sheet of music now."

Rod nodded his head. "Yeah, we're cool. We came to do a job, and we are going to do it well. Don't worry about us—worry about them."

Maria nodded. "I told Mikha we were going out tonight. He tried to play it off, but I don't think he knew we were here. Maybe his intel isn't as good as we have given him credit for. Anyway, look good tonight—we are going to paint Beale Street red."

"Aw, ma, do we have to?" he said, in mock disagreement.

"Yes, son, we've got bad people to impress. Go on, get out of here. I want to take a nap before we go out. I've got a lot of impressing to do. Don't forget about the calls. We can go to the bank about 4:00 P.M. Check with Helene about the branch manager. I don't want some flunky holding up our money. The account should be flagged already, but double-check. Thanks, partner, you're the best."

Rod gathered his notes, adding her new instructions to the inventory. "Yeah, I guess I am. Seems like I'm doing all the work."

"Yes, and you are so good at it. Good night," she called out over her shoulder. She retreated to her bedroom suite to rest.

At 11 p.m. she woke up to get ready. This was her night to make some noise in Memphis. She looked through her closet for the most appropriate outfit.

When Rod heard her knock on the door half an hour later he was nearly floored by her appearance. "Maria, they don't make them like you in Kansas."

"Why, thank you," she responded with a seductive smile. "You don't look too shabby yourself."

Agent Radford came close to crossing the line between professional admiration and the ordinary leer when he looked at her in her Maria-wear. His eyes feasted on the Roberto Cavalli outfit she was wearing. Several of her clothes had been procured from past lines or from fashions that didn't make the cut for the runways. This particular design came from a couple years back, when Cavalli really let loose. It was a soft leather black miniskirt and short jacket outfit, with matching black bra. Maria wore a see-through shell over the bra, leaving little to the imagination. The ultrasheer black hose and three-inch heels were enough to cause Rod heart palpitations. She checked her makeup, then was ready to go.

Rod closed his eyes, sending up a silent prayer. Maria's shoes made her reach six feet in height. She exuded sex appeal from every pore.

Maria spoke into her tiny microphone. "Okay, Helene, we are about to exit the front of the building. Walking out now. Do you copy? Do you have a visual?

Helene whistled loudly. "Damn, girl, you put us mere mortals to shame. I love that new look, and, yes, I have a visual and I copy you loud and clear. Why didn't you tell me about the magic Antonio worked? I would have gone to see my old buddy, too."

"Yeah, you might have told me that he was your old buddy before I got there, but I know how you like to surprise people."

Maria turned toward Rod, looking at him while answering Helene's questions.

"Anyway, thank you for the compliments. Do we have company yet? I think we are going to walk. There's no need to fight for parking when we are so close to the action."

Helene panned her remote cameras around the area, looking for people she could match to the intelligence photos she had in her computer system. "Give me a few seconds. We've got a possible. I just need to confirm."

Maria and Rod continued their leisurely stroll down Beale Street. It was Friday night, and the place was jumping. The night air was warm and sultry. Maria turned heads as she and her "bodyguard" took in the sights. They ducked into a dimly lit bar as their first stop of their night on the town.

A tall, lanky man entered the bar shortly after they did.

"We've got confirmation. Tall guy with dirty brown hair, black shirt, and blue jeans. He's been following you since you left the hotel. Right now he's on your six."

Maria pretended to be bopping to the music as she looked around to see the man following them. She looked at Rod. "Got him."

Helene responded, "Acknowledged. I'll keep a close eye on him. You guys enjoy Beale Street. Have a drink for me."

Just then three young men came toward the booth Rod and Maria shared. "Hey, sexy lady. Why don't you drop Paul Bunyan here and hang with us?"

Maria could smell the alcohol on the barely legal boys long before they reached the table. Rod looked at the three drunken young men in disgust. "Time to go."

Hmmm, the bodyguard, not the boyfriend, the man watching them thought.

She didn't want to make a scene yet, having just left the hotel. Maria tried to diffuse the situation before things got out of hand. "Boys as tempting as that may seem, *Paul* and I have business. Y'all have a good time now." She rose from her seat. One of the young men, who looked about twenty-three, fortified with liquid courage, moved to step in her way.

Now Maria was pissed. She grabbed him by the arm, twisted it awkwardly behind his back, and started for the door. Rod grabbed the other two hapless creatures and followed her. Not a word had been communicated between Rod and Maria, but they knew exactly what to do.

Once outside, the boys were given a good shove and told to go home before they really got into trouble.

Rod turned to her. "See what kind of trouble that outfit stirs up."

She smiled, "Uh-huh, that's why I wore it. Come on let's get something to eat, then go dance the calories off."

Rod sighed. "Yes, boss."

Helene who had been monitoring their actions, piped in with a comment. "Now that's what I like in a man—acquiescence."

"Yes, Helene, and that's why you don't have one," Rod retorted.

Maria smiled. "And now, getting back to the mission. Helene, what do you suggest in terms of possible hot spots?"

"Head up the block. There's a new club opening up. They'll probably have some snacks, and that way you won't have to pay for dinner. People keep talking about how hot the place is. I can't wait to see for myself," Helene told them.

The couple started walking through the streets again. Every few steps Maria would stop to adjust something on her outfit just to make sure the surveillance was intact. It was nearly 12:30 A.M. when they reached the club. The atmosphere inside indicated that it was definitely the night's hot spot.

Maria fell in love with the décor instantly. It was so Miami. Rod found them a table as soon as another couple vacated it. He asked her what she wanted to drink after they got settled.

"I'm going to splurge a little and have a Sour Apple, thanks."

Alex had just taken over the bar to give Ramon a smoke break when Rod came up to place the orders.

"Sour Apple and Cubano cocktail, please."

Rod looked closely at Alex. There was something

vaguely familiar about the man, but he dismissed it. He had more important things to worry about. Besides, he might have just been struck by how tall he was. He had to be over six feet four. Rod paid for the drinks, tipped the bartender, and headed back to Maria.

Maria looked around. It was a very nice club. The clientele looked to be mostly the yuppie/buppie type. The dance floor was filled with couples holding each other close. The music had a slow, jazzy feel. Just as Rod sat down, a man interrupted the music to make some announcements.

"Okay, folks, my name is Alex Milbon, I'm the owner of this fantastic club, Memphis Nights. We're going to do something a little special for you now." Alex nodded toward the stage, and the curtain rose on the band that had already started playing.

"Memphis Nights is proud to present musica caliente!" There was thunderous applause when the band began to play an uptempo salsa number. Maria jumped up, ready to dance. It had been a long time since she'd let her hair down.

"Come on, Rod." She was pulling him up to dance with her.

Rod gave her a blank expression. "Maria, I don't salsa. You're going to have to find yourself another partner."

Maria was dumbfounded. "I thought you had lessons last year?"

"Yeah, for the tango, not salsa. Sorry."

Maria gulped down the last of her drink and headed toward the dance floor. She would dance by herself. She swayed her hips seductively to the Latin beat.

Two men came up to her to sandwich her between them. She extricated herself from them and walked away from the dance floor. She moved more quickly when she noticed the murderous expression in Rod's eyes. He was walking toward her at a fast pace. This evening was turning into more than they had anticipated.

Alex rushed over to her to make sure that she was all right. The last thing in the world he wanted was one of the female patrons being accosted.

Alex tapped her on the shoulder from behind. Maria swung around, ready to do battle.

"Miss, I am sorry about that. No woman should have to put up with that kind of treatment. I assure you it won't happen again." Alex found her totally provocative in her leather outfit. It was hard to concentrate on his apology when he kept thinking of the ways he wanted to kiss her.

Maria looked at him closely. "Oh, my God!" Recognition slammed them both at the same time. Concerned about her cover, instinct took over. She couldn't afford to have the Russians think she'd lied. Maria drew back, slapping Alex with all her might.

He couldn't help himself. She was obviously undercover with her outfit. The flecks of gold in his eyes darkened before he pulled her into a fierce kiss. Every time she tried to pull back, he drew her closer, deepening the kiss.

"What the hell?" Rod and Helene said at the same time.

Alex released her, whispering in her ear, "It's nice to see you again, Agent Thomas. I like the new look."

Maria was breathing too hard to respond. Instead she stalked away, unsure when her knees would buckle from the earth-shattering kiss.

Rod looked at her, and then Alex. Before he made a move to pulverize the man, he wanted to know what was going on. He barked, "Helene, run a scan. Get me a name, now."

"I'm already on it. How's Maria, she looks like she's seen a ghost."

Rod was silent. He opened and closed his fists over and over, hoping to quell his anger.

Helene paused. She waited for her computer to spit out the information that she needed. "Hold on, I'm getting authorization. It is top level. Who the hell is this guy?"

Exactly my question, he thought. Rod made a valiant effort to hold his temper in check. It had to be more than macho pride that made him want to rip this guy's heart out, didn't it? How did this yahoo rate kissing Maria's pretty lips off? No, his anger was purely professional. It had to be. They had all agreed—mission first.

Helene finally obtained clearance to access the information she needed. "Got it. Whoa, he's in witness protection. His name is Alexandro Milbon. Leave him alone, and get Maria the hell out of there."

Rod went to where Maria was sitting. "We'll talk about him later. How do you want to handle our exit? Make your answer quick. We're being watched."

"You're my bodyguard. Do what you do. I'm headed for the door. Make it good."

Rod nodded his head. He searched the club until he located Alex sitting near the end of the bar. He got up after Maria left, then walked toward him.

A few patrons had noticed his purposeful stride. It became very quiet when Rod reached Alex.

Alex stood to his full six-feet-five-inch height. It was obvious he would not be intimidated tonight. "Can I help you?"

"Yes, you can. Stay away from my employer, Ms. Manez. She doesn't want anything to do with you."

Alex smiled, but there was no mirth. "Sure, just tell her that when she says that to my face, I will be happy to oblige." Alex turned to Ramon. "See that he gets a drink on the house. I've got some paperwork to do in my office." Alex turned to head for his office.

Rod called to his retreating back, "This isn't over yet."

Alex turned. "I certainly hope not. Tell Ms. Manez it was good to see her again."

The testosterone was freeflowing now. They had both staked their claim. Now, it was up to Maria.

When the altercation appeared finished, Ramon slid a brightly-colored drink toward Rod. "Specialty of the house."

Rod looked at it for a split second before downing the cool liquid.

Helene was buzzing in his ear transmitter. "That was just peachy. Can we go now?"

Rod was even more annoyed now and did not reply. Instead he started walking toward the door.

Maria was standing outside the club holding a ciga-rette. Her voice was cold when she finally spoke to him. "Nice, very nice. You know what else is nice? This is a Russian cigarette. Yeah, Ivan gave it to me. He told me I was an interesting woman and he looked forward to see-ing me around." Things were not working out the way they were supposed to. "We need to go. I've had enough for one evening. We're going to have to report this breach of security to Spates immediately. This case might just be over." She barely masked her disgust.

Rod gritted his teeth. He wasn't any happier about the turn of events. As her bodyguard he hadn't done a very good job. He wasn't even aware Ivan had approached her.

They started walking. She and Rod barely spoke to each other during the rest of the evening. Back at the hotel, both went to their rooms to figure out what exactly just happened.

Hours later, Maria knew it would be a sleepless night because she was so wound up. They had been caught off guard, and that was something to be concerned about. But that wasn't what was bothering her. She punched the pillow angrily. It had been three hours since the kiss, and her mind burned with the memory of Kevin's warm lips on hers. The touch was electric, sending currents of desire throughout her body. She wanted more.

Chapter 9

When Maria and Rod arrived at the safe house the meeting was already underway—the tension in the conference room was palpable.

Helene presented the information she had gathered. There was a brief pause to allow them to sit down and begin to review the briefing material. After a few more moments, Helene continued. "There have been several inquiries into Maria Manez's background. Her credit report, arrest history, bank account, and real-estate holdings have all been tapped into. They started poking around yesterday afternoon, and they've increased significantly since last night's fiasco. We've been able to handle everything without a problem, but we need to be very careful."

Agent Spates cleared his throat. The room became silent again. When he spoke, his deep voice resonated throughout the room.

"A year ago I was involved in the witness protection program, when Kevin DePalma was transitioned to Alexandro Milbon, and we placed him here in Tennessee. After my temporary duty, I returned to head this unit, and the case with Kevin proceeded on its course. I did not inform anyone in this room about Mr. Milbon's presence because frankly no one here had a need to know. There was always that one-in-a-million chance that agents would run into him here, but that was a calculated risk. I certainly never anticipated that he would pull a stunt like he did last night with Agent Thomas. You two provided quite a spectacle for the general populace of Memphis."

Maria flushed at that last remark. No one had to tell her how it must have looked. She remembered every second.

"McCoy wants a plan of action on her desk in Baltimore in two hours. I suggest you get something to drink and prepare to dig in. We've got a lot of work to do."

There were sighs and grunts as the agents around the table began to move around. Maria sat ramrod straight in her chair. *Kevin DePalma.* Willing her mind and body to cooperate, she kept repeating *Mission first, mission first,* to herself. She looked pale, and the dark circles under her eyes revealed her restless night. She remembered the sense of kinship she felt with Kevin as he watched Tangie walk out of his life. She saw the love in his eyes, the pain as he said good-bye. It served to reinforce her desire to protect her heart at all costs. Once bitten, twice shy.

Rod studied Maria's face. He watched her war with her emotions. There was more going on with this DePalma/Milbon situation than Maria was letting on. He had been working with her for the past two years on various cases and didn't know anything about him. *Don't worry, Agent Thomas, I will find out the rest of the story,* he thought watching her.

Rod went into the kitchen to find a cup of coffee. To his surprise, Spates had also provided sandwiches and other snack foods. He filled his plate, and one for Maria. Helene saw him struggling and came to his rescue. "I've got the drinks. Go on with the plates. I'm right behind you."

Rod mumbled his thanks and walked back into the room.

Rod looked at Helene, hoping she could shed more light on the situation. He and Maria usually didn't keep secrets from each other. They had known each other way too long for game playing. "What gives?"

Helene shrugged. Her friend had not confided in her, either. "I don't know, Rod, but I smell trouble. Make sure you have her back at all times. You only need to see the results of one Mafia contract killing to get it. Those guys mean business, and they are evil about doing it. Watch my girl," she implored.

Rod blew out a long, ragged breath. "You know I will. It makes it easier when you know all the players, though." *Are the Russians the only variable?*

Helene sighed, vexed about getting caught off guard. "I know what you mean. This is why we need to know who all the players are in this game. We could have avoided the club and Alexandro Milbon altogether. Spates made the wrong call, in my opinion. I think we needed to know."

Rod agreed, but his sense of duty wouldn't allow him to complain too much. "True, but it wasn't our call to make. We get paid to follow orders. Let's get ready to go back to work. McCoy will have our heads if we don't fix this."

Ivan was on the phone with Mikha, making his first report. "It looks like something was going down between Maria and the owner of Memphis Nights. I don't know what, so I am going to check him out, too."

Mikha was concerned. Eeverything hinged on him making the deal. "Let me know what you find out," he said tersely.

"Of course. *Da svidaniya.*" Ivan knew he would have few opportunities to prove his worth in Mikha's organization. Surveillance on Maria would be tight.

Chapter 10

Spates started the meeting after the team members rejoined him in the conference room. The other agents who had a more peripheral role were drawn into the meeting as well. Any change in plans would include them, too. Agents Steven Caldwell, Chantal McCorkle, and Max Wilson wondered what their next moves would be. It seemed that this was turning into a very strange case. Then again, there was no such thing as ordinary when working with the Special Corruption Unit.

Spates tapped his pen three times on the table, saying, "There are several issues that we need to address. First off, is this case still viable, and why?"

Helene spoke first. "Sir, if I may. Last night may have made the Russians want to check into the Maria Manez story more in depth, but I don't think the fact that they are running additional checks means that they are any more suspicious." She shrugged noncommittally. "Since Thomas has already been contacted in order to complete a small deal, I think Mikha is just being extra careful. They won't find anything out of the ordinary in her background, or Agent Radford's, for that matter. We've covered all of our bases. Now it is just a matter of keeping things on schedule."

Spates turned to Agent Radford. "What do you think?"

Rod lifted his brow a fraction. His expression was mostly impassive. "I think we are still a go, sir. We just need to be sure we have all the loose ends tightened up. If we are going to stop the Russians, they need to trust us. There will be no way to stop this gun pipeline if they won't deal. Besides, it will take too long to put another mission in place. And how many deaths will that cause? I say we move on. Treat last night like an unfortunate incident, and keep things in play."

Maria wanted to wait until the facts were in before making a decision. She wanted the case to continue, but not if there was too much risk to her team. "Before I weigh in, I want to know what all of you think."

Agent McCorkle spoke up. "We've seen no appreciable change in behavior. Mikha comes into the strip club three to four times a week. Some of the girls like him. Half the time they are so stoned that they don't care what he does. There are a few, though, who are dancing to support kids, not a habit. They hate to see him coming. When they resist he gets more turned on. He knows exactly how far to take it. He pays well, and some girls are willing to live like that. It turns my stomach."

She paused for a brief moment. "I say we do whatever we can to get this sick bastard locked up. The case is still viable, in my opinion. We just have to convince the Russians that there was a good reason for last night's incident."

Agent Caldwell spoke this time. "I agree, sir. Everything indicates that the deal will be a go. The case is still a go, I think. The guns are in a dock warehouse waiting to be loaded on a truck. This is the best shot we are going to get. Let's work with it."

Maria leaned back in her chair. This was still her mission. If her team members were willing to continue even with the increased risk, she was ready, too. She turned to her senior agent. "Sir, can we speak privately?"

Helene and Roderick sighed audibly.

Spates looked around the room. The agents weren't happy about being shut out again. But he granted her request. "You've got ten minutes. My office."

Maria followed him to his private office and shut the door. He motioned for her to sit down.

"Sir, I have an idea. It is just a kernel of one, so I didn't want to present it to the group."

"Go on, agent."

"Sir, is there a way we can bring DePalma in? I know it goes against policy, but there is precedent for such an action."

"Bring him in as what?"

"Well, that's my problem . . . I'm not sure. We would have to give him some sort of cover that the Russians would believe."

There was a good reason that Spates had been made assistant director. A plan germinated in his mind almost as quickly as Maria had posed the question. He had the framework, but McCoy would have to set things in motion.

"Join the others. I am going to run something by McCoy."

Maria nodded her head before leaving. The chain of command had to be followed on this one.

Thirty minutes passed before Spates rejoined the group, papers in hand. They anxiously awaited his decision. "All right, McCoy and I have considered several different scenarios. I want to thank each of you for your input. It made the decision to continue somewhat easier."

He disseminated copies of the new material to each agent. Maria's jaw dropped open when she read the new mission profile. Without thinking she blurted out. "You've got to be kidding me."

Spates spoke in a tone that brooked no resistance. "No, agent, I am not. This is the best way to keep the heat off the case. Now let's figure out how to bring him in."

Rod quickly read through the material. "Aw damn!"

An hour later Rod and Maria were back in their bureau car driving back to the hotel. They had a meeting to get ready for. The silence in the vehicle was deafening. Both needed time to work out their feelings.

As soon as she parked the vehicle, Rod jumped out. "I'm going to the gym. I'll catch up with you in a couple of hours."

Numbly Maria replied, "Yeah, see you." Her shoulders were slightly slumped when she entered the lobby. How in the world was she going to do this?

"Maria?"

She had a visitor waiting for her.

"I just wanted to say that I'm sorry about last night." Alex offered her a dozen red roses.

She froze for half a second. "How dare you show up here? I don't want your apologies or your flowers."

"There's no need to make a scene. Just give me five minutes to explain. That's all I'm asking for."

He moved toward her. Maria's breathing became shallow. He overloaded her senses. Again.

She couldn't be this close to him. She had to get away. She turned but Alex reached out to her. His touch seared her skin. There was no space, there was no time, and there was no air. Somehow his lips found hers. His tongue mated with hers, bringing forth soft moans from her throat. Passion electrified the air. He wrapped his long arms around her body and let his large hands stroke her back as he took her in. He kissed her to her very soul.

When he finally let her go, she reached back to slap him. He smiled and caught her hand in a single, swift motion. Passion ignited his eyes, making them appear sexier, sultrier. Maria was mesmerized. She wanted more . . .

He gently kissed the palm of the hand that sought to strike him.

"Your one chance to ever do that happened last night. You are going to only stroke me with these hands from now on."

His words were spoken softly, meant for her ears only. Maria flushed, a deep red coloring her almond skin.

He brought his face close to hers again, but this time he whispered in her ear. "We need to go to your room. I have my orders."

Maria's lips quivered in anticipation, but there was no kiss. She was jolted back to reality. They were standing in the middle of the hotel lobby. The bouquet was on the floor.

"Follow me," she managed after a few calming breaths.

Anywhere, he thought.

When they reached her room, Maria spun around to face him. "You want to tell me what you're doing?" she asked angrily.

Alex reached into the briefcase she didn't know he'd held. "I received this by messenger an hour ago. After reading it, I knew I had to come to talk to you."

Maria recognized the envelope and knew the contents immediately.

She nodded toward the suite's sitting area. She took off her designer pumps and sat down heavily on one of the couches. A headache was threatening to erupt behind her eyes. Alex sat opposite her.

"Okay. What does it say?"

Alex looked around the room before asking, "Is it safe to talk?"

"The room is swept by our people at all hours of the day. Talk."

Alex took a deep breath. "I've been informed that my actions with you last night, though quite enjoyable, may have caused a series of chain reactions that now jeopardize your case. And my life. I was told to cooperate in the manner set forth in that envelope, or take my chances with the Russian Mafia. Of course, it was a no-brainer. I'll take the Mafia."

Maria smiled. He had spunk. She had to give that to him.

Alex liked her smile. "That's better." He paused. "I'm sorry about interfering in your business. I'll do whatever you need me to do. Remember, I owe you my life. That means I am in your debt until I can repay the favor."

Maria sighed. She needed to ask this question, but she was almost afraid of the answer.

"Why do you keep doing *that?*"

"Keep doing what, Maria?"

"You know damn well what."

Alex moved toward her. She jumped off the couch. "Don't even think about it! Just answer the question."

He continued toward her. "The first time it was just happenstance. In the lobby it was opportunistic. Now I can't get enough of you."

Maria made a weak effort to push him away before she was swept into another soul-stirring kiss. He held her close as her knees buckled. Maria moaned as he continued his delicious assault on her senses.

* * *

Rod knocked softly on Maria's door, intent on calling a truce with her. He had no right to be angry with her; they were both there to work a case. He entered quietly when he didn't hear a response. He heard her moans before he saw Maria and Alex. The sight of Maria being so thoroughly kissed by Alex and enjoying it made his blood boil. The hour he had spent thinking and working out was all for naught; he was just as upset and tense now as before. He backed out the same way he came in, then went to the hotel lobby for a drink.

Ivan boldly approached Rod and sat next to him at the bar. He had seen Maria and Alex earlier in the lobby. "Not having such a good day, huh? Cheer up. There are plenty of other women. I know a good club I could take you to. The women there will do anything. Cigarette?"

Rod looked at him coldly. "I suppose there is a point to your being here. If you have a message, deliver it and be on your way."

"Testy, testy, as you Americans say. Yes, Mikha is satisfied with the arrangements. Be at this place tomorrow at 10:00 P.M. From now on, you communicate with him through me. Don't worry about finding me, I'll always know how to contact you." He turned to the bartender. "That one's on me."

Agent Radford took the paper, read it, then nodded his head in agreement.

"Let me know if you change your mind about the club. No man should look like that over a woman." Ivan smiled, showing a mouth full of crooked teeth. He lit another cigarette and walked away.

Helene had been monitoring the situation since Ivan entered the hotel. "I know you couldn't have planned that meeting, but I think you just helped the case out tremendously. I think Spates came up with a good plan, albeit a crazy one. Rod, friend to friend, I know you've always liked Maria, but I think you are going to have to back away from this one until this is done. I'm not sure she isn't in over her head, and as friends and fellow agents, we need to be there for her."

Rod had come to the same conclusion. He had come down to the bar to nurse his wounds, oblivious to anything else that was going on around him. If he had been on his game he would have noticed that Ivan was in the lobby. Emotion prevented him from being more observant. And that was too costly a mistake to make. "Yeah, you're right. Meet me in an hour," he said into his pin-sized microphone. "I want to talk to you. Figure out a safe place and let me know."

Helene responded immediately. "Mud Island, Civil War exhibit."

"Copy that. See you soon."

Rod left the hotel bar to head toward the meeting spot. He would have to lose Ivan, or at least make sure Ivan was unaware of his actions. Mud Island was the perfect place to get lost in the crowd. Ivan would have a difficult time keeping up with them. Besides, it didn't matter if he saw them together. Helene would just be a woman Rod met while taking in the exhibits at the museum.

Rod was looking forward to his chat with Helene. She could be a handful, but she was objective. Rod knew he needed a new perspective on the case. He had to find a way to keep his focus.

As he drove along the picturesque streets of Memphis,

the view from the car windows was beautiful. It was a lovely city, and by and large he was enjoying his time. He knew that he needed to talk to Maria about the case, but he wasn't ready to deal with her yet, especially if Alex Milbon was still in her room. He would talk things over with Helene first; talking to Maria this evening was soon enough. Tension knotted the muscles in his shoulders and neck.

He found a parking space, then headed toward the museum, where he paid for admission and the monorail fee. Some of the tension abated as he looked around the park. Seeing the riverboats had a calming effect on him. When he thought about the power of the river, the rich history surrounding him, it made him feel humble.

Rod had to be realistic. Why was he feeling hurt and angry? Had Maria ever given him the idea that they would one day be a couple? No.

Helene saw him before he saw her. She noticed that he looked to be deep in thought. She wanted to walk up to him and kiss him like Alex had done to Maria. She wanted to say, "Big dummy, you two are so wrong for each other. When are you going to see that?" But she couldn't. Rod had made his choice, and she didn't stand a chance with him.

Helene walked past him pretending to be thinking about one of the military exhibits. She studied the medals on one of the Confederate uniforms.

Rod smelled her perfume before he saw her. He looked around to see if they were being followed. Satisfied, he thought about his approach. He stood behind her as if to study the same exhibit. He leaned forward and whispered something for her ears only. Helene laughed.

She turned around and he introduced himself to her.

He shook her extended hand and they chitchatted about the uniforms and the Civil War in general. He invited her for a cup of coffee. She pretended to hesitate for a moment before agreeing.

They strolled along River Walk until they reached the Gulf Port Café. It was early yet, and there were plenty of seats.

Ordering coffee and dessert, they sat down in an out-of-the-way area by a window. Helene turned on a dampener, one of her many technogadgets, which would interfere with any attempts to record their conversation. She signaled to him when they could speak freely. He made sure to always have a coffee cup up toward his lips before he spoke. They wouldn't take any chances with lip-readers either.

Rod blew out a long, exasperated breath. "I don't know what's gotten into me. I almost blew it earlier today."

"You're human. Don't beat yourself up about it. I was never more than twenty feet away. I had your back. If Ivan had tried something we would have been on it." Helene hesitated. "Be honest with me, though. You and Maria have been playing this cat-and-mouse game for two years. How do you really feel? No bull."

Rod shook his head. He was still trying to figure that one out. "She's gorgeous and fun to be with, but we've never been more than friends to each other. You know that. You're her closest friend. I tried a couple of times, but she wasn't having any of it. Now here comes this Kevin guy from a case that I didn't work on with her, and the earth has suddenly tipped off its axis. I don't know if I should be happy or pissed as hell. "

Helene laughed. She was still smiling when she answered him. There was still the possibility that they were being watched.

"Well, buddy, you've only got a couple of choices here. You know how important this assignment is. The profile calls for them to date each other, and since you are the bodyguard, while you don't have to like it, you do have to deal with it. You can start to develop other interests, or you can mope. Maria cares about you, and I know she is not purposefully trying to hurt you. If I hadn't seen it with my own eyes, I wouldn't have believed that she could act that way with a man. We both know she has been closed off over the last couple of years—no dates, no emotional entanglements. Maybe this moment is about her."

Rod stared down at his cup of coffee. He liked it black and strong. "I just thought one day, who knows when, it would be with me."

It was Helene's turn to sigh. "I know what you mean. Well, Rod, this is fourth down. It may be time to back up and punt. Sometimes you just can't get it done, and the other team gets the ball."

"Oh, Helene, I love it when you talk football to me," he said facetiously.

"Well, what can I say, I am a woman with many talents. Are you going to be okay? I don't know if our talk has helped you any."

"Yep, I'm a Radford. We always land on our feet. Even after we punt." He reached for her hand. He felt it tremble ever so slightly under the pressure of his touch. "Thanks for being such a good friend."

Chapter 11

Alex sat in front of his bay window watching the water on the lake. If you asked him what color the water was, he would have no idea. He was deep in thought about one Agent Maria Thomas until he heard a knock at the door. He was surprised to see who had come to visit.

"Hey, Max, what's up?"

Max smiled. "Change in plans. The only thing you can count on in this job is that things will always change. I was at HQ when they told me about the predicament you found yourself in. Seems you will be joining our little gang for awhile."

"Have a seat." Alex motioned for Max to join him in the living room. "News travels fast. I didn't know you were working this case, too. Can you elaborate without having to take out your weapon?"

"I can tell you a little. Need-to-know information only. First off, do you have any questions about what the Bureau is asking you to do? You know you can always refuse."

Alex snorted, "Yeah, right, and just take my chances. No, thank you, I'll stick with the devil I know."

"Alex, believe me, this thing was approached from several different angles. Each scenario was dissected and put back together again by our analysts. The bottom line is, if we are to retain the covers that have been put in place and continue with the mission, we need to make sure that we don't give the Russians anything to be concerned about. Your part in this is just to keep up appearances with Maria. I'm sure you've read the dossier."

Max noticed the open folder sitting on the kitchen table.

"We just added a few nuances to your identity. There should be no way to connect you to your former life. We've established that you and Maria knew each other a long time ago. You walked out on her and now you want her back." Max leaned in for emphasis. "Alex, please be clear on this. We do not want you in any way to try to perform the duties of an agent. Your sole purpose is to give credence to the cover of Maria Manez. I hear, by the way, that you are becoming quite adept at kissing her."

Alex wasn't about to have a locker-room conversation about Maria. He stood up and walked toward the patio. He counted to ten before responding. In all fairness, Max had no idea how he felt about Maria. *Hell, I don't even know,* he thought. Alex sat down again. He rotated his neck and shoulders trying to work out the kinks. "I apologize. You have my full attention."

"Yeah well, you've got mine too. You need to know that you are going to be followed and your actions monitored by the targets. Inquiries are being made as we speak." Max held up his hand in reassurance. "Nothing we can't handle, but you need to know the depth of Agent Thomas's cover. She and her bodyguard, whom you've also met, are here to make a major purchase from Russian gun dealers. We are dealing with some pretty small quantities now, but the goal of this case is to get to the big deal so that we can shut them down.

"Trust with the Russians is shaky at best. They don't

even trust each other. This case has been long, difficult, and deadly. It is also Thomas's biggest case as team leader."

Max wondered how Alex would feel about the next part of what he had to say.

"Failure for Thomas right now isn't just about completing the mission. Failure could mean death. Other operations like this have ended horribly. I am authorized to show you the pictures, but I'd rather not, to tell you the truth."

Alex leaned back into the couch. He closed his eyes. The last thing he wanted to consider was Maria getting hurt, or worse.

"Max, what is it that you aren't telling me?"

"I'm telling you everything, man. I just need to be sure that you are hearing me." Max sighed heavily. "You and Maria are going to be a couple for the sake of her cover. You need to be mindful that not only are you going to be watched by us, but also by the Russians. We need you to look at this like it's a job. We are not looking for emotional attachment here. That will just complicate the case. We just need you to be around. Be seen with her; you know, all that romantic junk that women like. Hold hands in public, take long walks in the park, laugh at each other's stupid jokes and appear intimate when necessary. Follow her lead. She'll know when you two need to perform. Bottom line, pretend to be in love, but don't go there. You could get yourselves killed if they suspect something is not on the up-and-up with this deal and neither one of you picks up on that fact."

Max regarded him curiously. "Alex, am I too late in my warning about emotional entanglements?"

Alex jumped up to get a beer. With his back turned to Max, he swallowed thickly. He returned to the living area

holding the bottle. "Max you're right. I have been playing with fire. I won't do anything more to jeopardize the
case. The Bureau will have my full cooperation."

Max blew out a sigh of relief. "Thank you, Alex. It is always a sacrifice when you put your life on hold to go
undercover, as it were, but know that we appreciate this.
Getting these guns off the streets is of the utmost im-
portance."

Alex needed to hit something. It had been two hours
since Max left. It had been four hours since he'd held
Maria in his arms. He kept thinking what magical act
would stop him from claiming Maria as his own. He
knew from the first kiss that he wanted her. Wanted her
beyond reason. The second kiss confirmed his suspicions, and the third kiss in her hotel room let him know
beyond doubt that it was more than physical attraction.
He *felt* Maria, felt her spirit, felt her essence. How could
he walk away from that?

He was too restless to stay inside. He hadn't planned
on going to the club, but maybe it would serve to take
his mind off things. First though, he needed to work out.
He had to burn off some steam or he would lose it.

After thirty minutes on the bike, he started to feel
what he wanted. A little later he was lucky enough to be
able to join a pick-up game of basketball. He played ball
for another half hour. His legs weren't what they used to
be, but he was still able to show the young bucks something. He hit the shower to rinse away some of the funk
before he headed for the sauna.

Afterward, he dressed for the club and went to work.
It was well after 10:00 P.M. when Alex arrived. He was
clean shaven, dressed to the nines, and ready. He would

be discreet, of course, but he figured tonight was his last night to be plain old Alex Milbon for awhile. He would treat tonight like it was his bachelor party—only there was no bride.

Alex swaggered around the club, meeting and greeting the guests. He paid special attention to the ones he found attractive. He smiled, shook hands, and even danced with a couple of beautiful long-legged women, women who reminded him of Maria.

Maybe his idea was harebrained, maybe juvenile, maybe downright stupid, but he had to find some way to deal. He paid special attention to one young woman who was particularly stunning. "My name is Alex Milbon. Thank you for coming to my club. Are you having a good time?"

"Better now. You've done a nice job with this place. I like the use of color," she responded.

"You sound like you're into decorating."

She extended her hand to shake his. "My name is Joyce Ferrazi. I have a design firm downtown. We specialize in commercial interior designs."

"Yes, well, I'd love to see your work."

"Mr. Milbon, are you flirting with me?"

"Only if it's working. Would you care to dance?"

Joyce smiled at him. "Thought you would never ask."

He led her to the dance floor to dance to a slow, seductive jazz tune. She clung to him closer than he'd expected, and his body reacted to her nearness. He inhaled the fragrance of her perfume, intoxicated by the heady aroma.

Alex gave her a slow, gentle kiss and then excused himself. Taking another woman to his bed would not excise Maria from his system. He could sleep with a dozen women, but it wouldn't change the way he felt about her. He wanted Maria, but he wouldn't compromise her.

He left the club after saying goodnight to his employees and seeing to a few more guests. He thanked Joyce again for the dance and promised her referrals for her business.

Ramon stopped him before he walked out the door. In Spanish he told him. "Oh, Alexandro, I think you've done it now. Maria walked in looking for you while you were on the dance floor. She left as soon as she saw you. The lady didn't look too happy."

Alex nodded. "Gracias. Hasta mañana."

Chapter 12

Helene did not like the way things were progressing. *I've got to pull this rag-tag bunch together,* she thought. It was nearly 1:00 A.M. when she knocked on Maria's door, but she knew her friend was still awake.

"Come in, Helle," Maria said, without bothering to get up.

Helene used her key to open the door and walked in. She took one look at Maria, and her gut tightened.

"Okay, that's it. Put your guns away and scoop me out some of that ice cream. I'm going to get Rod. We are going to talk!"

Helene was so distressed about the way things were going she barged in on Rod without knocking. She was so concerned about her friend's mental state that it didn't occur to her that he might be busy. She gulped when she opened the door. Embarrassment flushed her face, she turned away quickly, but not before she got an eyeful of Roderick Radford in all of his glory.

"Helene, get out of my room," he barked.

Embarrassment did not dim her desire for every café au lait–colored, hazel-eyed inch of the man. Especially the area her eyes had just feasted on. The man was ten-plus inches of pure heaven. "I'm leaving," she roared back. "I need you, no, Maria needs you. Put some clothes on and come over."

Rod was angry, humiliated, and naked. "Just give me two minutes," he practically whispered.

Helene ventured one more look, licked her suddenly dry lips, and walked out of the room.

She stood in the archway between the two rooms. Desire coursed through her, threatening to tear her apart. The fire started deep in her core, and it was all she could do not to turn back around to Rod's room and show him what she could do. He could have her whole body if he'd simply ask.

Maria gave her a questioning look when she walked back into her room. Her friend's behavior was puzzling, but she was dealing with her own issues.

When Rod joined them wearing only pajama pants, Helene gave him an angry glare, which he ignored. She tried to settle her nerves by concentrating on the coolness of the ice cream. When she dropped a tiny bit on her thigh, Rod nearly lost his composure. He clenched and unclenched his fists. *Next assignment—I'm working with men.* When he could speak again, his voice sounded dry and hoarse. "Please pass the ice cream."

Maria looked from Helene to Roderick and then back again. *And I thought I had problems.*

She started slowly. "Helene, it is almost 2:00 A.M. and before you barged in on us we were having a perfectly good time by ourselves. So, your point is?"

Helene stole a furtive glance at Rod. He was studying his cookies and cream with great concentration all of a sudden.

Helene blew out a long and ragged breath. "Okay, I need to put this on the table. I am feeling like we are in grave danger of blowing this case. Blame it on the heat, blame it on the Memphis water, I don't care, but people, we have a problem. We are supposed to be the elite, the incomparable, right now, I feel like we are auditioning for P.T. Barnum." Helene pointed to Maria. "This one over here is cleaning her guns at 1:00 A.M. Rod is—"

"We get the point. We need to focus," he interrupted quickly.

"Rod over here is acting like anything but a bodyguard for a well-known gun runner, I was about to say before I was interrupted." Helene glared at him. "And I feel like I don't know who's on first. Okay, I admit it. I want to get back to D.C. so that I too can have a life, but we've got a job to do here. "

Helene continued. She was emphatic about doing whatever it took to get back on track. "Can we agree on that? I need to know that we are all on the same page here. Normally, I'd follow you guys to the ends of the earth, but not right now."

Maria was the one angry now. "I agree that I haven't been on top of my game, but I am still team leader and I'm still calling the shots. You don't need to worry about me anymore. I had my moment, but I'm cool now. This thing with Alex is just business. This case is my job. I'm cool, I got it."

"Helene, just do what you do," Rod said. "No more slip-ups from our end, and no more pep talks. We've got eighteen hours until mission time. Now, if we could finally get some rest. I'm beat, ladies."

Chapter 13

Ivan looked at the clock before he went to open the door. It was 4:00 A.M. *Mikha! Didn't that man ever sleep?* Mikha walked into Ivan's apartment as if he were visiting a friend at noon instead of in the wee hours of the morning. "Good morning. Tell me what you know about our American friends."

Ivan was angry, but Mikha paid well, and maybe if he stuck with him he would live to see forty. He scratched his head and walked toward the kitchen. He may as well get ready to make his report. Mikha wouldn't stop questioning him until he got all the answers he wanted.

Ivan grabbed a beer for Mikha and coffee and vodka for himself.

While the coffee was cooling, he found the files he'd organized. He put them in chronological order and prepared to make his presentation for Mikha.

They both sat at the small kitchen table. Mikha looked around Ivan's place. It was dark and cavelike. The man lived like a hermit, which was just as well because he was never home. Mikha drank his beer. He would save drinking vodka for when the deal was complete.

Ivan rubbed his tired shoulders, took a sip of coffee, and started talking. "Everything checks out so far. Word on the street is that Maria Manez is one tough *gaspazha*.

I've checked into some of her other deals; they all check out. She appears to be just another American out for the dollar. She likes to go first class. Her condo in Baltimore faces the Inner Harbor; rent is in the high four digits. Nice cars and good connections. She supplies most of the gangs. They don't mess with her, though. There's enough going on in Baltimore, with the drugs and prostitution and illegal gambling. I think she needs this deal, needs your connections, to gain a monopoly. She's ambitious."

Ivan cracked his neck before he continued. He was tired, but he would make the best of this. "She and her bodyguard are always together. She knows how to handle herself, though. I've watched her take on two guys with no problem. She was at this new club and apparently ran into what the Americans call a blast from the past. His name is Alexandro Milbon, the club owner. They had an altercation, but they seem to be working it out. The bodyguard wasn't happy. He seems to have the hots for her. It's a regular soap opera, but Manez is about business, from what her record says about her."

Mikha was silent, soaking up every word. He looked through the pictures that Ivan had taken. He was a little disturbed by the club owner, because his gut always told him to distrust what was new and unfamiliar.

"Tell me about *gaspadin* Milbon."

"He has been in Memphis less than a year. He bought this club, opened it for a few months, and then closed it down again to remodel. It is very Miami, like some of the places we've been together." Ivan gave him that crooked-tooth smile.

Ivan continued after not getting a response from his attempt at levity. "Far as I've been able to dig up, he speaks English and Spanish, spent a lot of time in Puerto

Rico. I am still tracing his family tree. Nothing sticks out. I think maybe he wanted Maria to go legit, but she likes what she does. He's never ventured too far from anything that wasn't straight. He's always owned clubs or restaurants. He doesn't go for drugs, whores, or gambling in his establishments. I think Maria is about as wild as he has ever gotten. From this photo, it looks like he wants her back."

Mikha's voice was hard. "Excellent. Now tell me how come you didn't know how long she had been in Memphis. You made me look bad."

Ivan was visibly nervous. "I was trying to deal with that situation in Texas. I got back here late trying to track down how we lost that shipment. It won't happen again . . . either situation.

Mikha's eyes narrowed. "*Da,* see that it doesn't. I'm going to get some rest. We deal at 8 P.M. I'll pick you up at six to get the guns. Get some rest now, I need you to be ready later on. *Da svidaniya.*"

"*Da svidaniya.*"

Chapter 14

"All right, people, this is the moment we've been waiting for. We've got three hours until deal time. Understand this is not the big deal, but if all goes well, we just might get there." Spates couldn't hide his excitement. Over twenty years in the business, and he still got excited with every case.

"Remember, we do this as planned. No Lone Rangers on this one. Everybody just stay on point. If something begins to look hairy it is and it will be Agent Thomas's decision to abort unless she becomes incapacitated. Helene will be listening and monitoring everything that's said. I'll keep command in Baltimore in the loop. You, each and every one of you, has done a fantastic job to this point. Let's get this deal done and finish it. I'll see you back here later for the debriefing. Be careful out there, and watch each other's backs."

Rod and Maria rode in their Bureau SUV back to the hotel. Helene followed in her specially-modified surveillance van. The meeting would take place in the warehouse district. Helene would arrive prior to the meeting to scout out the proper location to monitor the deal. She would alert Rod and Maria if anything appeared out of the ordinary. Her cameras and microphones were the latest in technology and would be impossible for Mikha's people to detect.

Ivan, Goran, and Mikha arrived at the warehouse at 6:30 P.M. They controlled a large portion of the storage area and they knew everything that was going on. They felt pretty safe conducting the deal relatively early in the evening. Mikha could taste success, and the flavor was addictive. He was psyched. This could be the beginning of his new life. Fear and narrow-mindedness would not dim his bright outlook of the future.

He greeted Goran and Ivan cheerily. They sat in his makeshift office. He pulled out three shot glasses and a bottle of vodka from a cabinet. After he poured he made a toast. *"Da dna."*

The three clanked glasses and then downed their drinks. When they were finished, the pallets were almost completely loaded.

Mikha said, "Comrades, now we count."

Maria stood in front of the mirror much longer than necessary. It wasn't vanity. She was willing the nervous jitters away. She had tried breathing exercises, counting to ten, imagining funny scenarios, but nothing had helped. She was scared. So many things could go wrong. She could let her team down and someone could get hurt. Negative thoughts swirled through her head, destroying her self-confidence. It had been awhile, but she bowed her head to pray. When she was finished, she gave thanks. She was ready.

Maria knocked on Rod's door to let him know that it was time to go.

When he saw her he spoke in Russian. "*Ga tova?*"

"As I'll ever be. Helene, t-minus thirty minutes."

"Roger that. We're here and ready to go. Agent Caldwell is in position. They just finished counting the guns. Everything is in order; he has ten thousand instead of the six that you agreed on earlier. Play around with him, but then pay him for the extras. He is trying to impress you and also find out if you have the money to handle it."

"Roger that, out."

The drive to the docks was short. They found the loading area that they had been directed to and began walking toward Mikha's office.

Before they were let in, Ivan greeted them at the doorway. Maria initiated the conversation in Russian.

"*Zdrastvuytye Vanya.*"

Ivan was pleased. "Good evening, Ms. Manez. You speak Russian well. Smart woman."

"*SpaSiba, Mikha gdye?*"

Ivan spoke as he frisked them both. Rod was silent during the interaction and simply glared at Ivan. Satisfied, Ivan let them come in.

He spoke to Rod when he passed by him. "What's the matter? You don't speak Russian?"

Rod smirked at him. "Only the important words like *astaf'tye minya f pakoye!*"

Ivan laughed. "Touchy . . . touchy." He deferred to Maria again. "Right this way. He and Goran are ready for you."

Maria nodded her head and followed him.

Goran and Mikha were involved in conversation when Maria and Radford entered the small space of the office. They stood up immediately and walked toward her. Mikha looked at Ivan, who gave him the signal that everything was all right. He greeted them enthusiastically now that he knew he wouldn't have to kill them. Introductions were made to Goran, and they sat down to business.

"Maria Manez, what an interesting line of work for a woman to be in, huh?"

Maria looked at him plainly. "It pays the bills." She looked at her watch. It was a delicate gesture made without impatience, but she got her point across. This was not a social call.

Mikha smiled. He admired her grit. "It must be your lucky day. It just so happens that I was able to secure more guns on short notice. Would you be interested in four thousand more product?"

Maria showed just the right amount of enthusiasm. "Of course, we are always interested in more. The demand always outweighs the supply." Maria crossed and uncrossed her legs. She gave Ivan, Mikha, and Goran a generous peek of her long legs.

Agent Radford stood in the corner watching. He smiled at her obvious play to control things.

She looked directly at Mikha. "What's your price?"

Mikha lit a cigarette. "I see this as an opportunity for all of us. We can begin to expand in the ways that we see fit for our individual operations. As a measure of good faith I am willing to make a slight reduction in the price. Of course, the more we deal in higher quantities, the more of a savings I can make for you."

Maria looked slightly impatient. "*Spasiba Mikha* . . . How much?"

"*Sto,*" he replied tersely.

Helene said into her earpiece, "Do that thing with your legs again. He is trying to play you. There's no way we are paying $100 per gun."

Maria shifted in her seat. Her short skirt rose up sinfully on her hip.

Mikha took a nice, long look before he spoke again. He cleared his throat. "Perhaps ninety dollars per gun?"

Maria spoke again, this time her tone wasn't friendly or delicate. "*Yirunda!*" She moved to stand up. Rod moved in closer. He appeared ready to do battle.

Mikha was concerned. He didn't want to lose the deal, but he also didn't want to give in too easily. "Maria, I've always said Americans are too impatient. Sit down, I'm sure we can come to some sort of understanding." He waved his hands dismissively at Rod. He was letting them know that there was no reason for concern.

Helene spoke to Maria again. "Wait about ten seconds. Let him think about his actions for a minute. I can tell he is anxious. He needs this deal much more than he is letting on."

Maria was abrupt. "Let me see the guns."

"Certainly, right this way. We've taken the liberty of loading them on this truck for you. Feel free to count them." He gave her his best solicitous smile. Maria tried to hide her revulsion. These were the guns that were killing kids all over America. She and Rod made a show of inspecting the weapons, taking apart and reassembling several different ones.

Maria said, "I'll take them. It's seventy-five apiece or I walk. I didn't get this far by being stupid. So, if you don't mind, I have a date tonight. Do we deal, or do I simply go dancing? You make the call."

Mikha looked at her hard and steady. She wasn't a pushover. He had to hand it to her. "We've got a deal. Shall we toast?"

Maria smiled, putting her hand up. "Yes, but just one.

I haven't quite developed the stomach for authentic Russian vodka, I'm afraid."

The three men laughed in delight. Maria Manez wasn't so bad after all. Mikha thought he would enjoy dealing with her in the future.

After the toast, the guns were reloaded into a truck that Maria signaled for, and the deal was complete. Rod unlocked the SUV to get the money and returned to the warehouse to produce the eighty thousand dollars for the deal.

Rod drove the truck back to the command center. The Russians could assume Maria's uncle was assisting her. Once the deal was completed, Helene moved on her way, too.

The debriefing would be held as soon as everyone arrived. Maria would head to Memphis Nights and then to the safe house once she knew she was no longer being followed. Mikha, Goran, and Ivan took the money and locked it in the safe. They were headed toward Beale Street, just as Maria was, presumably to go to Goran's club. She made sure that they saw her enter the club and then signaled Rod and Helene that she was there.

Everything worked like clockwork. Once the negotiations were complete, the work was done. Now the team had to prepare for the big deal.

Chapter 15

Alex had been holed up in his office most of the evening. He hadn't heard from Maria or from anyone else at the Bureau, and that was making him nervous. It took just about all of his resolve not to call Max.

His breath quickened. *She's here.* He didn't know how he knew, but he did. He quickly cleared the mess that was on his desk and went out to find her.

Maria was sitting at the bar toying with her glass. She was staring at the green liquid lost in her own world. He noticed that she was drinking a Sour Apple. He smiled. *Of course, what else would she drink?* They were connected in so many ways. He studied her as he got closer.

Something about the way she looked made his gut tighten. He sensed something was not quite right with her and he was glad that she had come to the club. He willed his body to go slowly. He didn't want to appear too anxious. When he finally reached her, his resolve failed.

She looked at him but was silent. Her body, her traitorous body, screamed for his touch. Maria didn't trust herself to speak when he was this close.

He stroked the side of her face. She gently nuzzled his palm.

He guided her off the barstool and led her to his office. He shut the door immediately and pulled her to him. He wanted to ravish her mouth, but he didn't. He'd promised Max, but that didn't stop him from holding her close. Her body trembled next to his. Alex had noticed that drawn look in her eyes. She was tense, and her body felt tight and anxious.

The evening had gone well by all accounts, but it had tested her. And now she was here with Alex. All Maria wanted was him, but that was not to be, either. Her time with him was borrowed. It wasn't real, so her heart and her body may as well stop craving him.

He spoke to her softly in Spanish. "It's all right now. You're safe. Stay with me as long as you can."

More tender words had never been spoken to her. She melted into his embrace. She inhaled his cologne and was intoxicated by the masculine scent. She forgot about the other night when she had seen another woman in his arms. For right now, in this moment, he was hers. Maria felt like she was home for the first time in her life.

Chapter 16

Maria arrived at the safe house a couple of hours later. She was emotionally drained, but pleased that things had gone well with Mikha.

When she walked into the conference room she was treated to a rousing round of applause led by Helene. She found herself buoyed by their enthusiasm.

"That was good work, gang," Spates told them. "McCoy sends her congratulations." He turned to Maria, teasing her. "Maria Manez knows how to negotiate." The team was in a good mood and feeling confident about the next phase of the case. Agents who had been in more peripheral roles also joined in the celebration: Chantal, who worked at Goran's strip club; Max, who was working with Alex; and Steven, who was assigned to the docks. It had taken everyone to make this moment a success.

Spates paused to let them celebrate before getting down to business again. "A team will be arriving tomorrow to catalog and store the guns. I appreciate the hard work in getting this far. So now comes the good part. It will probably take a few months for Mikha to figure out his next steps. We assume he will meet with Nikola again to set up an even more lucrative deal. I think he felt comfortable handling the small deal, but a larger shipment will require more manpower and much tighter security. Even though this last deal was successful, this is the time to stick to cover even more. Agent Thomas, you need to head back to Baltimore for a few weeks. It wouldn't look too good for you to make a deal and then hang around the city. You have your other business interests to concern yourself with, and Mikha knows that. He will be watching and listening, of that you can be sure."

It was nearly 2:00 A.M. and everyone was exhausted. Spates knew he couldn't ask them to absorb too much more information, so he prepared to close the meeting. "Okay, I think we can wrap it up for tonight. Everyone report in day after tomorrow at zero eight." A collective sigh of gratitude went up around the table.

"Everyone is dismissed. Thomas, I just need about five minutes with you."

She figured as much. "Sure thing," she responded.

Spates waited until she sat down. "How are you feeling? You look a little more than just tired."

She smiled; he had known her way too long for her to pull anything over on him. "You're right as usual, but I need to work it out on my own. I'll be fine. I always am. Thanks for caring—"

"You got it. You were the first female ever selected for the SCU—I made the nomination myself. You'll always have a special place in my heart. Doesn't mean you can run all over me, though."

Maria chuckled. "Like that could happen. Good night, sir. Thanks for everything; I'll make my arrangements to go back to Baltimore in the morning."

"Good enough, I wouldn't plan to be there longer than a couple of weeks. You still need to be visible here in Memphis."

What he didn't say was that she needed to maintain her cover with Alex. That fact was implied, but he didn't want to rub salt in the wound. Max had shared his concerns with him. Spates wanted to make sure that the two of them weren't in over their heads.

Alex looked at the clock. It was nearly 3:00 A.M., but he hadn't been able to sleep soundly. It took him a minute to understand the noise that he was hearing in his semiconscious state. The knock on his door was soft but insistent. He threw his robe on to answer it.

"Don't say anything. Just hold me. I don't want to think about whether or not this is a mistake. Just hold me."

"Come here, Maria, " he said softly.

He had done what he had promised. Maria awoke cradled in his arms, where she had spent the better part of six hours. She had been so exhausted when she'd arrived that he led her to the bedroom and tucked her in. She took off her clothes and he gave her one of his T-shirts to sleep in. They were both too physically and emotionally tired for words. After a few minutes, Alex heard her rhythmic breathing in the silence that echoed throughout his room. It was strange but comforting. No other woman had shared his bed while he had been in Memphis, yet her presence seemed natural.

It was past 9:00 A.M. when Maria finally opened her eyes. When she did she was treated to the delicious sight of Alex's muscled brown chest. She smiled before she kissed the smooth skin. Alex pulled her close, kissing the unruly curls that capped her head.

His arousal was evident through his lightweight pajama pants. Maria noticed again how wonderfully masculine he smelled. His long, strong body seemed to dwarf hers. She noticed for the first time too, how huge the bed was that they were lying in. *Must be a custom fit,* she mused. She imagined that a lot of things had to be customized to fit his large 6'5" frame.

Now, however, she was wide-awake and faced with a tremendous decision. When she looked up at him she saw the desire that flamed his eyes, the same fire that matched her own feelings.

Alex told her. "Don't start what you can't finish, I've been tempted enough already just having you here in my bed." His voice was husky and raw. "I want you too much to play games. But I think we both know that this is not the right time. There's too much at stake here."

Maria rolled over on her back and looked up at the ceiling. She knew he was right, but all she wanted right now was for him to quell the desire that threatened to consume her.

She closed her eyes to conceal the hurt that shone bright. She wanted him too, but the difference was she was willing to throw caution to the wind. Just for one day.

Hadn't she done enough in the service of her country? All she wanted was a little piece of happiness.

Alex studied her face. He loved her skin, her complexion a beautiful and flawless almond brown. He traced her lips with the pad of his thumb.

You can't do that and reject me too! Maria jerked her head away from his touch.

"Maria, don't shut me out. Talk to me. I'm just trying to do what's right. It's damn near killing me, but I'm trying."

Maria whispered, "I know, but it doesn't stop the pain."

If he stayed this close much longer he would break his promises to himself and to the Bureau. He decided that he needed to take matters into his own hands. He wasn't a monk.

"Come on, let's reduce this temptation. How about I make you breakfast? I'm a pretty mean omelet maker."

"Thanks, but I need to get back to the hotel. I have to go back to Baltimore for awhile . . ."

Alex sat up in the bed. The thought of her leaving disturbed him. "How long will you be gone?"

Maria sighed. "I don't know, maybe a week, maybe two. I just have to meet with the Baltimore folks and make sure everything goes okay with the log-in and disposal." She shrugged; there was no use in crying over spilled milk. They needed to move on with this.

"I'll take you up on breakfast if you throw in some bacon or sausage. I'm a down-home girl, you know. We need meat in our lives."

"You got it. Come on sleepyhead, half the day is gone. Let's get out of this bed."

"So tell me, what does a girl have to do to get into that sumptuous tub of yours?"

Alex gave her a mischievous grin. "Nobody is allowed in my private space, but for you, maybe I'd make an exception."

"Why, thank you, kind sir. I'm going to hold you to that later, but for now, I think I'd like that breakfast. I think I am famished. I don't even remember eating last night."

They walked toward the kitchen. Maria noticed that his use of neutral colors wasn't just in the bedroom. She sat at the counter while he started gathering ingredients for their meal. The space was not like she would have imagined, especially after seeing the club.

"So tell me about your color concept here. It is so different from Memphis Nights."

"Before I answer that, tell me if you like it."

"Yes, I do, it is very soothing. It's a good place to come back to. The club is so vibrant, but this feels more like a comfortable pair of shoes or well-worn blue jeans. It seems like a space you would never tire of coming home to."

Alex smiled. "Yep, that was my intention. The goal was comfort and relaxation. I imagine one day I will grow old in a space like this. I want to know that I'm not moving again, and it is safe to grow plants, put up pictures, paint the walls—"

"I imagine that this has been hard on you. Do you ever regret who you were?"

Alex was thoughtful for a moment. He'd had a lot of time to think about that question while in West Virginia. "Marisela taught me more than a few things when I was studying to be who I am now. I don't regret what was because it will stop me from appreciating what is. I have a brand new life ahead of me. How many people get to start over and be something that they never were? Sometimes I walk into that club and it's like I am a kid in a candy store. I don't think about the long hours, or about the time it takes to think of ways to keep the customers happy. I just go in there thankful for another chance. I don't want to sound like I'm preaching, but I've got a lot to be thankful for. I didn't end up like a lot of guys on those teams. Sometimes when it is very quiet I think about Bubba. What did he do to deserve to die the way he did? I escaped all that and I gotta wonder, why me? What do I do now?"

Maria listened to him with rapt attention. He was definitely more than just a pretty face. She admired his new outlook. "You know, you're different from when we first met. I just remember that lost puppy dog look you had before. I have to admit, something maternal made me want to reach out to you then. But you seem much wiser now. It was a helluva way to get there, but maybe you needed this to make you the man you are now."

Alex grinned. "I can accept that, but I am drawing the line at further kidnappings and torture sessions to grow. Give me the simple life."

Maria laughed. "Amen to that! You got any orange juice?"

"Um-hmm, in the fridge." He flipped the omelets again. When he didn't make a move to get the juice, Maria got the hint.

"Oh, I see how you treat your company—they have to fend for themselves," she said jokingly.

He gave her a chaste kiss on the lips. "I think you are way past company, young lady. Next time you get to cook. This is a fifty-fifty relationship, so get used to it."

Relationship. The word had a nice ring to it.

They settled into a comfortable silence while they ate. Alex had positioned the table so that they both could watch the water. The sun danced off the rippling waves, and ducks frolicked without a care in the world. Maria felt very content, and that scared the daylights out of her. Who was Alexandro Milbon to have her thinking thoughts of the proverbial white picket fence? Without realizing what she was doing, she rubbed her stomach. Would she ever bear children . . . his children? *You've got to get a hold of yourself, girl,* she told herself.

Alex interrupted the silence with questions about Baltimore. He needed to feel comfortable about her going. "Tell me about Baltimore."

Maria hesitated. It was an innocent enough question, but she needed to establish that they had boundaries. 'Why?" she responded simply.

"Because I want to know that you are going to be safe," he answered honestly.

"Alex, my safety is not your concern. I've been doing this kind of work for over ten years. I managed just fine without you. If you start trying to look over my shoulder, this will never work."

Alex was irritated now. He would be damned if he stood idly by and let something happen to her. He tried to temper his response. "So what are you saying? Don't call you, you'll call me?"

Maria glared at him. *What was wrong with him?* "Thanks for breakfast. I'm going to get ready to leave now."

"Maria, don't leave mad. I'm just concerned, that's all. Don't read more into it."

Maria crossed her arms over her chest. "I'm not reading anything. We have a job to do. I'll do mine, and you'll do yours. I'll tell you when something is going on that I need your participation in, and we'll take it from there."

"So coming here at 4 A.M. and begging to sleep in my bed was all part of the plan?"

That was the last straw. Maria drew her five-foot-ten-inch frame up against his. She spoke low and clear. "I came here last night because I wanted to be near you. It had nothing to do with the case, and everything to do with being a woman attracted to a man. This discussion proves to me beyond a shadow of a doubt that I cannot confuse the two issues. I will never come to you like that again, you have my word. It was unprofessional, confusing, and indicative of why we will not have an intimate relationship."

"Dammit, Maria, why are you acting this way?" Alex raked his hands through his hair. "I care about you! I don't want to see you get hurt. This has nothing to do with whether or not we are intimate. When I make love to you, it will be when you come to me. Trust me."

He caressed the side of her face with the pad of his thumb before walking away. Maria stood in front of the window watching the water for several more minutes. It took that long for her breathing to return to normal. She was incensed. *Of all the arrogance in the world! When we make love.*

Alex returned to the kitchen fully dressed. Maria turned when she heard him, prepared for round two, but the words died on her lips.

Damn! The man should be arrested for looking so good. He was a visual feast. The still-damp hair on his head curled gently into a wavy, dark mass. The gray that she had noticed earlier peeked out, giving him a gentlemanly appearance. His long, tall frame adorned in a cream-colored silk shirt and taupe pants gave him almost a Mediterranean look.

His gold-flecked eyes regarded her curiously. Who would speak first? Alex grabbed the keys off the kitchen counter. "I left some supplies for you in the bathroom. I'll be back in less than thirty minutes. Don't leave until after I get back. I'm going to get something for you."

With that he walked toward the door. It was obvious to Maria that he didn't expect a reply or an objection. Maria gritted her teeth, counted to ten, then walked toward the bathroom. She would be ready in ten minutes. She didn't take orders from him! Maria stalked to the bathroom and threw open the door. The soothing aroma of vanilla-scented candles filled the air. Alex had set up a vanity area for her. He'd left her a toothbrush, soap, lotion, and towels. He also put one of his oversized T-shirts on a ledge next to the tub for her to put on when she was finished.

Maria took off Alex's robe to step into his custom-made shower. She turned on the multijet showerheads and let the hot water soothe the tension that knotted her muscles. Twenty minutes later, she had washed her hair and had just finished brushing her teeth when she heard the apartment door open and close. She put on Alex's T-shirt, which stopped just above her knees, before going to greet him.

There was no mistaking the look of desire in his eyes when he saw her. Maria flushed with embarrassment. His heated gaze was incendiary.

Alex regrouped. "Do you feel better now?"

"I'm refreshed. I really do need to go now. I told Spates I was leaving in the morning."

Alex used a much softer tone than he had earlier. "I know, but before you do, take this."

Alex gently grasped her hand. The touch was electric, filling her with anticipation.

He resisted the urge to take her in his arms. This morning's confrontation had proven to him that their coming together would have to be her choice. He wouldn't push the issue, no matter how tempting she was. *Even in his T-shirt with nothing underneath.* "Here are two keys: a copy of the key to the apartment, and the silver one, which opens the doors to the club. The envelope has the security code information in it, as well as your vehicle pass. I'm sure I don't want to know how you managed to get in this morning, but this way you can come and go as you please. I've got to get over to the club now. I'm expecting a delivery. I'll see you when you get back from Baltimore. Have a safe trip."

Maria wanted to clear the air before her trip. He was being so sweet. Why did he have to make this so hard on her? "Alex, about this morning."

He shook his head no. "There's nothing to say about this morning. I'll see you when you get back. You know where to find me when you have something for me to participate in. See you later." Alex walked out of the apartment without another word. He had never been on the receiving end of the "Don't call me, I'll call you" line, but he supposed in time he would learn to deal with it. This was just a phase, after all. When the case was finished everything would go back to normal and he would have his old life back. Right?

Alex got behind the wheel of his car. He listened to his favorite Miles Davis CD on the way to the club. Scattered thoughts rambled through his mind. He would buy a sport utility vehicle over the weekend. He liked his car, but he needed to be higher up with more leg room. The Navigator, or maybe that new Aviator . . .

Alex continued his musings about cars, the gorgeous weather Memphis was enjoying, how well things were going at the club. Anything not to think about Maria's earlier rejection of him . . . Maria leaving today for a week . . . Maria . . .

Maria made arrangements to get back to Baltimore. It was going to be one helluva week.

She called Helene as soon as she got back to the hotel. The she packed her bags and prepared to go to the airport.

She met Rod coming in as she was leaving.

"What do you think you're doing?" he asked.

Maria was in no mood for round two. She'd had enough with Alex. "I don't know what your problem is, and at this point I don't care. I'll be in Baltimore for the next week. If you care to join me, let's go. If not, get the hell out of my way."

Rod wasn't backing down from this one. "I've been waiting for you all day. I didn't hear a word from you, and now you are ready to leave without me. How unusual would that look? We are supposed to be keeping up appearances. My bags are in the lobby. I didn't want to hold you up, so I thought I would try to be as ready as possible. I was trying to be considerate. When you have time, Ms. Manez, look up the word."

Several unladylike vituperative phrases escaped her lips.

With one eyebrow raised, Rod looked at her as if she had lost her mind. He wasn't going to deal with her like this. Rod turned on his heels to head down to the lobby. He ignored her outburst. *This too will pass,* he thought solemnly.

They walked out of the lobby and into the parking lot in complete silence. Rod retrieved his bags and loaded the trunk. He took her bag without a backward glance and started the SUV. They were at the airport in no time. Before they got out of the vehicle, he thrust a small bag in her hand and walked ahead of her to the terminal.

Inside the bag was a Barbie dressed in camouflage fatigues. On the card he had written a note in his script. It read: NOT EVEN KICK-BUTT BARBIE CAN HOLD A CANDLE TO KICK-BUTT MARIA MANEZ. GOOD JOB LAST NIGHT, ROD AND HELENE.

She let out another string of curses and shoved the card back in the bag. She sure had made a mess out of this day. She'd lost track of the fact these were her friends and they cared. Her Barbie collection was growing quite extensive. She loved the newest addtion.

When they arrived in Baltimore, Maria was eager to get back to her condo. She was tired of the hotel. She needed to feel connected to something of her own again. *Yeah, it was going to be a doozy of a week.* She could feel it. It was a typical summer day in Baltimore. Maria was glad that she'd cut her hair short. Once she arrived at her apartment, she dropped her bag with a loud thud. She was home. Sort of.

Maria walked straight into her living room. She stood enjoying the panoramic view of the harbor. She loved the view. Watching the water was calming. She felt better already. Examining what happened earlier in the day made her realize she had no excuse. She had behaved badly. She couldn't blame Alex or Rod. She had lost control of her emotions, and it was just a bad day. Probably one of many more to come with the way the case was shaping up. *You're gonna be a real joy during menopause,* she chided herself.

She went to her bedroom, stripped out of her undercover wear, and changed into a sports tank and shorts. It was hot as Hades and she would probably die of heat stroke, but she needed to burn off some energy. She put her fanny pack around her waist, strapped a .22 to her leg (which she hid with her socks), and started out the door. A mile into her run she realized why it was such a bad idea when the heat index was so high. She pushed on. Running down the streets along the harbor was one of her favorite routes. As usual there were tourists milling about, but she ignored them. She concentrated on her breathing, concentrated on just getting through. Her goal was to run three miles or bust. She'd stopped for water several times, but by the time she arrived back at her condo she felt her lungs would explode. *Definitely not one of my brightest ideas.*

She took a cold, then a lukewarm, shower, allowing her body temperature to become regulated again. The run had done her good. She hadn't really been exercising like she should in Memphis. The run and shower had helped her feel more relaxed and settled. After she finished, she put on an oversized T-shirt and plopped down on her bed to enjoy another one of her favorite pastimes. Her secret passion was needlepoint.

She found one and was in the zone within minutes. Her full attention was on making sure that each thread was precisely positioned, seeing how well she could focus on the detail that fascinated her. Maria was so focused on her project she nearly jumped out her skin when the telephone rang.

"*Hola,* Maria."

She recognized the voice on the phone and she was delighted. She had planned to call her favorite aunt as soon as she had a moment. She reverted to Spanish as naturally as she spoke English. "Tía Marisela!"

"Yes, little one. How are you?"

She put her needlepoint away again. "Whew, how do I answer that one? I guess I am doing okay. Got a few things that I am trying to work out." She paused. "I hear we know someone in common."

Marisela was enthusiastic. "*Sí,* Alexandro. I hear you two have met. How are things working out? You know he is one of my favorite people. After you, of course."

"Yes, tía, he speaks very highly of you as well. I saw him this morning. I suppose you know that, too. How do you always know what's going on? Never mind, I probably don't want to know. So, what do *you* want to know? You already know he is very handsome, intelligent, tall, luscious, and desirable. What else is there?"

"Get comfortable. I want you to listen to your older, much wiser aunt. There's always more to a story than meets the eye, and I want you to be prepared before you walk into a situation you can't handle so well. I have faith in you little one, but it doesn't hurt to be cautious."

Maria moaned.

Marisela ignored her and continued. "*Mi* Alexandro is very special to me. We spent a lot of time together before he moved to Memphis and so I think I know him pretty well." Marisela paused. "He's vulnerable. I think you two should be very careful. I know you have your own issues, too. This is a powder-keg situation—make sure if it blows up you two are wearing protection."

"Tía!"

"Don't tía me. I was talking figuratively. Get your mind out of the gutter. Be very sure of the path you follow. I don't want either one of you to get hurt. It has been awhile since he has been with a woman, and I know it has been awhile since you have shared the company of a man. Emotionally, this is a situation that bears monitoring. I wouldn't want hormones to get in the way of common sense. Now, I have said what all good aunts would say, so let's gossip."

That remark garnered a chuckle from her niece. "Tía, you have always been amazing. If it weren't for you, I wouldn't be doing this job."

"You honor me, little one. I am glad that you decided to follow in my footsteps. Of course you are much better at it than me, but that is a good thing. How is that very handsome bodyguard of yours? If I were just ten years younger, I'd go after him."

"Ten years huh. Let's try to add a few more numbers to that," she said laughing. "He is still very handsome and probably a little upset with me about now. I am making him an apology needlepoint. I snapped at him earlier today, and over the last couple of days I have been a real witch. I've been uptight and frustrated and maybe even a little scared. All new emotions to me, you know."

"What happened to my niece with all the *coraje*? You've always done a good job. You are an expert in so many things . . . so smart and always so good in school. When you are good at what you do, there is no need to be afraid. Confidence, remember that. Stop being so hard on everybody—including yourself. When you get back, think of it as a new start. Go back there and kick ass."

"Tía!"

"Yeah, yeah . . . I got to go now. Juan is calling again. Call me every now and again. Tell me about you before I hear it from other people."

"Good night. I'll call you when I come back this way. When my business is done in Memphis. Gracias, tía."

She thought about her argument with Rod. She knew she should apologize. It was very late in the evening, and it had been a long day for everyone, but she dialed Rod's number anyway. She wanted to get a fresh start with the team, and there was no time like the present to do that.

"Rod, it's me. I know it's late, but I need to talk to you. First off, I'm sorry. I would say I don't know what got into me, but I know different. I think I have things under control again. We did good work, and I thank you for being there for me. Second, thank you for the doll. I love it. Third, I'm making you something, so come by for breakfast."

Rod laughed, "if you were calling to apologize why did you threaten me with your cooking?"

"I'm serious. Let me make it up to you. I have more apologies to make in Memphis, but I figured I should start with you."

"Apology accepted. I'll see you in the morning. Get

some rest." Rod was still laughing when he hung up the phone.

It was a nice sound for Maria to hear. It seemed like ages since he felt comfortable enough to tease her. She didn't want to lose his friendship. They had shared too many years, too many good times together.

She took a few calming breaths before picking up the phone again. She had to be careful how she handled this next call. She nervously dialed Alexandro's number. It was almost 1:00 A.M., but she figured he would just be getting home from the club.

She was disappointed when she got his voice mail. She put the phone down dejectedly. There was always tomorrow.

Maria left a message for Helene, checked her doors and windows, and then prepared herself for bed. It was nice to be able to use her own toiletries in her own bathroom. She looked around the room. It wasn't as fancy as the one that Alex had designed, but it was nice.

So, everything comes back to you, Alexandro Milbon.

Alexandro played another game of Doom on his computer. It was a perfectly mindless way to occupy his time and keep his thoughts off Maria. He realized too late that the phone was ringing. He knew it was her before he checked the caller ID screen.

He shut down the computer and retired to his bedroom. After he had gotten comfortable, he picked up the phone to call her. She answered on the first ring.

"Hi," she said.

"Hi, yourself. Everything okay?"

"Yes. No, I'm sorry for being such a jerk earlier. I didn't want you to go to bed mad at me. I was wrong for the things that I said."

"I'm sorry too. I didn't mean to insinuate that you are

not competent. I'm here when you need me. When you want me."

Hmmm, you mean like right now? she wanted to say, but held her peace. There was no need to make the situation any more difficult. "Thank you. I got a surprise call from Tía Marisela. You made quite an impression on her. Tía is selective who she takes under her wing. Consider yourself honored."

"Tía?"

"Yes, she is my father's aunt. He is actually a few years older than she. Let's just say she was a wonderful change-of-life baby. I think that contributes to her crazy sense of humor. She helped me see things more clearly. I didn't tell you about her earlier because it didn't seem important, but you know what, I want us to have an open, honest relationship. When I get back, there are some other things that I want to discuss with you. I know why I'm up so late, but what were you doing?"

Trying to figure out how I am going to sleep in this bed without you. "Missing you. I was playing a video game trying to get tired enough to go to sleep," he answered. Alex took her hint, deciding against pressuring her for more information. He would let Maria determine the pace of their relationship. At least she was interested in talking . . . sharing.

"Well, I've got a big day ahead of me tomorrow. I'll call you again before I head back to town. Goodnight."

"Goodnight, Maria."

Chapter 17

Fortunately, the week seemed to fly by. Rod and Maria were on their way back to Memphis as soon as they tied up the loose ends with the guns. Maria had been very visible on the streets, supposedly moving her product and establishing new contacts.

Ivan had subcontracted surveillance on her to another office. He preferred to stay in Memphis and monitor Alex. The reports would be compiled and reviewed before they were willing to conduct further business with Ms. Manez.

It was Saturday afternoon when Maria and Rod flew back in. The team met with Spates and then went back to the hotel to prepare for phase two. It was a waiting game now. Mikha would call when he was ready to deal again. In the meantime, Spates suggested they continue to be visible in town, maybe even initiate contact with Mikha later in the week, just to nudge things along.

Maria, Rod, and Helene decided on a night out on the town. Helene would accompany Rod as his date. It seemed like a good plan. Besides they hadn't really had the opportunity to celebrate their small victory. This was their chance.

Maria looked through the expansive collection of clothes in her closet. She tossed several outfits on the bed, hoping the right combination would catch her attention. She would leave the leather in the closet tonight. It was too warm, and she had decided that she wanted to soften her edge this evening. She would have liked nothing better than to put on a T-shirt and jeans, but she had to be somewhat presentable. She wasn't in the mood for haute couture though. She sat on her bed sorting through several garments.

Her hair was starting to grow out a little, giving her hairstyle a little more softness. Maria wanted an outfit that would match that style. She finally settled on a two-piece ensemble. When she looked at her reflection in the mirror, she was very pleased. She had achieved the exact look that she had strived for. She was applying her lip gloss when Helene knocked on her door.

"Wow! I like it. You are certainly going to knock someone's socks off tonight. I know best friends aren't supposed to be jealous, but if I just had a couple of your inches I would be so happy."

Maria looked at her friend and chuckled. "I don't know why you are complaining. You look fabulous, and you know it. I know one bodyguard who is going to be pleased to have you on his arm tonight."

Helene tried to quell her excitement. "You really think so? We've played games for so long I don't even know if he is remotely interested. Seems like he only has eyes for you."

Maria noticed the touch of disappointment in her friend's tone. "I know I said that I was going to stay out of this, but you need to know that nothing has ever happened between Rod and me. Sure, we've flirted and talked trash, but that's as far as it has ever gone. After my brief affair with Eric, I swore I wouldn't date anyone else from the office.

"That was entirely too much drama for me, and besides, I knew that Eric was on the rebound. I just didn't care, and I was the one who got hurt. That's a road I would think carefully about, my dear. You and Rod have to work together for many more cases to come. How much are you willing to risk?"

Helene sighed. "I know, but every time I see those eyes and that body, I just go carnal. The lust takes over where careful analytical skill used to be. Girl, the man just does something for me. Trouble is, I've been waiting for him to do something *to* me!"

"Helene Maupin, you are truly crazy, girl. Come on, let's see if Mr. Handsome is ready." Roderick was treated to a visual feast when Maria and Helene appeared at his door. "In the immortal words of that famous philosopher, Johnny Gill, my, my, my." His hazel eyes twinkled in delight. "You two look ravishing tonight. Are you ready to set Memphis on its ear?"

"Yes, our handsome, ravishing escort. I love your suit. Looks like a new acquisition, am I right?"

He twirled around to model the Armani suit for them. It was an olive green that perfectly complemented his skin tone and eye color. With it he wore a taupe-colored blended silk shirt and a printed green, cream, and taupe tie. Helene barely suppressed the urge to lick her lips. Just looking at him made her mouth dry.

"This suit doesn't make my butt look big, does it?" he said in a falsetto that was supposed to mimic a woman's voice.

"See there, everything was fine until he opened that mouth," Helene joked.

Maria shook her head. "Yeah, you had us going for a second. Keep the comments to one syllable and just look gorgeous for us. We want all the little hotties to be jealous."

The trio laughed and joked all the way to the club. The atmosphere was very festive, which was much appreciated and much needed after a tough few weeks.

They were sure Ivan and Mikha were enjoying themselves too. Part one of their deal was complete. Now everyone had time to relax before phase two began.

They arrived at Memphis Nights shortly before 10 P.M. It was a sultry evening with the tangy, sweet smell of purple irises in the air.

The club was moderately crowded, but they were able to find a table in one of the conversation pits with little trouble. Maria looked around for Alex. She couldn't wait to see him again after missing him for a week. She hoped he appreciated her scaled-down outfit.

Alex arrived at the club later than usual. He went directly to his office to get a jump on some of his paperwork. Taxes were going to be a bear this year, but that was good. It meant he was in the black. He'd had a long week without Maria and wasn't sure when he would see her. She hadn't called when she said she would, and he figured she had gotten caught up in the job. He needed a little pick-me-up, which he hoped the customers wouldn't mind. The live band wasn't on the calendar for another couple of weeks, but he wanted to hear some salsa tonight. He called a local band he knew was in town to ask for the favor.

He didn't emerge from his office until the band was scheduled to go on. He liked to introduce the live acts because it helped him feel more involved with the patrons in the club.

As soon as he walked toward the bar he felt her presence. Maria and Rod were shaking it up on the dance

130 Katherine D. Jones

floor. Alex watched for several minutes, enjoying the sight of her. She was especially lovely tonight. He admired the outfit that she wore, loved how she could be sexy and demure at the same time. Tonight she wore a cream-colored silk haltertop with a floor-length taupe-colored skirt. The skirt hugged her hips, then flared out, exposing the small expanse of skin between her breasts and midriff. Alex imagined how soft the skin was there. He felt familiar urges pulling him toward her. He watched until his hands burned to touch her. When Rod went to dance with Helene, he made his move.

"Would you care to dance?"

Maria's heart beat in double-time. She had been looking forward to seeing him all evening. She took his outstretched hand as he led her farther out on the dance floor. They danced to a few slow jazzy tunes. It gave them the opportunity to be close to each other. Maria loved being in his arms again.

Alex reveled in the scent of her warm vanilla sugar bath gel. Vanilla was one of his favorite scents, and she had it on from head to toe. He wanted to kiss her everywhere she wore it.

Maria was enjoying herself very much. Tonight there was no tension, no uncertainty clouding her decisions. Tonight she was at peace and allowing herself the freedom to just exist.

Alex noticed that she was freer, too. They executed intricate dance moves, moving to the beat in perfect time. No matter where he led, Maria followed. They made a striking pair on the dance floor, and they knew it. His assistant manager introduced the band and soon the dance floor was filled with people doing the latest Latin dance moves.

Ivan walked in shortly after Alex and Maria had begun

dancing. He noticed their chemistry and thought they seemed to be perfectly suited to each other. He also noticed that the bodyguard seemed to have moved on, too. He was sitting at the table with a lovely young woman enjoying drinks. He had seen them on the dance floor, too. The group seemed to be very cozy, and for some reason that worried him. He wouldn't feel comfortable until the business with these folks was done and they had gone back to their respective places of residence. Ivan was the naturally cagey type, which made him a natural at ferreting out security problems. If something turned out to be wrong with their business, he would find that out.

Maria saw Ivan before Roderick. She nodded to him and Helene from the dance floor. They followed her gaze to where Ivan was sitting. Everyone had the heads-up. It was showtime. She pulled Alex close. "You in the mood to kiss me senseless? We've got an audience over there at the bar. See him, black shirt and western-style blue jeans? Laugh like I've just made the funniest joke."

Alex did as he was told. Maria thoroughly enjoyed the sound of his baritone voice rumbling in laughter. He followed that with a sensuous kiss along the curve of her jaw. Then he gently nuzzled the back of her ear. Maria heard herself moan. She pulled him closer, willing him to give her more of him. She used her hands to direct his lips toward her waiting lips. The kiss was soft at first, becoming deeper as the hot tide of passion rose between them. Alex deepened the kiss, wanting more of her. He tasted the sweet fruity champagne she had been drinking. His hands caressed the exposed skin on her back. He was starting to appreciate the return of the halter top. All at once she was soft and delicate and strong and muscled. She intoxicated him. He felt he would never get enough.

He spun her around in an exaggerated dance move when he noticed her tattoo for the first time. It was a broken heart on her scapula. He made a mental note to ask her about it later. Every time he spun her out of a move he drew her to him for more kisses.

They were making a scene on the dance floor. Ivan watched in amusement.

Maria was the first to break away. She looked up into his intense brown-eyed gaze. "I think you follow orders very well. But I think we can stop now."

Alex smiled down at her. He still had five inches on her even with the added height of her three-inch sling-back shoes. "But I was just getting warmed up," he protested.

"Let's go home."

Alex looked at her, stunned. He didn't want to mistake her meaning. "Are you sure?"

"Do these eyes look like they are kidding?"

"Can you give me a few minutes to lock up? I'll be right with you."

Maria nodded. "I'll let Rod and Helene know that I'm leaving with you. This is strictly for appearances' sake, of course."

"Of course," he answered dryly.

Maria ordered another glass of champagne from the bar and drank it with Rod and Helene while she waited for Alex. "I'm going to be leaving soon. Do you two kids think you'll be okay without me?"

Helene piped in immediately. "The better question is do you two think you'll be okay without a chaperone. Remember you've got surveillance on both ends, no pun intended."

Rod laughed. Helene always had the quirkiest sense of humor.

"This is just for appearances. I'm sure it won't get out of hand."

Rod and Helene looked at each other with doubt.

An hour later Alex and Maria were pulling through the security gate of his complex. Maria started to have second thoughts about the decision as soon as they reached the door. His pull over her was so strong—did she really have the willpower to stop?

Alex was nervous, afraid to hope for more. "We're here. How do you feel? I noticed you drinking champagne. Are you going to have a hangover in the morning?"

Maria smirked at him. "I had two drinks. I think I can handle myself better than that. If anything, I'll sleep like a baby. So don't mind me if I start to snore."

"And just what makes you think that I'll even notice? I don't think I'll hear you from the couch. I hear that it is very comfortable."

Maria regarded him coolly. "You wouldn't dare put me on the couch!"

"You betcha. I am not going to be tortured again in my own home. I barely slept a wink with you in my bed. Since I need longer sleeping accommodations it is only natural for me to sleep in my own bed. You're only about five-feet-ten inches tall. The couch will be perfect for you. While you were away, I bought you some gifts which I will show you in the morning, but for now—goodnight." He headed for the front door.

"Alexandro Milbon, don't you walk away from me!"

He chuckled as he sauntered away from her. She would have to get used to separating the man from the job. She couldn't turn him on and off like a faucet. They would have to come to some sort of understanding about the best way to handle the case. Alex walked into

134 *Katherine D. Jones*

his bedroom and locked the door. He wasn't sure if it was protection from her or protection *for* her.

His dreams were filled with visions of her in various positions; just having her close sent his libido into overdrive. It would be a long night no matter where she slept.

His couch was extremely comfortable, but Maria fumed nonetheless. How dare he reject her again. She wasn't going to take much more of this. Her nipples strained against the thin silk fabric of her halter. Although he gave her linens, this time he didn't bother to give her anything to sleep in. Maria went into his guest bathroom and took a quick shower, after which she returned to the couch wrapped only in her towel. She had no choice but to sleep in the nude.

A few hours later, Alex unlocked his bedroom door to check on Maria. He thought he might do well to purchase a day bed for the second bedroom, which he currently used as an office.

The air conditioning was doing nothing to combat the warm August air. He had taken off his nightshirt earlier and was sleeping in a simple pair of boxers. He wanted to see if Maria was too warm as well.

Alex felt like a voyeur watching Maria as she slept in the nude. She had pulled the sheet half way down so that her beautiful brown breasts were exposed. Alex licked his lips when he saw the rise and fall of her nut brown areolas as she breathed. Her breathing was light and steady, just as it had been when she was in his bed. She looked so peaceful, so desirable. He wanted to taste her.

He knew that she had taken a shower earlier; her wet hair had dried in a cap of thick curls. He took a chance on touching her. He ran his fingers through her silky curling hair. It was as soft as he imagined it would be.

Maria inhaled his masculine scent the minute he entered the room. She had always been a light sleeper and was never one to be caught off guard. It took all of her concentration just to remember to breathe again. She waited. What would he do? She felt the moisture pool between her legs. Her breathing became more erratic when he touched her hair. Didn't he know that was one of her more sensitive areas? She moaned in response.

Alex was surprised by her reaction. She was incredibly passionate. He knew their lovemaking would be explosive. He continued touching her, moving his hands to caress her lovely breasts and teasing the buds of her nipples. They were taut now, begging to be suckled.

Maria was on fire. She moved her hand from the pillow and made a slow path toward her feminine center. The sheet was removed in the process, showing Alex every almond-colored inch.

Alex had hardened to the point of pain. He had to leave or he wouldn't be responsible for his actions. He stopped caressing her breasts and moved toward the kitchen. Gripping the kitchen counter hard, he forced his breathing to return to normal. Alex made himself a Sour Apple and one for Maria too.

He let the tart, cool liquid ease his dry throat. He let his gaze fall again to the sleeping figure on the couch. She was so beautiful. *You are going to be the death of me, woman!*

He would sneak one kiss before going back to bed. When he returned to Maria on the couch the sheet was on the floor. He put her Sour Apple on the end table next to the couch.

Maria's hand was gently, with ever so slight motions,

moving up and down her feminine core. Alex was instantly jealous. He didn't think before he moved. Suddenly his hand replaced hers and then it was replaced with his mouth. He showered kisses along the insides of her thighs until her moans became louder and more intense. He tasted her moisture; she was even sweeter than he had imagined. Alex used his tongue to penetrate the engorged flesh of her lower lips. Over and over he licked and sucked until she arched her back and pulled him to her greedily.

Maria was fully awake now, but she still felt like she was dreaming. She reached out for him; she wanted him inside her more than she wanted air. Alex continued his sensual assault, pushing his tongue deeper inside her until he could suck her completely. Maria was pushed over the precipice almost immediately. She screamed out his name as she came to an explosive orgasm. Her body shook and rocked for several minutes after.

When she opened her eyes, Alex was watching her as he stroked himself. Maria shook her head no and motioned for him to come to her. Maria moistened her mouth with a sip of the drink that he had prepared for her. Then she positioned her cool wet mouth to receive him. She treated him to the same pleasure that he had given to her. In minutes he was trying to pull back.

"Maria, you feel so good I don't know how much longer I can hold it. You've got to stop."

She did, but only long enough to tell him to shut up and come back to her.

Maria continued her ministrations on his heated body until he roared his own orgasm. Blinding white light signaled his release. It was much more powerful than he had imagined it would be. Their sharing had proven to be much more intense and potent than each could have fantasized. It was going to be tough not to get addicted to each other. The fragrance of their passion hung heavy in the hot air.

Chapter 18

Rod stood in the doorjamb of the hotel room watching Maria. He thought for several minutes before he spoke. "You sure you know what you are doing?"

Maria laughed. "Hell no, but I thought I would give it a shot anyway. Are you cool with this? It won't change our arrangements. I'll drive to meetings myself, and you and Helene can ride together."

Helene. A twinkle tickled his eyes when he thought about the sexy little minx that she was last night. He hoped she realized how much he had enjoyed her company. Rod shook the thoughts from his head. "That's fine. I'll talk with her about that later on today. We were going to meet for lunch. Will you need any help with your bags?"

"No, I left Alex a note this morning. Hopefully, he will be here soon. So, how was the rest of your evening with my best friend in the whole entire world that you'd better not hurt?"

"Maria, I am offended. I would never do anything to hurt Helene. Besides I am not going to try anything with her. She's turned me down flat and I'm not opening myself up for the drama and pain of unrequited love. I think I've had enough of that for one lifetime."

Rod hesitated before saying more. "I don't want to be

politically incorrect here, but I heard some rumors at
the Academy about her. I've never seen her with anyone
except you, and that's another reason that I've decided
to leave well enough alone."

Maria looked at him. *Men could be so dense sometimes.*
Helene was nothing short of heterosexual, but an ob-
noxious would-be suitor had started a rumor while the
three were at the Academy. Once the ball got rolling,
Helene didn't feel it necessary to do anything about it.
Let people think what they wanted to. Besides, to her
way of thinking, she was given the space and distance to
concentrate on her studies. Maria couldn't believe that
sensible, intelligent Rod actually believed that garbage.
The man was on his own on this one. She wouldn't confirm or deny. He would just have to work things through
himself.

"Well then, just enjoy each other's company. Have fun
at lunch. I'm going to finish packing, then order room
service. I'll catch you guys later. This afternoon I'll stop
by to see Spates. He probably won't like it, but he'll get
over it."

Alex woke up feeling better than he had in weeks.
He'd made a promise to Max and the Bureau, but as
soon as the mission was complete, he knew he would
have Maria. He wouldn't do anything now to stand in
the way of the case. He could be patient until it was re-
solved, but after that all bets were off.

Last night had proved to him that he loved her more
than he could have thought possible. He had already
recognized the physical connection that they shared, but
he had never wanted anyone like he wanted her. He'd
realized that she made him complete. It was about more

than sex, it was spiritual for him. He loved her; every fiber of his being knew it.

He wanted to wake up to her every morning, come home to her every night. He didn't know if he would have to move again, but whatever it took to be with her—he would do it. His life didn't mean anything without her in it.

Common sense prevailed, though. He knew, unfortunately, this was not the right time to do anything about being with her. They had to wait until the time was right. He suspected that she felt just as strongly about him, but they would have to temper their expressions for the sake of the case. Alex would never be satisfied with just part of her. He wanted their coming together to be complete, whole, just like their feelings for each other.

Alex took care of his basic hygiene needs before going to find her. He didn't know if she'd had to leave early or if she would still be sleeping soundly on the couch. Entering his living room, his spirit sensed the emptiness. She was gone. Alex walked dejectedly to the kitchen. He consoled himself with the knowledge that he would see her later, hopefully at the club.

Maria had left a note for him on the kitchen counter. Alex read it quickly, then put it down again. *Damn!* He would call her as soon as his nerves settled down.

Maria was starting to get nervous. She knew that Alex had to be up by now. He would need to get over to the club to finish his paperwork soon. She checked her watch for the umpteenth time. Maybe he wasn't coming. Maybe she shouldn't have asked to go home with him last night. Maybe last night meant more to her than to him. Maybe he thought she gave her body to every man.

She should have told him how much she loved him before.

She almost jumped out of her skin when the phone finally rang. Answering quickly, she said, "Maria Manez."

"Maria, so good to know that you are back in town. I trust that things went well at home?" She recognized the voice on the other end.

"Goran, I didn't expect to hear from you so soon. I trust that all is well?"

"Yes, very well. Mikha would like to meet with you now, if you are available, of course."

Maria hesitated for half a beat. They still didn't trust her, so she would have to be careful. There was no time to contact Rod and Helene to pull them from their lunch date. She was on her own and felt exposed without her team in place. She was reluctant to contact anyone; the Russians had probably tried to bug the room or her phone line. She hoped her voice sounded as cool as it was supposed to. Her stomach lurched in protest. "Sure, I need a little time to pull myself together, but I can make it. Where does he want to meet?"

"My club in one hour, then. We look forward to seeing you again. *Paka.*"

"Yes, see you later, Goran."

She took several minutes to unpack her bags. She couldn't show up to a meeting in the blue jeans and sweatshirt she was wearing. She sighed, knowing whatever her personal plans, they would have to be put off until later. She took a shower and scented herself with expensive designer perfume. Warm vanilla sugar was only for Alex.

She dressed for the weather, expecting another warm and sultry day in Memphis. When she was done, she was satisfied. This ought to give them something to look at, she thought.

She brushed the natural curl out of her dark brown hair, using styling gel and mousse to give it a sleek appearance. Her makeup was nothing short of dramatic, especially for an afternoon look, but she figured, why not? She was giving them textbook Maria.

She wrote a quick note to Rod and Helene: *Meet me at Goran's club now.*

She slipped her feet into her red slingback shoes and headed for the door. She opened it just as Alex was about to knock.

His brown eyes darkened when he saw her outfit.

"Going to work?"

She wasn't pleased with his tone. She arched her left brow before responding dryly, "So what was your first clue?"

Alex chuckled. He loved her fiery spirit. He took her hand. He wanted to kiss her, but he didn't want to ruin her makeup. He was becoming a real sucker for red lipstick, especially when it adorned the lips of one Ms. Manez.

"Come on, let's go."

Maria stood her ground, but she didn't release her hand from his. "What do you think you're doing?"

"I am going with you. I don't see Rod or anyone else with you, and I'm not letting you go anywhere looking like that by yourself. So I repeat, let's go."

Maria pursed her lips and started walking toward the elevator. Alex had to let go of her hand or risk twisting her arm. She would always be difficult, that much he knew.

He let her go down in the elevator, but he opted for the stairs. He was waiting for her in the lobby when she arrived. Maria smirked at him and tried not to let him see that his antics had amused her. When he joined her by her side, she gritted her teeth before addressing him again.

"You can go home now or go to the club. I'll be fine. Did you see my note?"

"Yes, I did, and I'd like to talk about it later. Right now, we've got a meeting to go to. Perhaps you should focus on that."

"Alexandro Milbon, leave me alone," she whispered.

Alex swept her up in a passionate kiss. They seemed to provide erotic entertainment for the hotel staff every time they were in each other's presence.

Alex broke the kiss before things got out of hand. He whispered back to her, "Never."

Maria shook her head and sighed. She shouldn't give in to him, but the fact of the matter was if they were seen together like this, it would only help her cover.

Finally she said, "Fine, but I'm driving."

"No you're not."

"Alex!"

He continued walking until he came to his new vehicle. He had settled on a black Navigator with black leather interior. The size of the SUV perfectly suited his large frame.

Maria was fuming. If he thought he was going to come in and take over her life, he had another thing coming.

He looked at her while opening the doors to the vehicle. "Maria, I love you. Now shut up and let's go."

Her heart stopped. "What did you just say, Alex?"

He looked at her before getting into the car. He held her gaze for several seconds before responding. This wasn't the time or place, but he had let the cat out of the bag, so he couldn't leave her hanging. "I think I said, Maria, I love you. Now, shut up, we need to go."

"In that case, I love you too, you arrogant, chauvinistic—"

"Thank you. I think that just about covers it. So, where are we going?"

"Goran's club. Mikha wants to talk. Are you going to let me take the lead on this, or am I going to have to put a bullet in you right now?"

Alex smiled at her. "Keep the safety on. All I want to do is get you there and watch from a distance. When the rest of the team shows up, I'll just disappear. I'm not here to get in your way, *querida*, I just want to make sure that you are safe."

"I suppose I should be grateful for my knight in shining armor, but I have been doing this for a number of years. I can take care of myself. Promise me that when we go in there you are not going to do anything foolish."

Alex held up three fingers in a scout salute. "I promise."

They arrived at the club in less than fifteen minutes. Ivan, who seemed to take pleasure in frisking them both, greeted them at the door.

Alex gritted his teeth. He'd promised Maria he would behave; however, Ivan was making that difficult. He would have liked nothing better than to show him a few tricks that he'd learned along the way.

Maria smiled at Ivan. "Darling, next time you touch me like that, be sure to buy me a drink first. There's only one man that gets to do that for free."

Ivan laughed in amusement.

"Always a pleasure to see you, Maria. Goran and Mikha are in the office in the back. *Señor* Milbon stays with me. We watch the ladies."

The club had started to fill up. It was time for the 1:00 P.M. show to start. The music was cued up, and half-dressed waitresses began circulating around the room.

Maria turned to Alex and nodded her head yes. Alex shook his head no. They looked at each other, neither one moving, neither one blinking.

They were at a standoff until Roderick appeared at the door. "Hi, boss, I got your note. How's everybody doing?"

Alex spoke first. "Everything is cool now. Boss needs you for a meeting, and I need to get back to my club. Maria, I'll see you later."

Alex pulled her to him to whisper in her ear, "I'm sorry. I know I didn't do what I said. You can punish me later." He kissed her possessively before walking out the door.

You'll be punished all right! she thought wickedly. She would teach him to mess with her emotions, then try to bully her. Rod noticed the spark in her eyes and decided he was glad not to be in the shoes of Alexandro Milbon tonight.

After Alex left, they got down to business. The meeting with Mikha was interesting. He just wanted to feel them out. Maria felt like she was being tested and she had grown tired of the game. Just minutes into the meeting, she made her exit.

"Enough of the games. I can give Ivan here my itinerary so that he can stop following me around. I know what I am doing. When I need more guns, I'll call you. Until we need to transact again—don't call me. When you can handle *my* business, you and your cronies will know where to look."

She stood up to leave the office.

"Maria, this was just a little getting-acquainted chat.

We are preparing a very large shipment of product for you. Surely you can understand our caution?" He gave her an oily grin.

"Maybe you don't understand my caution. Don't play games with me. If everyone just does what they are supposed to, life will be just peachy."

Ivan was alarmed by her tone. He stood up to move closer to Mikha.

Maria said, "Oh, what now, am I supposed to be intimidated? Ivan, if you ever touch me again like you did today, I will slowly break each of your fingers and—"

Rod cleared his throat. "I think we're done here. Contact us with the shipment details." Rod was sure Mikha hadn't had time to work things out with Nikola. He wanted to make sure that he had suppliers to go to before he brokered the deal with the senior man.

As soon as they left the club, Maria held her hands up.

"Don't lecture me. I am tired of having my chain pulled by that slimy SOB."

Rod chuckled, "Who was going to lecture? I was going to compliment you. That was good thinking to have Milbon with you. Helene and I would never have forgiven ourselves if you had gone in there alone."

That was the icing on the cake for Maria. Why was everybody so damned excited about Alex being with her? she exploded. "And just what the hell was untrained, unarmed, uninformed Alexandro Milbon going to do?"

Rod shook his head slowly. "Don't blow a gasket. I wasn't trying to insinuate that you couldn't handle it, just that I felt you were safer. You know, safety in numbers? Now, can I have the keys?"

"I didn't drive, moron. Alex did."

Rod ignored her outburst. "Cool, shall we call Spates to let him know about the latest developments?"

"Sure, give him a call and tell him we need to meet this evening." She put a hand on his shoulder. "I'm mad at Mikha and Alex, not you. I'm sorry. Again, just let me blow off some steam and I'll be fine. I need to go swimming or do something else to burn off this energy. Call me later, I'm going to the fitness center."

Maria stayed in the water until every bit of tension was erased. Much later she went back to her hotel room. After giving it more thought, she realized her anger was just a mask for the hurt she felt. Wanting to be with Alex despite the costs was unnatural for her. Maria was used to being in control of her emotions, her situations, and her life. Alex made her consider giving up everything.

After showering, she returned her room to normal, unpacking the bags she was once ready to take over to Alex's place. They had a lot to work through, and last night had simply complicated matters more. Another issue, of course, was their profession of love. So the million-dollar question was, what do you do after the morning after?

Chapter 19

As soon as Maria returned to her room, Rod contacted her through their transmitters with a message. "Hey, Spates called. We are being summoned. How soon can you be ready?"

"Let me grab my purse and I'll be right with you. How are you feeling?"

"I know my lazy butt is going to sleep well tonight. I think I may have overdone it working out today. My new motto is, to each his own. Besides, after watching him today, I think you guys are made for each other. I think you will be doing a lot of needlepoint for him," Rod teased.

"Such a lot of help you are. Let's go. Is Helene already there?"

Just then Helene joined the conversation. "No, Helene is in her trusty, dusty surveillance vehicle enjoying the drama that is the life of her friends. You definitely got your hands full with Alex, girlfriend. Aside from being gorgeous, he is no pushover," she added for Maria's ears only.

"Hey, girl," Maria said, "I'd almost forgotten about you. Seems like I haven't seen you in a bit."

"Yeah well, remember to turn off your pen transmitter when you need privacy. You sounded like you had fun last night. Don't worry, I erased the tape. It won't be a part of the case record."

Maria stopped walking and almost tripped over her own feet. "Helene, are you serious?"

"Do you want me to repeat what I heard? It was very hot. Calm down, my hush money is very reasonable."

Rod was curious about their conversation, but didn't ask. The look on Maria's face told him it was none of his business.

Maria looked over at Rod. Her cheeks were flushed a deep crimson. She couldn't believe she had been so careless. Alex was definitely dangerous for her concentration. "Helene, we'll talk about this later. As your rater for this assignment, I'm sure we will come up with a good way to deal with the situation."

Helene chuckled at her friend's idle threat. "Oh, my goodness, she threw out the 'evaluator' card. Girl, it must be love. I told you my hush money was reasonable. Tell that handsome bodyguard hello. I'll see you guys in about thirty minutes."

The meeting lasted less than two hours, which was a record for Spates. Each agent's position was reevaluated, and possible scenarios were thrown on the table. No changes in the mission profile were made. Rod and Maria reported on their contact with the Russians earlier in the day and talked about the increased need for security. After some discussion it was felt that Ivan was intent on finding something. There was some concern over Helene's position. Max was called in to do more surveillance. He would apply for a bartending job at Goran's club to keep a closer eye on them. If that didn't work out, he would become a regular patron.

The meeting concluded with everyone feeling more than ready to tackle the big deal and move on. Stings that took a long time were the most risky. It was hard for the agents to be in character for too long without feeling antsy.

Maria and Helene spoke briefly after the meeting. Rod waited in the Bureau car.

"I don't know why you are so worried about this," Helene said. "You know I'm not going to say anything."

"I know that. This isn't an agent talk, this is a friend talk." Maria sighed heavily, the breath of air escaping in a long ragged stream. "Helene, I love him. I know it goes against all that is supposed to happen, but I love him with all that I am. I am frazzled when I am with him and stressed out when we are apart, but being together is so much more fun. To make matters worse, he says he loves me too." She threw her hands up in resignation. "So, now what do we do?"

Helene looked at her friend carefully. "Sweetie, I'd say be very careful and make sure every move you make is for the case and not for personal pursuits," she reminded her.

Maria and Rod returned to the hotel for some much-needed rest. Maria intended to take a short nap, but after her earlier workout she slept for a much longer time. When she awoke it was in the wee hours of the morning.

She freshened up and got herself ready to visit Alex's place. It didn't take long to get ready or to arrive there.

Warm vanilla sugar. Maria's signature scent wrapped around Alex like a warm blanket. Slipping into the sheets, she snuggled her body against the contour of his. He moved to bring her closer, before they both settled into a deep, comfortable sleep. Talk would wait until the morning . . .

The tantalizing smell of bacon and eggs woke Maria up. She made herself presentable and went to find Alex in the kitchen.

"Good morning, sleepy. How are you feeling?" he asked.

"I'm doing very well, thank you. I could get very spoiled in your bed. It is so comfortable. I can see why you didn't want to give it up the other day." Maria smiled at him. She loved the sight of Alex in the kitchen.

He turned back to his cooking. "You hungry?"

She smiled. "Always. Is there anything you want me to do?"

His tone was so polite it was flat. "Sure, you can put those biscuits in the oven. We'll be ready to eat in about ten minutes. You want some coffee?"

Maria responded, "Yes, I'll get it. You want me to freshen your cup?"

Again, he displayed no emotion. "No, I've got it."

Maria put her hand on her hip. "Okay, I think that about covers the Cleaver routine. We need to talk. Your choice: now or later?"

"I need to eat."

Maria raked her hands through the brown curls covering her head. "That's fine. I'm hungry too."

They ate in companionable silence for several minutes. Maria was more than hungry; she was famished. Alex watched her, amused that she could put away so much food in so little time. Probably came from working so many strange cases and being in harrowing situations. That last thought concerned him. He really didn't like the idea of her working under the threat of violence. He had definitely turned into the male protector. He had never thought of himself as the alpha-male type before, but he knew for Maria he would gladly give up his life to keep her safe. She had completely turned him around. He wasn't the same man he was before meeting her.

When they were finished, he moved the dishes to the side and took her hand. He followed her gaze, "I'll do them after we get done, unless it will be too distracting for you?"

Maria looked at him sheepishly. "Yeah, I'd rather get them out of the way. To me it's like sitting in the bedroom with the bed unmade. My mama would have a fit."

Alex laughed. His mother had been the same way. "Okay, we clean, then we talk. But after this, no more distractions."

In no time they were sitting in his living room on the couch that they seemed to favor so much. Alex began. "Maria, I meant what I said earlier. I do love you. I think it was destiny that brought us back together again. You're my connection to the real world. You have given new meaning and purpose to my life."

He looked toward the kitchen counter, recalling the events of the previous day. "When I read your note telling me that you wanted to move in, part of me rejoiced. But then the other part of me, the part with good sense, knew that it was a lousy plan. I would love to wake up to your beautiful face every morning. Lord knows, too, that I would love the opportunity to make love to you every night, but we both know that we have a greater responsibility here. We can't be selfish. Let's just get through this, no matter how tough it is, and then make our plans."

Alex paused, looking into her brown eyes. He wanted to make love to her in the worst way, but he couldn't. Not yet.

Maria listened quietly. She had come to the same conclusion. "Yesterday afternoon showed me a thing or two. It didn't get ugly with Ivan and the gang, but what if it had? I would have drawn you into a situation where you could have gotten hurt. Alex, if anything had happened to you because of me, I would never have forgiven myself. I love you too much to have that on my conscience." She paused, steadying herself against the negative thoughts that clouded her mind. "I think we need to come up with an alternate plan."

Alex crossed his hands over his chest. He wanted to remain neutral even though he didn't like the turn of the conversation. "What are you suggesting?"

Maria exhaled. "Maybe I should talk to Spates about changing the course of this assignment. I haven't really thought this out; maybe we should have a public blowout or something to let them know that we are over. Ivan would stop following you and keeping tabs on your life. Maybe then you could get back to normal."

Alex leaned his head from side to side, trying to release the tension that had begun to build at the base of his neck. The thought of not being with her was worse than the possibility of any danger he might be in. Finally, he said, "I don't know if I can accept that. What happens after the case? Are you ready to move on to the next case without so much as a backward glance? I don't think you can."

"Alex, all I know is I have a job to do, and you complicate it. My happiness is irrelevant. I have a mission to complete, and that comes above all else."

Alex moved toward her. He was angry and the kiss that he swept her in proved that. His lips were hard and demanding. Maria pushed him back. He didn't budge; the kiss was becoming more insistent, more passionate, more loving. Maria melted in his arms. She wanted to hate him for the way he made her feel, but she couldn't. Alex was right. She couldn't just walk away from him. Case or no case.

When he finally released her, he looked into angry eyes. They were a deep shade of brown now, the fury evident in her dark orbs. "You can't control me, Alexandro. Don't ever try to bully me like that again. If you love me the way you say you do, respect me."

Her eyes shone with unshed tears. "I'm leaving now. I'm willing to do what needs to be done, even if you're not. It's my reputation and my head that's at stake here. You just got caught up in the circumstances. I would be here working on this case with or without you."

Alex shook his head. "I wasn't trying to bully you. I just want you to know that we are connected. You can't just walk away. I respect you, but you need to quit hiding behind your job. Be a woman and stand up for what you want. What we have is between us, not the Bureau. No, I am not an agent, but does that mean I don't have any sense? You are treating me like less than a man. I can deal with a lot of things Maria, but that's not one of them." His chest heaved with emotion. "Make up your mind, because before you walk out that door I want a commitment from you one way or another."

Maria was incredulous. She rose from her seat to pace around the room. She looked at him long and hard before speaking. "A commitment from whom? From Maria Marisela Thomas or Maria Manez? You want blue jeans and a tank top, or tight designer wear? Do you even know who I am, what I have to do in my job?"

She baited him, waiting for him to explode. "Alex, a commitment for what?"

Alex's gaze was equally as intense. He refused to buy

into her defenses. He wanted an answer from her today. His voice was low and husky when he spoke again. "A commitment to love me, a commitment that we are going to see this case through together or a commitment that when you walk out that door, you don't walk back. No more late-night crawling into my bed. No more teasing me and playing with my emotions. The next time you are bold enough to get in between my sheets, be bold enough to make love to me. Or stay away."

Maria shivered. Her body betrayed her. She was responding to his words in ways that her mind did not want to. She felt her heart rate increase, her palms begin to sweat. His pull over her was too strong, and she knew she would somehow have to regain control.

Maria walked toward the kitchen where she had left her purse. She withdrew the key and parking pass that he had given to her earlier and placed them both on the counter. She looked at Alex for several seconds. Then without another word she walked out the door.

Chapter 20

Alex felt his heart breaking with every step away from him that she took. He had meant every word, but he didn't expect it to hurt so much. He prayed her walking out the door didn't mean her walking out of his life forever.

Maria just made it to her government vehicle before the tears began to fall. She was angry with herself again. She hadn't shed tears over any man in over three years. Now, here she was, in charge of a major operation, crying like a baby! She had to walk away before she allowed him to destroy what she had worked for longer than a decade. Damn you, Alexandro Milbon, she thought miserably. She had to pull herself together before going to see Agent Spates. Things were going to have to change if she was to complete this mission.

Maria had changed into her favorite pair of blue jeans and put on a simple white tank top. With her white canvas sneakers, she could easily pass for a woman half her age. Her only makeup was berry-tinted lip gloss; this was a far cry from her usual glamorous Maria Manez look.

Spates knew something was amiss the moment he saw her. She would come to him in her own time if she wanted to, he decided. He was relieved when she asked to speak to him privately.

Maria spoke softly. "Sir, I think we need to reconsider adding Milbon to this case. When he accompanied me to Goran's club, things could have gotten really sticky. I don't feel comfortable letting him continue on with us. He doesn't know enough about what we are planning to be a threat to the mission. Besides, I don't think that Ivan or Mikha are too interested in him. And we have other agents who can keep an eye on him, like Max or Steve. I think we made our point with his cover. It's time to move on before something nasty happens."

Spates listened quietly.

"I'm proposing that we have a very public fight, and then let Mikha and the gang figure that we are no longer an item. It lets Milbon off the hook, and me, too. I can concentrate more on what I have to do, instead of having my worries compounded by watching out for his safety."

Spates looked at Maria, his eyes sharp and assessing. His worst fears had been confirmed as he listened to her. She and Milbon had gotten too close for comfort. She was admitting in her own way that she couldn't handle having him involved.

"Agent Thomas, is there something more going on than you are willing to say?"

Maria turned away. "No, sir. I just think that this is better all the way around."

Spates responded casually. "I'll talk with McCoy. Any changes now will have to be approved by her. We'll confer and get back to you. In the meantime, continue as you are."

Maria groaned inwardly. That's the last thing she wanted to do. After her meeting she sulked back to the hotel. All she wanted to do was to lick her wounds in peace and quiet, but Rod was waiting for her when she returned.

She was glad to see him, she needed a pick-me-up. "Hey buddy, can you do a favor for an old friend?"

Rod gave her that easy dimpled smile of his. "Sure thing, since you asked so sweetly. What can I do for you?"

"I'm thinking that I need a trip to the fabric store. I need a major needlepoint fix. You game for a little excursion?"

"I'll be ready in five. Knock on my door when you want to walk out."

He hoped he would not be the recipient of any more of her creations. His place was starting to look like a Christopher Lowell throwback.

They talked as they shopped. "Rod, we've worked together for more than ten years, so we know each other, right?"

Rod looked at her skeptically. "Yes—"

"Am I losing my mind? Why can't I seem to get a handle on Milbon? I have never allowed emotion to get in the way of my ability to do my job before. Why now?"

To be clear, he asked, "Friend to friend, or agent to agent?"

"Friend."

He shrugged matter-of-factly, "I wanted to dislike the guy. I admit I was a little jealous in the beginning, but I know better now. You and I have flirted, but there hasn't ever been anything between us. You two have real chemistry. I can't tell you what to do, but in his shoes I'd want you to stick it out. I say work the case, then figure out a way to be together."

Maria smirked. "Is everything so cut and dry with you guys? I want to do just what you're saying, but I don't know if I can."

Rod smiled, "You'll figure it out, and then one day I'll be coming to you for advice."

After two hours of talking, looking at fabric samples, and shopping, they were on their way back to the hotel. She had purchased several needlepoint projects and a couple of skeins of yarn to crotchet an afghan.

Alone in her room, she thought about her conversation with Alex. What did he expect her to do? She didn't know how to play the weak, vulnerable female, and she wasn't about to start learning now. She would play her cards right, do what she was supposed to do, and eventually close the case. That was all that was required of Agent Maria Marisela Thomas.

Spates mulled over the situation with Maria for about an hour before deciding on a course of action and finally calling McCoy. He steepled his hands together. He usually loved any opportunity to talk with McCoy, but not today. "Yes, this is regarding operation Red Takedown. We may have a problem with Thomas. No, she is performing well, at least for now, but I'm concerned about her objectivity about the new plan.

"I think she's fallen for our civilian asset, Mr. Milbon. Right now, things are going as planned. Everyone is safe and secure, and our folks on the inside, McCorkle and Caldwell, have not been compromised. Thomas came to me requesting that we change the cover for Milbon. She would like him removed from the profile."

McCoy was thoughtful. She wanted to support Maria in any way that she could, but changing the scenario now would only bring more suspicion. They needed to stay on track and not give the Russians anything more to be concerned about. They were getting too close to closing this case out for slipups. "I'll tell you what. I have to go to Denver tomorrow for two weeks. Tell Agent Thomas that you missed me and that a decision will have to be postponed until then. She can distance herself, but there can be no change in plan for the moment. Hopefully in two weeks we will be well on our way to putting these thugs away for a long time. I know of a great Siberian gulag that would welcome their presence. When I get back I will take a trip to Memphis and have a little chat with her. She's very special to me, as I know she is to you, but we want this case to be successful."

Spates welcomed the support. "I agree that we shouldn't go messing with the parameters of the operation now. She'll be disappointed, but in a few years she will thank us for helping to make her a stronger agent."

Chapter 21

Mikha was in much better spirits now. The deal with Maria had gone well by Russian standards. They had been able to move the product, and now they had room to make other deals.

His satisfaction over the deal could only be compared to the satisfaction he'd had with his last two ladies. On some level he knew he was perverted and depraved when it came to women, but it didn't stop him from enjoying his little games.

Lately he had been watching a cute little number at Goran's club. She seemed to be on the periphery, never really out in the forefront, and he'd taken more than a little interest in her. He'd spoken with Goran about her and was given her basic background. He told Mikha her name was Sunny and she came into the club looking for a job because she was new in town. She spoke Spanish well, saying her Cuban parents were recent immigrants to Miami. She'd run away from Florida looking for a better future in Memphis.

Goran had hired her because she was pretty, desperate, and homeless. That usually made the woman a good candidate for his strip clubs or other business ventures. Mikha thought about her exotic Cuban features, finding himself turned on by the prospect of seeing her again.

She barely spoke to him when he came into the club and seemed almost spooked by him, Mikha noticed. She was always close, but chose to serve the other customers their orders before him. Maybe it was just that he had a reputation. Mikha thought she was unusual, which made her either a challenge or a danger. His instincts told him to watch her for a few more days before deciding. In the meantime, he had business to conduct.

He had called a meeting at his apartment with Ivan and Goran to talk about next steps and was waiting for them to arrive. Mikha looked out the windows of his apartment while he waited. The view of downtown Memphis reminded him of Odessa. Unlike Odessa, however, in Memphis, he had a shot at achieving his goals. Maria Manez was his ticket to success.

Ivan arrived first. He did a general surveillance sweep of the apartment, more out of habit than necessity. Goran arrived a few minutes later and was pleased to find that his compatriot had straightened up his act. Still, worry furrowed his brow. He knew Mikha was about to upset the proverbial apple cart. The man was never satisfied.

After a round of Stoli the meeting began. As usual, Ivan discussed security issues. "Everything about Maria Manez checks out. I did some checks on her bodyguard and on the boyfriend. I don't have any tangible reason to suspect they are not who they say. My gut is not totally convinced, but not enough to stop doing business. I will continue my checks, and if they are dirty, maybe they will eventually slip up. I've followed her, paying special attention to the places where she spends most of her time and the people she meets with."

Ivan shuffled papers and photos around the table. "There are a couple of people that she has been seen with on more than one occasion. The bodyguard has a new girlfriend, and Maria and that woman seem very friendly. Everyone has met Maria's boyfriend—not a factor. He seems like a man in love and love can make you dangerous, but he left her before and will probably do it again. She's not going to change, and he won't ever fit in to her world. He doesn't seem on her level, way too straight. He won't even allow drug use in his club."

Mikha leaned back in his chair, sipping his drink contentedly. Nothing Ivan reported so far was cause for alarm.

Ivan continued. "One point of interest. She also has an uncle whom she sees quite regularly, and his place is a fortress. I suspect he is somehow involved in her business, but he is very cagey. I can't even seem to get a good photograph of him. I've tried several different tactics, but he doesn't let anyone get through the front door. That intrigues me. Of course, if anything more develops I will keep you posted."

Mikha and Goran listened thoughtfully, each attaching risk to what Ivan reported. In their line of work everything had to be assessed and considered before the next move was made.

Goran had little to add. "As for me, business goes well. I have no complaints. People love the dancers, the music, and the alcohol. Business is good without the guns."

Mikha had come to his own conclusions and was now ready to let the group in on his plan. He needed their cooperation, if not their approval; it would take a team effort to be able to pull off what he had in mind. It was time to contact Nikola Mudiuranov.

Mikha leaned in over the kitchen table where the three were sitting. His tone was serious, giving no indication that what he was about to say was up for discussion.

Goran thought that he would lose his lunch. This was the source of his persistent stomach irritation. He could only pray that Nikola would go for a deal. He had originally said for them to schedule a meeting in a couple of months. Mikha was trying to advance that timetable. Messing with Nikola got you two things: either his respect, or his wrath. They had no way of knowing which way the wind would blow for them.

There was heated debate in Russian as the trio decided the best way to handle things. Mikha disagreed with Ivan and Goran, who recommended caution and a chance to find out more information. They wanted to be sure their new business partners were trustworthy. In the end, Ivan and Goran bent to Mikha's will. Mikha wanted to go for the big deal with Maria. It would garner over two million dollars in resale value, but they would have to negotiate with Nikola. No one could move that amount of merchandise without his approval. He ruled with an iron fist, but to Mikha's way of thinking it was an old fist, one ready to be lopped off, and he was more than willing to do that in order to achieve his goals.

They met Nikola three days later. Mikha, Goran, Ivan, Viktor, and Gregor were escorted into Nikola's private office in his warehouse. Mikha was struck by the fact the office looked exactly as it had months ago. It was still dark and musty. And it still held the equipment he secretly fantasized about owning one day.

Nikola appeared amused by Mikha's desire to meet. They toasted with vodka after the initial greetings were made, and soon after the meeting began. Nikola spoke first. This time there were no pleasantries exchanged; he simply came to the point. His voice was strong and clear.

"I hear things, Mikha, about you making deals with the American woman. Is this true?"

Mikha hoped Nikola wouldn't begrudge him his ambition. Although his palms were wet with sweat, Mikha tried to remain cool. *"Da,* Nikola Mudiuranov. I felt if I hadn't met with her, I would've run the risk of losing the deal. I'd like to think I'm in the position now to sell more guns and make a lot more money. I'm not content to have such a small operation any longer. Surely you can understand that?" Mikha looked around boldly. If Nikola had been content for small deals, he wouldn't be a wealthy, respected man.

Nikola followed his gaze. He knew Mikha was ambitious, which pleased him, but he now he was in a quandary. The young man had deliberately disobeyed him and gone after a deal that he hadn't sanctioned. So, did he punish his impertinence or reward his tenacity?

Nikola narrowed his small eyes and set his thin lips in a grim line. His voice was low and gravelly. Mikha had reason to be nervous now. Nikola was a man known to make his enemies suffer. A former Mafia capo, he felt he had to maintain face at all times.

"Mikha, what is it that you propose, and what do you want of me?"

The younger man saw this as his opportunity. "When we spoke earlier, we discussed increasing our gun-sale operation and moving our base of operations here to Memphis. I'd like to do that now. I think with this American woman, Maria Manez, we can greatly increase our sales and profits. She could open up a significant pipeline for us all along the East Coast. Our sales numbers have been fine on the West Coast and in other regions, but our area of greatest opportunity comes from the east. I'd like to look into doing a multimillion-dollar deal with her. She says she can handle the volume. To move so many guns, we would need your dock connections as well as police protection. I don't want to take the chance of my merchandise, *our* merchandise, getting hijacked."

Nikola nodded. "I'd like to meet with your American woman." He smiled at his own cleverness. "Set up the meeting for three months from now. I have business to take care of in Canada. You wait until I get back before you make any more moves with her. If I like her, we do business."

Nikola assessed him coolly, shaking a gnarled finger at him. "I am not an unreasonable man. Your impudence is forgiven this time. I am not so old that I don't understand the impatience of youth. We make a deal for one hundred thousand guns."

He rubbed the back of his fat hand across his mouth. "I don't want them in my warehouses anymore. You take your finder's fee and begin operation as you see fit. I take thirty-five percent. *Da?*"

The deal was unjust and they both knew it, but Mikha checked his anger. He would take being treated like an insolent child. For now. "*Da,* Nikola. I will contact her to schedule a meeting three months from now. *Spasiba.*"

Mikha stood up to leave. Nikola motioned for him to sit again. He would dismiss him in his own time.

When the two men were facing each other again, Nikola reached for his hand. He held it firmly, his left thumb in a viselike grip. He bent Mikha's thumb back, almost breaking it. Ivan and Goran watched intently, wondering how far this scene would go. Mikha refused to give in to the pain. He accepted that Nikola felt he had to take some action. He remembered what it was like growing up in Odessa and Moscow, willing his mind to go blank. Nikola could do whatever he wanted to him. He had been caught behind enemy lines as a soldier in Afghanistan. He'd suffered much worse than Nikola could ever do to him now.

Several tense minutes passed before Nikola let go. He smiled his satisfaction when he noticed Mikha's grimace as he let go of his hand. "You wait for me to return from Canada." He stood up, signaling that the meeting was over. His bodyguards walked over to escort Mikha and his entourage from warehouse.

Mikha waited until he was in the privacy of his own home before he called Maria. He wanted to savor the moment by himself. Despite the problem with Nikola, he had been successful. Soon he would be able to start his own organization in Memphis. This was good news, no matter the sacrifice. He wanted to celebrate. Later he would go to Goran's club to see if Sunny was available.

Chapter 22

GUNSHOT VICTIM FOUND IN NORTHEAST
SCHOOL SHOOTING IN THE DISTRICT
SHOOTING VICTIM DIES IN SOUTHEAST.

It seemed the headlines were always the same. The number of shootings was increasing, as were the fears and heartbreak. Maria read the latest facts and figures and despised Mikha more for his role in the continuing saga of gun deaths in the district, as well as around the nation. She had been back in the city for a week. She was miserable, depressed, and irritable. She missed Alexandro more than she thought possible.

She kept up the pretense of her undercover assignment, often going to the most dangerous and depraved neighborhoods in the city. She wanted to feel connected to those she was working so hard to save. Those who knew her as Maria Manez either welcomed her presence or resented it. After a couple of hours on one such trip, she was emotionally exhausted. She shouldn't even be in the area unless under the pretext of making sales. She got back in her car and drove back to her condo near the harbor. She hoped that she could sleep tonight. Her eyes were drawn and puffy from sleep deprivation. It had been a long, lonely week. Rod was out of pocket for a few days at Quantico. She was on her own and at her wit's end. *Now what?*

When Maria awoke early the next morning, she knew she needed to contact Spates as soon as possible. She packed a light bag and made her reservations before calling him. He couldn't say no. She wanted to leave as quickly as possible. Last night had been miserable, and she didn't want to endure another endless evening looking out of her bay windows at the Baltimore skyline.

The September weather was beautiful; the cloudless starry skies seemed to mock her. She was on top of the world by most standards, but it wasn't real. Her body craved something more.

Coffee in hand, she dialed his number. It wasn't quite 8:00 A.M., but she knew Spates would be going at full throttle.

"Spates," he answered simply.

"Hello, sir, it's Agent Thomas. I need a favor. I need to go off line for a week. I need to spend some quiet time alone before going back to Memphis. I thought a trip in the country would do me good. I've done just about all I can for a while, anyway. Ivan has a whole month's worth of material to report on. My report, by the way, will be on your desk by tomorrow morning." She was talking too fast and she knew it, but she couldn't slow down. She was so keyed up she felt like she was on stimulants. Maria finally took a deep gulp of air while she waited for a response.

Spates was very proud of what she had accomplished. Any request she made would be granted as long as it was reasonable. He smiled to himself. He knew his agents. Maria always talked faster when she wanted something, but was too nervous to ask directly.

His response was slow and measured. He hoped to

help calm her down a bit. "I think that's a great idea. Why don't you make it two weeks? Rest, relax, spend some time doing some of that crafting that you are so famous for." He chuckled to himself, careful not to offend her feelings. She enjoyed her tough-girl image. He wouldn't let her know that she was as highly regarded for her weapons and other skills as for her capacity for friendship and caring.

Maria hesitated. Two weeks sounded heavenly, but would that be too long away from the case? She decided she would change her reservation to extend the time, but if she started getting stir-crazy she could always return sooner. "Sounds great. I'm heading to Solomon's Island. I'll check in with you as soon as I get settled in. I am sure there are some fish down there with my name on them," she joked.

That area of Maryland was one of his favorites, too. "Sounds good to me. I want a souvenir."

"You got it, sir, thanks."

"You're welcome. Have a great time."

She left a message for Roderick, loaded up her Maria Manez Bureau car, a red Ferrari, and soon after was on I-95S headed for St. Mary's County.

She looked forward to strolling along the riverbanks, fishing, and cooking over an open fire. Going off line would guarantee her that Ivan or anyone else from Mikha's organization wouldn't be following her. The Bureau would make sure they were occupied during her absence. She was going to relax and have a wonderful time being plain old Maria Thomas again. No makeup, no designer clothes, and no pretenses. Just blue jeans and T-shirts.

The traffic headed toward the island was light. She had picked the perfect time for her trip. Most of the rush-hour traffic was gone, and as she suspected, the trip didn't take more than a couple of hours. The Ferrari handled like a dream. The suspension and steering were taut like she liked them. She enjoyed the power of the sleek engine under her body. *Out on the open road,* she thought. *This is more like it.* She smiled for the first time in several days.

Ramon knocked on the open door before entering. "Hey, boss, what's shaking?" Alex was wading through the paperwork on his desk. But his concentration was not on receipts, inventory, or sales. Business had been great lately. The weather was sunny, breezy, with just the right amount of humidity. People seemed to enjoy hanging out to all hours when they came to the city. Tourists loved coming to his club. Each night they had to turn people away to stay within the fire code, but as Alex sat behind his mahogany desk he found it difficult to find pleasure in anything right now.

He watched the condensation on his martini glass while absently circling the rim with his finger. His Sour Apple did nothing to calm his tense nerves, did nothing to stop the ache in his heart for Maria. Unlike before, he wouldn't try to seek solace with another woman. He would give her time and space, and hope she'd be back. Eventually. He just had no idea how long he could hold out.

Ramon continued talking to Alex. "You work too hard. After the Labor Day rush you should consider taking a short vacation. Max and I can handle this place for a few days. I gotta tell you, you are starting to look a little rough around the edges."

Alex looked up from his paperwork. "What are you

trying to say? You wouldn't be angling for my job, would you?"

Ramon laughed. "No, you can keep it. I see the way you are always doing paperwork. I think I will pass on that. Just want to make sure that I don't find you passed out on the desk one day."

Alex shook his head. "You're all heart, man. I'll think about it. If I decide to do it, I'll let you know."

After Ramon left, Alex sat in his chair, thinking. He longed to talk with someone familiar so he could feel connected. It had been a long time since he'd thought about his former life in Virginia. Right now, he would love to be playing basketball with some of his buddies. He wondered for the first time in a long while what some of his old friends were up to.

Or maybe this nostalgia could be attributed to the fact that he missed Maria and there wasn't a thing he could do about it. Before Ramon interrupted, he had been troubled by the memories of their last meeting. She had made her position clear and he would abide by her decision, no matter how wrong he thought she was. Being without her these last several days had made him think of domestic things. Settling down, children, and the white picket fence. He didn't want to be domestic. He wanted to be hard and strong and totally unaffected by her leaving. Instead she had him strung out and waiting and acting like a wuss.

Alex slammed his fist on the wood desk. "Dammit, Maria, why are you so stubborn?" he said to the empty office. He knew he was losing it. Ramon was right. He needed a fresh perspective. He called the one person who just might be able to help.

He reverted to Spanish immediately. *"Hola,* Marisela."

"Alexandro! Is everything alright?" Concerned peppered her tone. It was unusual for someone in the Witness Program to call their handler, but then again, Alex had never played by the rules.

The sound of her voice was reassuring. He trusted Marisela more than anyone else in the Bureau, with the exception of Maria, of course. "Yes and no. I just needed to talk with someone familiar. I guess I am kinda missing my old life." Alex hesitated. Maybe he shouldn't have called. His voice sounded defeated. "I'd like something. . . . I don't know what I am looking for."

Marisela knew, but she didn't know if he wanted to hear it. "I hear very good things about you, *hijo*. The club is doing well, thanks to your business ideas. I love the fact that you are doing a Latin night. Of course, I think you should do it more often than once a month, but who am I?"

Alex was warmed by her sense of humor and wit. "How are things going with you? You still giving Juan a hard time?"

"No, that old goat is still giving me a hard time. I wish he would retire. After thirty-eight years, he's making *me* think of retirement. But anyway, what's going on with you and Maria? I hear you two are playing footsie in Memphis."

His laugh was warm and rich. She'd always had a way of cheering him up. "You do have a way with words. I want to play more than footsie with Maria, Marisela, but she's fighting me. I think she is too concerned about her job. Right now, I don't think she has room in her life for both." His voice faded. "I don't want to lose her, but she's pushing me away. I don't know how to get through to her."

Marisela heard the pain in his voice as Alex spoke. Reflecting on her conversation with her niece not long ago, she'd heard the same in Maria's. She would like nothing better than to see the couple together and happy. With no children of her own, her job had become her life. And now her niece and Alexandro had become a very special part of that. She chose her next words carefully.

"Alexandro, my niece can be very stubborn, especially when she thinks she is making an honorable choice. Her sense of duty and responsibility run strongly through her. Don't ask her to compromise who she is. Let her know that you will always be there for her. She needs you more than she wants you, and it's your job to show her that. Maria will give up all personal gain for her job. Know what you are up against, and decide if that's a battle you are prepared to fight."

She paused. "I have to admit when I first heard about you two I was wary. Now I'd say you two were made for each other. You're both bossy, temperamental, strong-willed, and just loving enough to keep each other straight. I think you are very lucky, *hijo*."

Alex smiled to himself. He agreed. He was very lucky to have found Maria again. She was everything that he ever wanted in a woman, and then some. Alex finished his conversation with Marisela and then prepared to make some other calls.

Only Maria could keep him coming back when he swore he wouldn't. He'd made his decision. He dialed her cell phone number first.

He was frustrated when he couldn't reach her. That night, he went to bed again with Maria on his mind. It would be another restless night.

The next morning brought new decisions and fresh insight. He was glad for his conversation with Marisela. When he arrived at the office, he told Ramon and Max that he would be out of town for the next few days. He went to his office and took a few minutes of quiet time before making his next phone call.

"Agent Spates, this is Alexandro Milbon. I need some information from you. When you asked me to help with the case, I did so, albeit with hesitation. I know how hard you guys work and how much you put it on the line every day. If it hadn't been for you I would be dead right now. So I am asking you to trust me. I need to be with her. Tell me where Maria is."

Spates recognized the strangled tone of his voice. He was a man on the edge. Funny how love could make you lose your mind like that. *Dammit, these young agents are going to make me lose all my hair!* "Milbon, I'd like to help you, but she's asked for a little down time. I can't say that I blame her; she's been working very hard and she deserves it. If she didn't tell you where she was going, I don't think that it was an oversight. She wants a break. From everything."

Anger boiled just beneath the surface. Alex was having difficulty breathing. "Agent Spates, perhaps you don't realize how important this is to me. I'd better explain."

It was eighty-five degrees and summer showed no sign of relenting so that fall could be ushered in. Maria strolled along the exhibits of the Calvert Marine Museum at a leisurely pace. She had always enjoyed finding out how things worked and examining their history. She supposed that's what had made her such a good crime scene investigator when she first joined the Bureau. She needed answers and she would do whatever it took to get them. Long hours, uncomfortable situations, and diabolical crimes were just par for the course. The museum filled her with the same kind of wonder.

Marine life offered humans a way to look at the environment the way it was several million years ago. She was fascinated by the way fish and water mammals adjusted and evolved to ensure their survival. After strolling for an hour, she went on the lighthouse tour. The view was spectacular, but she realized living in the cramped quarters took more dedication than she thought she could ever muster. The gentle breeze off the Patuxent River felt heavenly. She wished she could sit and watch the water all day, but the tour was only half an hour. A few stomach rumbles later, she knew it was time to move on anyway.

Maria left there to go in search of some good barbecue. Her time in Memphis had spoiled her. She asked a couple of the locals where they would recommend that she eat.

Her time away was well worth it. She had spent a week in the warmth, surrounded by peacefulness. It was too soon to imagine heading back to Baltimore. She called Spates to confirm that she would take him up on his offer for an extra week. She also asked about surveillance and reported she hadn't seen Ivan anywhere. Spates confirmed he was still in Memphis and wouldn't be bothering her for the next week.

"You're free to enjoy yourself. You might want to check out the Navy Recreational Center. You can probably get a room on the water. I have some connections if you are interested."

Maria was excited. She could go fishing at the facility, too. She had managed to read, do some crafts and go swimming, but she hadn't managed to sleep under the stars like she'd wanted. She enthusiastically agreed to the offer. She felt freer still knowing the Russians weren't watching. She looked down at her T-shirt and shorts and grinned. They wouldn't recognize her anyway.

She packed an overnight bag with a few essentials and told the hotel staff she would be back before the end of the week. They were to hold her messages until her return.

True to his word, Spates had arranged for her to be housed at one of the Navy cottages. Maria was delighted. She had a wonderful view of the water and full facilities. The cottages were two- and three-bedroom units, complete with separate living and dining rooms. She had enjoyed the hotel, but was now able to cook for herself in the full kitchen.

With her map of the Center, she struck out to find a good spot to camp. She was going to rough it tonight and then return to the cabin in the morning. She'd had to make a choice to either camp or have a cottage. She knew that she probably looked silly, but pitched her tent right next to her cottage anyway. She listened to the waves all night, enjoying the smell of the water; the sound of its lapping helped to relax her soul.

Maria wondered where her life was headed. Was she a FBI lifer, like her aunt Marisela? She was looking at another ten years before she could even think about retiring, and even then she would be much too young to stop working. What did that leave? A husband? Kids? She had a couple more years to go before that dreaded thirty-five when she would be considered mature for having children. She had never been pregnant, and at this point didn't even know if it was possible. She couldn't assume that she would be able to pump out a couple of babies just because she wanted to.

Maria got comfortable in her tent, turning off her

lamp and enjoying the darkness. She listened to the frogs singing, the water, and the breeze gently swaying branches of the trees. Soon all was calm. Soon all thoughts of the future gave way to a complete and restful sleep.

Chapter 23

In the morning when she awoke, she returned to the cottage. She'd smelled food and assumed it was the neighbor's. She walked in the door rubbing her back, which was stiff from sleeping on the hard earth. As soon as she pushed open the screen door to walk inside, she let out a blood-curdling scream. "Alex what in the world are you doing here?"

The smell of bacon wafted through the air. He looked at her disheveled appearance and chuckled to himself. He was silent as he cracked four more eggs for their omelets.

"You've got grass in your hair," he said, finally.

Instinctively, she raked her hands through her tangled mass of curls. She knew she must look a fright, but that's what he got for surprising her. Her eyes burned a steady hole through him.

"Answer me, Alexandro Milbon! What are you doing here? I came here to get away from it all, so how did you find me?" *To get away from you,* she thought, but wouldn't say. Why was her heart fluttering at the sight of him?

He ignored her questions. His only response was, "Toast?"

He pulled four slices from the loaf, then put them in the toaster while she glared at him.

He successfully resisted the urge to grin; she probably wouldn't appreciate it.

Finally he said, "Let's just say that I have friends in high places. If you want me to leave after breakfast, I will, but I had to see you again. I didn't like the way we left things. Didn't like what I said to you. That's not my style. I came here to apologize."

Now her heart thudded in her chest. She muttered something about being right back and exited the room quickly.

Maria looked at her reflection in the bathroom mirror. It was worse than she had expected. Assorted bits of grass and leaves were scattered through her hair for decoration, and her face had a few red splotches from insect bites. Her mouth felt like cotton and her body felt like a truck had hit her.

Maria felt a shudder of embarrassment. She thought, *If he still wants you after seeing you like this he should have his head examined*. Her lamenting was cut short by her appetite. Her stomach reacted noisily after another whiff of the bacon Alex was cooking. But she couldn't go back this way. She opted to take a quick shower before returning to the kitchen. When she was finished, even she had to be impressed. Five minutes flat, including the hair washing. She was ready to face him now.

His body would always have the same reaction to her. He had smelled her light scent while he was cooking and it drove him crazy. The scent of warm vanilla sugar trailed into the room, and he knew she was near. He didn't know if he could make good on his promise to himself to leave after breakfast. He knew he wanted nothing less than all of her. His body begged to make love to her. His groin tightened in the most uncomfortable way whenever she was near. He needed a distraction.

When Maria fully entered the room, she could see that he was placing pancakes on their plates. She appreciated his efforts for her. "Everything looks great. What do you want me to do?" she asked cheerfully.

He found it difficult to look at her without wanting to touch her. "I've got everything under control. You look great, by the way. Your time away seems to be agreeing with you."

Her almond skin flushed a deep bronze. He made her feel beautiful even when she wore blue jean cutoffs and a tank top. She walked into the dining room of the cottage. If he was trying to seduce her, it was working. He had set the table and even put white roses in a vase for the centerpiece. Maria looked at him in wonderment. She had plenty of questions for him, but they could wait. For now she would eat and enjoy his company.

Alex joined her, bringing the rest of the food to the table. He reached for her hand before blessing the food. The warmth that spread through her because of his touch felt good.

Maria sniffed. "This is delicious as usual," she told him.

This was her territory and she planned on making the rules. "This morning I am going to catch some fish for my supper. I am not the best in the kitchen, but I can make a mean fish over the fire. I had planned on walking along the Riverwalk today. Maybe even have lunch at Solomons Pier."

Alex snickered.

Maria loved to see the twinkle in his eye when he was amused. He was even more devastatingly handsome when he smiled that devilish grin.

"Great. After *we* clean up the kitchen I'll grab my gear and be right with you."

She gritted her teeth. "Are you always going to be this insufferable? I told you what *I* was doing. Don't remember inviting you, though." She took another bite from her omelet while she waited for his response.

He wasted no time in spreading it thick. "Maria Thomas, I would be honored if you would allow me to spend the day with you. Although you are ornery at times, I enjoy your company tremendously. I promise I'll be a good boy. I'll even bait your hooks if you want me to."

She snickered and pretended to consider his proposal for several minutes. She ate her bacon and buttered her toast. The man was truly a marvel in the kitchen, she thought. Her breakfast usually consisted of cold cereal or an energy bar. She loved being pampered by him.

She reached for his hand over the table. Her tone was much softer when she answered him. "Thank you for coming, Alex. If you don't mind following my agenda, you are more than welcome to stay with me. But this is the last day I do dishes. If you chose to cook, you clean up. I came here to get away from it all. I'm on vacation from my life, as I know it right now, anyway." She sat back in her chair when she was finished. Alex was pleased. He would do dishes, toilets, ironing, or just about anything else to be with her.

Agent Maria Thomas had transformed into a fresh-faced young woman while on vacation. Looking at her, he almost felt like he was robbing the cradle. This care-free, casual girl-woman had replaced the elegant designer-clad woman he had come to love in Memphis. It would be interesting to see whom he liked best.

"You're right. I invaded your space. I'll clean up this

time. Get your gear, I'll be ready for you in a jiffy. Don't forget your sunscreen. It will probably take us a while to get enough for dinner. This is kind of late to start fishing."

Maria wrinkled her nose at him. "A good fisherman can fish anytime, anywhere. Thanks again for breakfast."

She readied herself, and after she'd brought her supplies into the living room, she went back to the kitchen to help him dry and put away the dishes.

Twenty minutes later they were loading up the SUV he'd rented. He had come prepared and she was impressed with his selection of rods, reels, and hooks. She tried to gently examine his equipment without appearing to study it or look over his shoulder.

Alex laughed to himself. She wasn't exactly subtle, he thought as he watched her from the safety of his sunglasses. She definitely had some control issues, but that was okay, he figured. A few months, or years, of butting heads, and they would learn to compromise. He wasn't giving up without a fight.

The drive to the pier was a very short one, in fact. It took them longer to load and unload their supplies. The tourist season was just about over. Sunset Pier was mostly empty, so they had their choice of fishing spots. True to his word, he baited their hooks while Maria set up the portable chairs and table. Minutes later, with a cooler between them, they had their rods in the water and were enjoying the breeze off the river.

Her heart sang with delight. Yes, this was the feeling she was after. The warm sun danced off the blue water, the breeze ruffled her hair, and she was with Alex.

He was supposed to be keeping his eye on his fishing pole, but instead he watched her. A strong feeling of contentment washed over him too. There was no place in the world he'd rather be than right here with her.

The sun had given her hair highlights throughout the summer, and now the brown streaks were more pronounced.

Maria knew that he was watching her. She liked it too. No one else had made her feel so beautiful, so cherished.

But she needed to know what he was up to. "I have some questions for you," she said lazily.

"I knew you would. What do you want to know first?" he responded casually.

"How did you know where to find me and what made you want to?"

"You know the answer to both those questions, so are you just making conversation?"

"Are you always going to be this maddening?"

"I want to kiss you."

She smiled, but continued to look straight ahead at the water. "Can't. We're fishing right now."

Alex shook his head. "I guess I should be asking you if you are always going to be difficult too."

Her line began to shake violently. She had to stand up quickly before she lost her rod. Maria whooped in excitement. Several moments later, wiping the sweat off her brow, she reeled in a very large darter fish. She reset her line and cast her lure thirty feet out into the water before she sat again. "Well, guess I got my dinner for tonight. I suppose you will be making hot dogs for yourself," she gloated.

"Such churlish language from such a pretty mouth. The day is young and there are plenty more fish in the river. Just be patient, *querida*."

An hour later they had five good-sized fish in their

catch bucket. They packed up the equipment and supplies and headed back to the cottage.

In the car he told her what she wanted to know. "When I couldn't reach you, I called Spates and I made him an offer he couldn't refuse. I hopped in the car late last night after getting a pass to come on post. When I drove up I noticed your tent. I called out to you, but when you didn't respond I correctly assumed that you were sleeping in it. You left the door unlocked, so I kinda made myself at home. I checked on you a couple of times during the night, but you were so out of it that I didn't want to disturb you. I brought my things in and took a shower and hit the sack myself. You are so beautiful when you sleep."

At his comment Maria's skin felt flushed and heated; the warm air had nothing to do with the increased temperature she felt. He had a way of turning her tough exterior to mush. *He was going to be very difficult to keep at bay,* she told herself, but she needed to try. She moved the conversation toward safer ground.

"When I left I wasn't trying to worry you. I just needed a little time to myself. It has been a crazy year. I felt myself coming unglued, and I didn't like that. The good news is that in a few months this thing will be over and I should have some down time before being called into action again."

Alex felt a familiar burning in the pit of his stomach and his gut tightening. Whenever he thought of her moving on or participating in another dangerous situation, he wanted to stop her, but after talking with Marisela he knew that would be a mistake. The Bureau meant so much more to her than just a job. She had a right to choose her own path, especially one that she had worked so hard to forge. He wouldn't try to com-

pete with something that was such a big part of her life—
his only choice was to learn to live with it.

Conversation ceased when they reached the cottage.
They unloaded the car and went about preparing for the
rest of the day. She felt hot and sticky from her time on
the pier so she went to freshen up. When Alex heard the
shower water turned on he resisted the urge to join her.
Being so close to her was going to be tougher than he
thought. His body reacted violently to her whenever she
was near. He groaned as he headed toward the bathroom in the second bedroom to take a cold shower. *At
this rate he wouldn't have to worry about being sexually frustrated. He would die from pneumonia,* he thought miserably.

After completing her shower and moisturizing her
body with her favorite scent, she debated with herself
over what to wear. She had been in shorts and a tank top
during most of her stay, but now she wanted something
a bit more feminine. She put her blow dryer on the
highest setting and styled her slightly damp hair in a
bob. In the eight months she had been in Memphis, it
had grown out to her chin in the front, while the back
was still a little shorter. By the time they reached their
destination it would be completely dry in a mass of wavy
curls.

After her marine tour the other day she'd picked up
the cutest sundress on sale. She didn't want to give Alex
the wrong impression, though. She fingered the soft gar-
ment before she made her decision. It was perfect, with
the texture and feel she wanted.

Alex had changed into a pair of black tailored slacks,
black soft Italian leather shoes, and an olive green short-
sleeved brushed silk shirt. She almost felt underdressed
in her easy silk sheath and low-heeled sandals. The dress

reached her ankles and the simple lines framed each curve.

Alex looked at her appreciatively. Maria saw, but ignored the gleam in his eye, more because she didn't want her body to respond to him, than for any other reason.

"You look nice. Ready to hit the Riverwalk? There are about half a dozen places that I want to stop into." She secretly congratulated herself on her acting skills. He had her body in overdrive, but she managed to stop herself from pouncing on him.

He responded to her with the same affected aloofness. "That shading of taupe brings out your tan and the highlights in your hair nicely. I like the red Maria-wear, but neutrals look just as nice. So, do I get to ride in the Ferrari?"

She stopped to pick up her purse from the dinette table. "Nope." She tossed him the keys. "But you get to drive it."

"You sure? I was looking forward to seeing you behind the wheel."

"We've got plenty of time for that. Don't mess up my 'do by driving too fast. Let's go. My stomach is starting to rumble, despite that wonderful breakfast that you fixed. I guess we should stop by the grocery store on our way back for some snacks, huh?"

He held the door open for her. "Lead the way. Your wish is my command."

They drove down Solomons Island Road for several minutes, then parked near the boat rental. The sidewalks of the Riverwalk were filled with casual strollers. Lovers walked hand in hand. Mothers pushed baby carriages. Teens laughed and teased each other along the wide boardwalk. Some looked at Alexandro curiously.

His six-foot-five stature commanded attention. With his custom-made clothing, many looked to see if he was someone famous. Whenever female onlookers became too bold, Maria would move closer to him or seek his hand possessively. He chuckled inwardly. *Women.* He wasn't complaining however; any time he could be closer to her was fine by him.

They worked their way down to Solomons Pier, stopping in several souvenir shops, the Harmon House Shops, and Carmen's Gallery. Alex accepted each bag without complaint. He knew how some women liked to shop. She was in her element telling him how she just had to have item after item. He loved the sparkle in her eye when she found some new trinket. She bought souvenirs for everyone in her family, including Tía Marisela.

He noticed her admiring an Austrian crystal train set. She studied each piece before moving on to other figurines. She could more than afford the cost, but her more practical nature won out. The price tag was four digits, so she passed.

They finally arrived at the restaurant laden down with bags after what seemed like hours of shopping and strolling. The car was located at the opposite end of the pier, but Alex insisted on taking the packages back to lock them in the trunk right after he'd ordered.

Fifteen minutes later he was back. His long strides were seemingly unaffected by the previous weight of the bags.

They shared a window booth with a spectacular view. They watched the boaters, folks on jet skis, swimmers, walkers, and diners. Maria had always been fascinated by human behavior and she was having a ball people watching. She had enjoyed her dinner of very tender and juicy filet mignon and lightly breaded fried shrimp. Alex had enjoyed steak and lobster.

"Now, that was good food!" she acknowledged. I'm going to have to come back here before I leave at the end of the week. I almost dread going back to Baltimore."

Alex listened, absently plucking a crouton from her salad. He didn't even want to think about going back to Memphis without her.

"I feel so relaxed here," she continued. Was it the atmosphere or the company?

He looked at her intently. "I have a question for you."

She noticed his brown eyes took on a smoky quality when he was serious.

He started slowly. "I'm not going to ask you for more than you're comfortable with, but I need to know that we are the real thing. I guess I'm asking for exclusivity. I'm not willing to be intimate with anyone else, but I can't assume you feel the same way. In my mind, you will always be my Maria."

She chuckled. "Is that all? Alexandro, I don't want anyone else but you. I am very content being your Maria," she added softly.

"You mean everything to me. I know that I am repeating myself, but I have to say it again. You look so beautiful in that dress, I am having a hard time concentrating on anything but you."

She saw the desire smoldering in the soft brown depths of his eyes.

Again, she retreated to safer ground; the topic and the intensity of his gaze were beginning to unnerve her. A few more minutes and she would be in his arms, where she longed to be anyway.

"I'm glad we'll have a late dinner. I'm sure that I will

be hungry again after I finish my swim. I need to stay in shape. How do you keep so fit? It must be hard for you to keep a schedule with your hours."

"Sometimes, but with my height and build I have to make the commitment. Laziness is not an option for me. I try to work out at least five times a week without fail. I'll go swimming with you, if you don't mind. Maybe I can get in some laps. Besides, I need to practice my strokes."

She tipped her face to the sun. *Men!* "You can tag along as long as you promise to behave. We can swim at the navy Aquatics Complex, which is very nicely equipped, or if you're game, we can hit the beach. You brought your trunks too. You really are a Boy Scout. I'm impressed."

His eyes burned with invisible flame as he spoke to her. "And yet there's so much more that I'd like to share with you. Are you ready for the walk back to the car? I don't think that I can sit much longer."

She stood up, stretching as she did. "Yep, I've got to get this body back in the gym. I feel the old bones creaking."

Alex reached for her hand. "Come on, old woman. Lean on me for support. I gotcha."

They walked hand in hand to the car, continuing their light banter.

"So tell me, why were you sleeping in a tent outside a perfectly good two-bedroom cottage?"

She laughed. "I know, that must have looked strange. I really wanted to go camping, sleep under the stars, and all that good stuff. But, I would've had to give up my reservation for the cottage. I decided to have it my way and do both by sleeping outside for one night. It was great, too. It reminded me of one of my first field assignments." She chuckled again at the memory of how she looked when she first entered the cottage and Alexandro was in her kitchen.

Alex marveled at her. *What couldn't she do?* "Tell me you can play a little basketball and we'll get married today."

She tipped her head toward him. "I've been known to drive it down the lane and in for a dunk a time or two."

He smiled, taking her hand in his. *There was so much to love about her,* he thought.

Returning to the cottage, they found the sun was still bright in the afternoon sky. Maria sat on the porch reading and watching the water for several minutes, allowing her stomach to settle before they went for a swim.

He stayed inside, giving her time and space while she read. An hour later he went to see if she was ready.

He found her on the porch with book in hand, sound asleep. He watched her silently. His heart filled with love. He would never get enough of her. He pushed a wayward tendril of hair away from her face. She stirred but did not awaken.

He reminisced about the night they shared on his couch. *Better leave while you still can,* he told himself.

When she awoke the book was in her lap and the temperature had dipped. She shivered and shook herself to get the blood circulating again. Swimming would wait until tomorrow.

She called out to Alex, but was greeted with silence. She went back into the house to search the rooms; she thought perhaps he had been taking a nap too.

A car door closing brought her attention back to the front of the house. She met Alex coming through the door with two bags full of groceries.

"I picked up a few snacks while you were napping. Do you feel better?"

"Yes, much better. I don't think I realized how much I had been running on empty. I could sleep and laze around for another week, I think."

She watched him unpacking the bags. "Thank you for picking up goodies. So, what did you get?"

He smacked her hands as she tried to inspect the bags. "Down girl," he said jokingly. "I've got this under control. You just go entertain yourself while I take care of this."

"Pass me those chocolate Oreos, and you've got yourself a deal. I hope you hadn't planned on eating any. They are my favorite cheat food."

"So, chocolate is the way to your heart? No can do, though. They are a part of my dessert surprise. Have an apple while I get things ready for us to make dinner. I am holding you to making your fire fish."

"That's fish over the fire, thank you. I'll be really good if you just let me get two."

Alex grinned at her. He stopped putting the food away to look into her eyes.

He pulled her to him and whispered in her ear, "I'm all the chocolate you will ever need," before crushing her lips in a passionate kiss. His tongue mated with hers until he heard her groan. His arousal was evident instantly. She melded her body along his, crushing his chest with her throbbing breasts.

How could she have waited so long to do this? Her body craved this. No, demanded this. Her senses were on overload. Familiar heat spread throughout her body and she felt moisture pooling at her core.

His long fingers caressed her back, stroked her hair, and finally, when he felt she couldn't stand much more, he began to pebble her nipples. Her back arched, giving him greater access. She enjoyed his touch for several seconds before moving his hands.

He stopped long enough to give her a questioning look.

Desire pounded through her body. Her dark brown eyes had taken on a smoky color. "Follow me," she practically ordered.

"*Querida,* are you sure?"

"No."

"We can wait."

"I can't."

They went to her bedroom. The bed was large, with several floral pillows on top of the comforter. She tossed them to the floor, hurriedly disposing of anything that would get in their way.

Alex tried to slow his breathing. He wanted her so badly he hurt.

She drew him near, planting kisses along his neck and chest. He enjoyed her light touch. He drew her face to meet his. Her lips were swollen from his earlier assault, but she didn't seem to mind. Their mouths met again. These kisses deeper and more intense than before and she felt like her knees were going to give way. Maria felt as if she were melting under an intense flame.

His body ached for her touch, and soon he wouldn't have the good sense to turn back. Moving the relationship to intimacy would make it harder for both of them back in Memphis. He still wanted more than she said she was willing to give. For now, this would have to be enough.

She stepped back long enough to pull her tank top over her head. Her nipples yearned for his touch again. The tawny buds jutted out, anticipating his caress.

Alex took off his shirt and loosened the buttons on his

trousers. He didn't remove them though. That would be up to her. She lay down on the bed, but not before taking off her cutoff shorts. Long legs and lace blurred his vision.

He inhaled the scent of warm vanilla sugar. It was everywhere that he touched her.

He removed her thong underwear with the pad of his thumb. He licked her nipples one at a time, and she arched her back for him, demanding more. He took in one firm bud and suckled until she called out his name. Her kisses were hard and demanding—she wanted all of him right now. She massaged his stiff member with one hand while she stroked his ripening nipples with the other. She sent him spiraling with sensation.

She reversed their positions, slowly climbing on top of him and pushing the fabric of his pants down, allowing them to drop to the floor. She found his sex with her mouth and began to tease him with soft, then hard, licks. He shook his head no.

"Not this time, sweetheart. I want you too bad. I don't know how long I can hold out. I want to pleasure you."

He rolled her on her stomach. He rained kisses down her neck, spine, and buttocks. His tongue found the wet cavern between her legs. He sucked gently, keeping her pinned beneath him. *She wanted to take control again, but not tonight,* he thought.

He positioned her on her back again, allowing her to suck his nipples before beginning his own ministrations on hers. She was so wet and so ready for him. He found it hard to concentrate on anything but being inside of her.

"Alex. Please. Now."

Slowly and seductively, his fingers ignited her special spot and gently brought her to her first release. She screamed his name over and over; her pleasure was pure and explosive. Her heart pounded in her chest, causing her breath to come in short gasps. She would never get enough of this man.

Alex waited for her to recover before he reached down to his pants pocket and withdrew a black foil packet. She read extra large on the package and glanced down at his well-endowed sex through hooded eyes before he entered her. He was much more man than she'd ever had before. She received all that his six feet five inches and two-hundred-twenty-five pounds had to offer.

"I love you, querida," he whispered softly to her.

"*Te quiero*, Alexandro. Love me . . ."

He entered her slowly to allow her to adjust to his size. Undulating her hips, she took more of him with each sway. Soon he completely filled her. She was so tight. So wet. She felt so good.

His voice was deep and husky when he spoke to her. "Oh, baby, you make life worth living."

Finding the perfect rhythm, they stroked each other lovingly. He changed the position so that she was on top. He grabbed her lush bottom and controlled the rhythm from under her. She offered her nipples, which he suckled greedily. He pushed into her farther and farther. She felt the first signs of another release bubbling up. "Alex. Oh, Alex," she moaned.

He increased the tempo, connecting with her most sensitive spot. They continued loving each other at a frenzied pace. He moved faster and deeper with each stroke. He loved the feeling of her closing in around him. His body began to shake.

Minutes later, Alex took one last gulp of air before exploding into her. He growled her name as his body convulsed in an energy-zapping orgasm.

Tears streamed down her face, as simultaneously she felt the release of her second orgasm. He completed her, made her feel like a woman; she never wanted to lose this feeling with him.

Her body continued to quiver, shattering the hard shell that she had so carefully built around her heart. She was his, and he was hers. There could be no turning back.

He brought her sweat-slick body down on top of him. They lay chest to chest for several minutes, allowing their breathing to return to normal. She thought her body would never stop trembling. Her orgasm seemed to go on and on. Somewhere in the recesses of her mind she thought it should be illegal to make a woman feel that good.

Alex kissed her hair, her forehead, her face. "Thank you, *corazón*. I don't know how I'll ever be able to leave you again."

"I don't want to think about that now. I feel too good." She adjusted herself so that she could stroke him again.

"Oh, you wicked woman. Are you trying to kill me?" he teased.

"Never. I want you around for a long . . . *stroke* . . . long . . . *stroke* . . . long . . . *stroke* . . . time."

Alex moaned, enjoying the feel of her. She was getting to know his body very well. "My thoughts exactly."

Chapter 24

She and Alex spent the next couple of days shopping, reading, exercising, and loving each other completely. Everything else in the world had ceased to exist in the cozy world that they had created for each other. Maria had never felt so free and content, and Alex found himself thinking about forever.

Mindful to give each other personal space, Maria was reading a magazine on the back porch of the cottage. She walked into the kitchen, drawn by a tantalizing aroma. "I know that smell. Oh, my goodness, *tía* Marisela. No one makes *carne frita y tostones* like *tía*. Tell me you followed her exact recipe and I'll marry you right now," Maria gushed, licking her lips in anticipation.

Alex watched her in amusement. He would love to take her up on the offer. He found thoughts of marriage to her more and more appealing.

"She wouldn't let me cook with her or touch her precious kitchen gadgets, but I managed to pick up a few tips and recipes during my time with her." He placed a drumstick on a plate for her to taste. "What do you think?"

Maria closed her eyes, sighing in satisfaction. The chicken was better than *tia's*, if that was possible. "I've got my dinner. What are you going to eat?" she teased. "Alex this is divine. Can I clone you?"

He looked at her through sultry brown eyes.

Too bad she was just joking about marriage. She had to admit she was blissfully happy playing house with Alexandro, but the fact remained, she was an agent of the FBI on a major case.

Alex's heart grew heavy when he thought about leaving Maria. He loved their time together, but he knew it was only temporary. After the next night, he made the decision to return to Memphis. The longer they were together, the harder it would be to break away. One of them had to be practical, so he figured it might as well be him.

They sat in front of a campfire on the beach. The flame flickered in the cool September night air. He held her between his legs, rocking her to the gentle beat the river played against the rocks.

She listened to the hard thud of his heart beating against her back. She sensed that something was wrong. "What's on your mind, sailor? You've been quiet most of the night," she said.

Alex kissed her hair then hugged her closer. She felt his withdrawal. They hadn't talked about how long he would spend with her, but at that moment she knew he was leaving. "You're leaving in the morning." His warm breath stirred longing in her. She wanted to be with this man always.

Alex had to tell her. He spoke softly in her ear, quietly, comfortingly. "I need to get back. I hate leaving you, especially since you won't be returning to Memphis right away, but I've—"

She turned around to put her fingers to his lips.
"Shush. . . . You don't have to explain anything to me.
This wasn't planned, and we can't do anything about
what's already done. No regrets, my love," she sighed.
"Let's not talk about it. Just hold me, Alexandro."

"Reach into my pocket. I have something for you,"
Alex said.

Trying to lighten the mood, Maria, said, "You frisky
old dog, you!"

"Get your mind out of the gutter, woman. You'll get
that surprise later. Now be a good girl and reach in."

She reached around to him. "Okay, but it better not
bite," she teased. Maria put her hand in his left jacket
pocket withdrawing a gift-wrapped ten-inch-long box.

"Oh Alex, you didn't have to get me anything. You've
done so much for me already."

She gave him a quick kiss before she tore into the
wrapping paper. Her eyes widened with joy when she
opened the top to the box. Inside was the crystal train
set from the Riverwalk store. Emotion choked her voice.
"Alex, it's beautiful. I was that transparent, huh? I love it!
Thank you, sweetheart."

"You're quite welcome. I want you to think about me
whenever you see it. My love sparkles for you brighter
than any crystal ever could." He hugged her tighter.
"Thank you for being you, *mi querida*."

She turned her body to be able to cup his face in her
hands. She looked deeply into his brown eyes. "Me is all
I know how to be. Are you sure you're ready for the life
of an agent?"

He took his time answering. It was the same question
he continued to ask himself. "No, but I sure am going to
try." His hands lightly traced a path over the soft skin of
her breasts.

Moaning, she only half protested. "And you call me wicked. Love me, Alexandro Milbon." Her breasts surged at the intimacy of his expert touch.

"Forever and always. Let's go inside."

She loved the husky quality that his voice took on when he wanted to make love to her. "I'm way ahead of you," she crooned.

Morning came all too quickly. They spent the night in each other's arms, making love and reveling in the feel of their closeness. Alex was the first to get up. He made Maria a simple breakfast of waffles and bacon, which he put in the microwave. She did not stir from the bed, but pretended to be sleeping while he cooked.

Maria didn't want him to see her like this. She struggled against the tears that threatened to spill over her lashes. He would be leaving any minute, and her heart knew it.

After he had packed up the car he found her on the patch of beach in front of the cottage. She sat stone-faced on a rock even though he knew she had heard him walk up. He put his arms around her from the back, and she leaned into his embrace. He let out a long, woeful sigh. He would have to leave soon or he would make a fool of himself, begging her to let him stay.

The case wasn't over yet and this was not their time. Doubt worried the recesses of his subconscious. *What would she want? Did she believe in forever, like he did? If he proposed would she turn him down?* "Look at me, *querida*."

Maria shook her head. "No. I can't. Just go." The first teardrop fell softly on her cheek.

He felt the rigidity of her body. He pushed, "Look at me."

She shook her head again. "No. If you love me, don't put me through this. Just go, Alexandro."

He heard the hurt and pain in her voice and respected her wishes. He held her tighter. "I'll be in Memphis. Call me when you get back. I'll be out of sight, but I'll never leave you, Maria. I love you."

She nodded her head in understanding against his broad chest. He planted one more kiss in her hair. She whispered her response. "I love you, Alexandro Milbon."

He longed to show her all the love and passion that he had stored for her. Slowly he released her and walked away. He didn't turn around; he wouldn't be able to leave if he did. He knew how much she hurt, because he felt the same way. Alex walked quickly to his car and backed out of the driveway.

Before he made it to the highway, the first teardrop fell softly on his cheek.

Chapter 25

Alex had been back for over a week. He hadn't heard from Maria and it was driving him up the wall. But with one look at the newspaper, he knew why it was so important for Maria to finish this case. The news had been filled with more gun violence. Kids shooting kids, adults shooting kids, and now there was talk of another gang war. The world seemed to be going crazy.

Alex sat at his desk under the pretext of doing paperwork. He had stared at the same sheet of numbers for fifteen minutes. He was no closer to making sense of what he was looking at now than when he first started. His concentration was only on Maria.

He just wanted to hold her in his arms. Maybe he shouldn't have gone to Maryland, it was much easier to deal with the separation without having to remember their nights of passion. The way she felt to him, the way she called his name, the way she said she loved him.

Frustrated, he needed to blow off steam. His work would always be there. Unfortunately, it didn't go anywhere on its own.

Ramon was setting up the bar for the festivities that night. They would be having a special on margaritas.

He looked concerned when he saw Alex coming toward him. The man didn't look so good. "You okay, boss?"

"Yeah, just need to stretch my legs. Do you need anything from me?"

Ramon shook his head. "Nope, everything is cool here. I'm just waiting for the ladies," he grinned.

Alex attempted to return the smile. "Then I'm going to take a breather. I'll be back in plenty time to help beat them off of you. This bar seems to be a magnet for the lovelies."

A flash of humor crossed Ramon's face. "Yep. And I'm not complaining a bit."

"Page me if you have a problem. I'm going to get some exercise."

"Sure thing, I'll catch you later."

Alex drove around in his black Navigator, trying to collect his thoughts. When he spotted a music store, he pulled into the parking lot. He was pleasantly surprised to see the store sold sheet music. He walked toward that section and scanned the selection. It had been years since he'd picked up his saxophone. When he lived in Virginia he used to play frequently. He had even been invited to do sets at clubs, but he never followed up on it. He loved to just sit and create with the instrument. He and the keys and the notes became one. An hour later he had several purchases under his arm.

He returned to his vehicle to continue his drive. Her name lingered around the edges of his mind. The passion he felt for the music was similar to the one he shared with Maria. They had become one. Their souls inextricably connected, which made his next decisions all the more difficult. Alex knew that he would have to find a way to let her do her job without interfering. But how could he do that and manage to stay away from her?

How could he leave her alone when his body and soul craved her for survival?

Helene called Maria shortly after she returned to her suite at the Peabody. "Hey girl, I see you decided to take the AD up on his offer for a two-week break. Are you ready to get back to work?"

"I am, Helle, but I have one favor to ask. Could you please beg Antonio to take me for a massage and trim tomorrow?"

Helene laughed. "Sure thing, but I am going with you, and you're treating because I want to hear about everything that happened. You don't get to go off-line for two weeks and not give up the details."

Maria pretended to protest. "Are you trying to get in my business again?"

Helene responded in her usual quirky way. "Of course. Girl, if you know what's good for you, I'd better hear all the juicy details. Rod told me that a couple of weeks ago one Alex Milbon disappeared from Memphis. Reports are that he was seen in Maryland having a good time with someone who looked surprisingly like you."

"Okay, twist my arm," Maria said laughing. "I guess I could use some girl talk about now. Call him, and then call me back."

Helene made the call and with a little cajoling was able to convince Antonio to give both of them Personality Spa and Salon specials. She called Maria back with the good news.

Maria had a few questions of her own. She wondered if her two friends had made any headway while she was away. "Now *chica*, tell me what has been going on with you and my bodyguard. Quid pro quo."

Visions of café au lait muscles floated through Helene's mind. She cleared her throat before answering. "We'll talk tomorrow. I have to run now," Helene responded. Our appointment starts at 8:00 A.M. and we'll be there most of the day. I don't want you to be grouchy, so don't hang out too late tonight. Are you going to Memphis Nights?"

"All day?"she whined. "Okay. I was just planning to read tonight anyway. It's too soon for me to go out. I need to get acclimated again. Get back in character and concentrate on what I need to do."

Helene agreed. "I hear you. My surveillance duties were pretty boring without you to spice things up. Call me later if you need anything. "

Maria was grateful to have her as a friend. She settled in for the evening after taking a long, hot shower and putting on a pair of silky pajamas. She sorted through the intelligence and surveillance reports that Spates had sent an FBI messenger to bring to her. She would meet with Spates in a couple of days.

Maria thought about the request she had made of Spates. Would he grant a change in the profile so that Alex would be protected? She would find out the decision in a day or two. Could she really hope to be able to accomplish the mission with everyone returning home unscathed? Her goal was to get in and make a quick strike. She wouldn't let her first job as team leader become her last one.

Her mind burned with the memory of her magical time with Alex. She had spent the better part of two days just trying to pull herself together after he'd left. Finally she had been able to convince herself separation was the only answer. It had to be.

Now that she was back in Memphis, her fingers

yearned to dial his number. If she called, then what? She would have to tie herself down to keep from going to see him. No. It would be better to leave him alone until absolutely necessary.

After a fitful night, she woke up in time to meet with Helene. She was so tense and upset, the least little thing would make her snap. The masseur would have his work cut out for him. The best she had been able to muster was a black velour sweatsuit. It wasn't exactly her normal Maria-wear but she didn't have the energy for much else. Helene greeted her at her hotel door with coffee and a cinnamon roll. It wasn't the same as her breakfasts with Alex, but it was enough to kickstart the morning.

It took only one look at Maria to know something had gone terribly awry on her recent vacation. Helene blurted out, "Oh, dear. I guess this is truly an emergency."

Minutes later they were greeted at the door of Personality by Antonio. The spa was in full operation even though it was barely eight. He took one long look at Maria and knew it was going to take all of his skills to bring her back to life. The first thing he did was throw out the remainder of her coffee and called for one of his assistants to bring her a chai tea. Quickly.

Antonio looked at Helene and shook his head. He mouthed to her that she owed him big time. Helene snickered at him before the two were ushered off to change out of their clothes. Tea in hand, they moved quickly toward their first service.

Antonio sighed. It would be a long day.

During her transformation, Maria was poked, prodded, kneaded, ripped, dipped, and soaked. If she didn't feel better after all that, she wouldn't have a pulse. Antonio made sure that he had provided her with every comfort and treatment available. Her skin glowed, her hair shone, and her body felt incredible.

She hugged Helene when they finally left the salon. "Girl, this was worth every penny! I think that I am addicted to that deep-tissue massage. I would kiss Antonio if I didn't think he would like it so much," she joked.

Helene grinned. "I know. You look fantastic. Let's go lounge by the pool. We only have a few more weeks of good weather, so we need to take advantage of it while we can. Besides I have a lot of reading to catch up on. You up for some more relaxing?"

Maria nodded at her friend, glad that she had thought of it, too. "That sounds good. I tried to read while I was in Maryland, but I didn't get too far."

They took the short drive back to the hotel where they planned on sitting by the pool.

Maria changed out of her sweats and put on capri pants and a T-shirt. She searched for a book to relax with while Helene waited in the suite's sitting area.

"So, *chica*, tell me all about Maryland, and please don't spare the details," Helene said while flipping through a magazine.

Maria had debated about how much she would share. She knew Helene would needle her until she was satisfied.

"Give me a sec, I'm almost ready." Book in hand she joined Helene on the couch. "Well, he surprised the heck out of me when he just showed up at my cottage—I'll tell you that much. Girl, I had grass in my hair, bug bites on my face, and I was a mess."

Helene laughed, imagining her sophisticated friend looking a fright.

"I had to make a mad dash to the shower to get myself together, but he didn't seem to mind. That's the problem, you know. He makes me feel so comfortable all the time. I can't stay mad at him for long, and he knows how to push all my buttons. I'm used to being in control and knowing how to get my way."

Helene was amused. "Serves you right! It's about time you found a man that doesn't get intimidated by your personality. He doesn't know about your skill with knives, does he?"

Maria wagged her finger. "No, and don't you dare tell him. We'll save that kind of information for after the honeymoon," she teased.

"Do you realize this is the first man you've ever joked about marrying? You've got it real bad for Mr. Milbon, don't you?"

Maria stared off into the distance. After a long sigh she said, "Yes, I do. He's everything, Helene. I have never fallen so hard and so fast for someone and known that it was so right. I mean aside from absolutely lousy timing I know this could work, but—"

Helene interjected. "Why the buts? Just let that be enough. I'm jealous that you found someone to love and someone that loves you so much. Girl, be happy and take it for what it's worth. Let tomorrow worry about tomorrow."

Maria stared at her. "Okay, will the real Helene Maupin please stand up? Where did all this philosophizing come from? What happened to 'don't jeopardize the case' and all that good stuff? What did Rod do to you while I was gone?"

Helene blushed. *Not everything that I wanted him to do,* she elected not to say. "See, I am trying to be supportive, and you are treating me like this. So I've had a change of heart, big deal. I just think we could give our whole lives to this job and walk away with nothing. I think we deserve some happiness along the way. We are doing the best that we can to make the streets safer, to protect the public from the maniacs and crazies. Is it too much to ask for a little love in return?"

Maria studied her friend's expression. Helene had fallen for Rod much harder than she had realized. *Oh boy,* she thought, leaning back in her chair. "I suppose you have a point, but I don't want to lose my edge. I need to be able to focus. I think it is best if we just slow down and take a look at this later."

Helene's voice had a hard edge to it when she spoke again. "Maria, we are not talking about turning in a report or scheduling a briefing. We are talking about the man you love. You don't *table* love!"

Rod's firm knocks on the door stopped further conversation. He barged in without invitation when he didn't hear anything. When he saw Maria he greeted her cheerily.

"Hey there, stranger. How are you? What are you guys doing, and can I join you?"

Helene shot Maria a warning look.

Maria stood up to hug him; it seemed like eons since she had seen him.

Rod continued, his hazel eyes twinkling. "I missed you, partner. Hope you didn't get into too much trouble while you were in Maryland. It took all my energy and effort to keep this one in line while you were away. She didn't know how to behave without you to watch over her." Rod pointed at Helene. He continued playfully, "She is such a handful. I had to take her out to lunches and dinners, a couple of concerts, and out dancing just so she would have something to do."

Maria arched her eyebrows at her friend. "Do tell, what else did you two kids do whilst I was away?"

Rod gave her a devilish smile. "I'm sure not what you did while you were chillin'."

Maria pretended to pout. "Hey, I was a perfect angel. I resent the implication that I don't know how to carry out the duties of an agent with decorum and honor."

Rod and Helene both rolled their eyes. "Right!" they said in unison.

Rod sat down to make himself more comfortable. "So what's on the agenda for today? Are we going to the club tonight?"

Maria ignored the question. She wasn't ready to think about seeing Alex just yet.

Noticing the awkward silence, Helene told Rod that they had planned on reading by the pool.

"Great, let me just grab a book and we can go down together. You can tell me the plan for the rest of the evening once we get down there."

The rest of the evening, Maria thought. She had been trying not to think about Alexandro and how much she would like to spend the rest of the evening in his arms. She missed him so much that it hurt.

Chapter 26

The trio spent a lovely afternoon and evening pool-side doing more gabbing than reading. As the sun began to set, Rod wondered aloud about the evening's entertainment again.

"So what do you have planned, Ms. Maria? You've been away for awhile and I think it's about time you showed your face around town."

"I've been thinking about that," she replied. "I think we should go to Goran's club. Let's get in Mikha's face for a little bit. What do you think? You guys ready to muscle in on some Russian crooks?"

"You have such a devious mind, and I like it. Count me in," Helene agreed.

Rod wasn't too sure that he wanted to go to a strip club with two women, but he would do his duty.

"Uh, you ladies sure you want to do this? It could be a little crazy in there. Am I going to have to take my boxing gloves?"

Maria laughed. "No, Mr. Foreman, leave the gloves at home. We'll be fine. We are just going to show up and order a couple of drinks. Nothing serious . . . just checking things out. Besides, if we are lucky, maybe we will run into some of the other players. We may be able to start gathering intel on some of their activities too."

"Good one. My girl is always thinking. You could learn a lesson or two from her, Radford."

He grinned at Helene, his eyes telegraphing more than mere mirth. "I'm sure I could, but I'd rather learn them from you."

Helene felt her temperature climb. Heat practically burned her cheeks. She saw desire in his eyes directed toward her. She felt panicked. What the hell was she to say to that, or was that the point? For once he had left her completely speechless.

He grinned to himself. *Score one for Roderick Radford.*

Maria interrupted their interlude. "I'm not going to have to referee for the two of you, right? We are going to have a good, clean night of fun out on the town."

"Sure, no problem. We know how to behave," they both agreed.

"This has been lovely, but I am going to go upstairs to rest before our shenanigans later on," she said. "Ladies and gentleman, we are out to make a statement. Dress to impress."

She left Rod and Helene at the pool making eyes at each other. *You two are real nutcases, and I thought Alex and I had problems,* she thought walking back into the lobby.

Maria rested, or at least she was in the bed for a couple of hours. She hadn't truly rested since Alexandro. He was a drug to her. She craved him, needed him. Everything reminded her of him, but she had made up her mind. The case came first, love later. His leaving the way he did proved to her that he felt the same way. He couldn't stay with her any longer knowing that they wouldn't be together in the same way once they were back in Memphis.

A rumble deep and low in her stomach reminded her that it had been awhile since she'd had something to eat. She ordered a chicken Caesar salad and iced tea. That would tide her over until they went to the club. They would probably order a light dinner after their festivities.

By the time her food had arrived, twenty minutes later, she thought about calling Alexandro again. He was never too far from her consciousness. What would she say? *I love you, but now just isn't a good time for me?*

Rod's distinctive knock broke her from her reverie. She hadn't even started to get dressed, so she hoped he didn't expect her to be ready.

"Come in," she called.

He wasn't dressed to go out either, so she felt a bit relieved.

"What's up?" she asked.

He blurted out. "I don't think Helene is a lesbian. I don't care what the rumor mill was at Quantico. She looks at me real sexy sometimes, like maybe she is interested in me too."

Maria put her hand to her mouth and laughed out loud. One look at Rod's face, and she laughed longer and louder. She stopped when he turned on his heel to go back to his room.

She put her hand out to stop him as soon as she composed herself. "Rod, wait, I'm sorry. It's not just you. I was sitting here thinking about how much I wanted to be with Alex. I'm laughing because the four of us are so damned pitiful. Come on, don't be so sensitive."

He hesitated. "You're her best friend. Maybe I should just keep my mouth shut."

Maria motioned for him to join her in the sitting area again. "Don't be silly. Besides, the truth is you are her best male friend. Just talk to her. I know she can be a real wiseass, but you know she just does that to protect herself. The woman is brilliant, and she can handle most situations, but when it comes to the personal stuff, she, like the rest of us, is severely lacking. You are going to have to decide if you want to try to break through that tough exterior. Helene Maupin does not come easy, my friend."

Rod nodded his head in agreement. "Trust me, I know. After this case I am going to take three months off and hike in the Himalayan Mountains or something. I have had enough drama for one lifetime."

Maria put her hand on his shoulder. "We're only getting started. Stick around. The ride gets bumpier and wilder, but that's when the fun begins."

He noticed her untouched salad and made a move toward it.

She caught his hand before he could spear a piece of chicken. "Hey, get your own. Why do all the men I know try to steal my food?"

He looked at her curiously. "Yeah, so are you saying you are ready for life to become even crazier than it is now? Does Alexandro know what a wild woman he is hooked up with?"

Maria shrugged her shoulders. "We'll see. I am hoping that I won't have to see him again until after the case. I've decided that I am not going to call him or go by Memphis Nights unless I have absolutely no choice. It's too hard seeing him, and I'm not sure I want to keep tempting fate by becoming too attached. Besides, who knows where our next assignment will take us?"

Rod nodded his head in agreement. "Yeah, you've got a point. Our next gig could take us anywhere. The prep time alone could be from a couple of weeks to a couple of years. Makes it kind of hard to really look at long-term relationships. I guess I need to get in the love 'em and leave 'em mode."

"You'd better not; besides, that's not your style. We can't sell our souls for this job. I just don't know if Alex and I are meant to be right now. But I am going to do everything I can to get through this case so that I can find out."

Rod gave her a wry grin. "I guess we're quite a pair. Let's say we get ready to go out and find out what these guys are up to."

Maria smiled. "Go on, get out of here so I can get ready, then. I may have to pour myself into the outfit that I have in mind. With the cooler nights, my leather is ready for action again."

They made it to Goran's club a little after midnight. Helene had found a table a distance away from the main entertainment. She could do without adding more grist to the mill where Rod was concerned. She inhaled his cologne and felt herself weaken. *Why did he have to be so handsome?*

Rod appreciated the scandalous little red dress that hugged Helene's every curve. It skimmed the tops of her knees, exposing just the right amount of shapely leg.

Maria watched the two for a few minutes before clearing her throat loudly. At the rate they were going, they would never notice that she was standing right next to them. Now she knew how they felt when she and Alex were together. It always seemed that nothing else mattered.

Finally, Helene noticed the perfectly wicked black dress Maria wore. Another Roberto Cavalli that hadn't made it to the runway. It was definitely not an outfit for the faint of heart. The dress stopped midthigh and had a crisscross design in the back. The front had a midsection cutout that showed off her pierced navel, which she'd had done specifically for this mission. Little was left to the imagination, and that's exactly what she'd wanted.

Mikha noticed them right away. He openly admired the outfits that the women were wearing. He loved their exposed flesh. It made him want to touch it. He felt himself getting aroused from looking at them, even though he had been watching strippers all night.

Mikha picked up his drink and made his way over to them. "Ms. Manez, what brings you and your friends to our little neck of the woods? Though I am not complaining at all, what with the nice view."

He leered at them both, making Maria cold inside. His admiring gaze felt nothing like a compliment, but she had his attention, and that was her goal. "We were in the neighborhood, so we thought we'd stop in for a drink. Nice crowd you have here."

"Yes, well, Goran likes to keep a more upscale establishment than a lot of other gentleman's clubs in the area. We believe in the total package. This should be a place where a man can bring his woman. So tell me, why are you here alone? Or were you looking for some company?"

Maria smelled the alcohol on his breath and her stomach lurched. His company was not what she had in mind, not intimately anyway. She looked at Rod and Helene before answering. "I'm not here alone. I'm here with my good friends, old and new. What do we have to do to get a drink around here?"

Mikha turned toward the bar and nodded his head. Within minutes, they were given VIP treatment. Mikha sat down with the trio, making himself comfortable. "So, Maria, how did a nice girl like you get into such a rough business as this?"

"Who said I'm a nice girl?" She responded low and deep. Her voice had taken on a sultry quality.

Mikha looked at her curiously. *Was she trying to seduce him?*

He nodded to her. "You know, me and you could make a good team. With my connections and your connections we could move as much merchandise as we want without waiting on outside resources."

Maria casually took a sip of her drink. "I'm listening."

Rod and Helene made a show of ignoring them and talking to each other or watching the show. The girls on stage seemed to be trying to outdo each other with intricate acrobatic moves.

Mikha had clearly surpassed his limit and the alcohol was doing the talking. "It's just something I've been thinking about. If you truly can keep up with the demand, then I can supply you with all the merchandise you would ever need. I mean, I am working on a way to break free of my associates, become my own boss. Are you interested in a little exclusivity?"

"I'm not interested in dying," she stated calmly. "I'm not trying to get caught up in some turf war. We can talk about this maybe after you have the details worked out."

"Such little faith, Maria. Have I ever let you down? I'm talking about a good move for both of us, but I need a commitment before I can take any action. Maybe we can talk about this later. Perhaps in a more private setting?"

Maria sat back, giving him a good view of the swell of her breasts. In his inebriated state Mikha wore his lust with gusto. "Ms. Manez, you are lovely. We could have a good time together. No business, all pleasure."

"*Nyet*, Mikha. I don't mix business with pleasure."

He boldly ran his hand along her thigh. "Are you sure?"

She firmly grabbed his hand before answering. She put enough pressure on his fingers to let him know that she was serious, but not enough to hurt him. "*Da*, Mikha, besides, you know there is someone else and I am always faithful in my relationships, if for no other reason than for practicality."

Mikha shrugged off the rejection. "I had to ask, you understand, of course? So, how is the club owner from Miami? I am surprised he let you out of his sight."

"Alexandro is fine. We have a mutual understanding when it comes to business affairs. He does what he does, and I do what I do. Our relationship is stronger when we both know our place."

"Touché. Let me buy you a drink?"

Maria spoke to Rod and Helene for the first time since Mikha sat down. "Would you guys care for more drinks?"

Both declined. She turned back to him. "I'll have a Black Russian," Maria instructed.

He laughed before going to the bar for her.

"Nice work, boss." Rod complimented her.

"Thanks, so did you guys learn any new moves? That was quite a show on-stage."

Helene blushed. She had been studying some moves she would love to do on Rod. "The dancers were certainly entertaining," she said.

A momentary look of confusion passed over Rod's eyes. He had been enjoying Helene more than the show, but had he gotten the wrong impression from her again? "Yeah, the show was great, almost as good as watching Maria Manez in action."

Mikha sent a waitress over to their table with Maria's

drink. "Hi, my name is Sunny. Just call me if I can be of further assistance."

Maria nodded her understanding. Agent McCorkle, who had been posing as a waitress in the club, had something to report.

Rod felt deflated. His evening with Helene had taken a decidedly sour turn. "So, are you ladies about ready to go?"

"Soon as I finish my drink. I haven't had one of these in years."

Maria mulled over Chantal's situation. She felt bad the young agent had to spend so much time in the pit with Goran and Mikha. Depending on Agent Mc-Corkle's report, Maria would figure out a way to get her some R & R from the club from time to time. Prolonged exposure to Mikha and Goran wasn't good for anyone.

Rod drove them back to the hotel and then Helene drove over to her accommodations. She was in a house close to the Peabody where she could monitor what was happening with the team. The group said their good-byes and then retreated to their private spaces. And that's where the trouble began.

Maria was jittery. It had been an interesting night, full of the usual twists and turns of working with Mikha and Goran. She learned more about their operation with every meeting; each new day brought the discovery of another piece of the puzzle. And yet she sat on the edge of her bed in her hotel room wishing she was any place but the Peabody waiting for the call she knew wasn't coming. Thoughts of wanting to be with Alex tore at her insides.

After an hour of torture, she gave up the fight. Without alerting Helene or Roderick, she jumped in her car and headed to Memphis Nights.

The club would be closing soon, and most of the patrons had already left. It was after midnight and Ramon had made the last-call announcement. Alex walked out of his office, his restlessness too much to bear. The deejay had slowed the tempo, playing one of his favorite slow, sensual salsa songs.

Maria saw him before he saw her. He was so wrapped up in the dance, he hadn't sensed her presence. He turned around when he felt her stare, like a metal bore, through his back. She had jumped to conclusions. Alex excused himself from his lovely dance partner, catching Maria just before she reached the exit.

When he caught up with her, her eyes were bright with unshed tears.

"Maria, wait. It's not what you think."

She glared at him, shaking her head in disbelief. Not trusting her voice, she remained silent. Her breathing was in short gasps. Thoughts of betrayal overshadowed the truth.

They stood watching each other for several minutes. Alex's anger bubbled to the surface. She was the one who had set the terms. "Don't look at me that way. It was just a dance, Maria."

The tears fell, but she didn't care. "How could you, Alex? And how dare you say it was just a dance? I have eyes. I know what I saw. If you two had been any closer I'd have advised you to get a room." She turned to leave, her body shaking in anger.

Alex raked his hands through his hair in frustration. "Dammit, it was just a dance. Nothing happened, nothing was ever going to happen, and you know it. Don't play games with me, Maria."

She stopped. She pointed a long manicured finger at him, jabbing him in the chest as she spoke. "I'm not the one playing games. I came here tonight to tell you that I was wrong, that I miss you and that I—"

Alex interrupted her, his anger punctuating every word. "Don't say it. Don't say you love me when all I see is hurt and pain in your eyes. If you loved me, you would trust me. You would be here with me. Instead you're dressed in expensive designer clothes no bigger than Band-Aids, going out all over Memphis. What do you want me to do? Wait by the phone for your call? A call that may never come?"

"Alex—"

"No, you started this, so let's finish it. What's it going to be, Agent Thomas?"

Her eyes narrowed in defiance. She placed a hand on a scantily clad hip and met his icy glare head on. "You're right. Maybe I have been playing games. I should never have played house with you in Maryland, never have shared my body or my bed with you. I was wrong. I gave in too easily. My mistake. Trust me, it won't happen again."

He closed his eyes, his breathing shallow and uneven. "I'm sorry. I didn't mean to put you on the defensive. Can we just talk about this calmly?"

She threw her hands up in the air. "I've said all I'm going to. Have a nice life, Alexandro Milbon."

"Don't do this, Maria. Don't walk away from us. If you do I won't be here when you come back."

"Don't worry. I'm not coming back."

This time he simply watched as she walked out the door.

Chapter 27

Nikola sat on the porch of the rustic old lodge. He had taken a few days to himself for a personal retreat. Watching the river as it meandered along its way, he was seemingly unaffected by the chill in the air. Winter was coming soon; the cloudy skies confirmed this as fact. The grayness seemed to match the weary feeling in his bones. He didn't want a showdown with Mikha, but he also wasn't ready to retire. He would have to choose soon, though; the young man seemed determined to force his hand. At least they weren't in Moscow—if that were the case, one or both of them would be dead. Nikola sighed, his breath coming out in a puff of fog. He longed for a cigar, but his doctor would have a fit. Signs of continued smoking would show up during his next appointment.

His bodyguards regarded him warily. The two men suspected that they would be looking for new employment soon; Nikola wasn't looking so good. The cancer was spreading faster than he wanted to believe, and it would only be a matter of months before he wouldn't be able to run his business.

Nikola cursed silently. Just when everything was going well and the business was successful and continuing to grow, he had to get sick. Maybe he should just hand over the reins to Mikha and be finished. He could do worse in a successor. Mikha would make sure that everything continued to go well. Maybe.

However, if he quit now, that would mean that he would have to admit defeat. Nikola didn't like to lose. His thin, dry lips formed a grim line. The cold was beginning to sap his strength. He would go back in to warm up. Besides, he had another four weeks before the meeting with Mikha and his gunrunning friend. He had folks on the inside at the Bureau who were checking into Maria Manez. Mikha might think he was cautious, but Nikola had been in the game long enough to check and double-check information. He hadn't survived in his line of work over thirty years by being careless. Something about Mikha's deal bothered him. His gut hadn't steered him wrong in all these years. He would be patient.

Mikha slowly opened one eye at a time. The sun had been up for hours, but he had not been able to pull himself out of bed. He'd had too much to drink last night and tipped his hand with Maria. He must have sounded like a desperate drunken fool, he lamented. It was time to come up with a new strategy. Nikola would be calling soon, and there was no way he wanted him to get wind of what he was planning. The old man would have him shot.

Mikha tried desperately to remember what happened. There was Maria. After that, nothing. He looked at his hands. They hurt like he'd punched a wall or something. Grimacing, he checked for other bruises. There was a nasty purple and black bruise on his side, which he had no recollection of. Something was very wrong.

Mikha rose slowly. The room started to spin. He sat on the edge of the bed, gulping in air so he wouldn't pass out.

Papers, mail, clothes, shoes, and knickknacks were strewn around the room, he noticed, as his vision slowly came back into focus. If he'd had the energy he would be furious. Instead he looked around at his ransacked belongings in disbelief.

Mikha started looking around. Had he been robbed? How did someone even get into his place? He had several locks on his doors. Memphis was relatively safe, but he had a business to protect.

He fought through the pain in his head and body to search his apartment. What he found made his blood run cold.

When more feeling returned and his coordination improved, he dialed Goran's number. As soon as he picked up, Mikha spoke to him in rapid Russian.

"Goran, get over here now. I'll explain when you get here. Call Ivan too." He hung up the phone and sluggishly paced in the living room until they came.

Goran and Ivan arrived at his home a short time later. They looked at Mikha with flat expressions. What had he done now?

Mikha looked scared and confused, which worried Goran even more. He explained his discovery. He'd found several thousand dollars of counterfeit money in a case in one of his closets. He only opened the case because he didn't recognize it. There were also printing press plates and several well-known trademarked products. Mikha knew that counterfeiting would carry a federal sentence if discovered. They had to help him.

What they heard they didn't believe. Both were convinced that he'd decided on another money-making scheme without Nikola's consent.

"I swear to you, those are not my plates and money." Anxiety choked Mikha's voice. "I don't know how those things got here," he said deliberately.

Goran noticed for the first time that Mikha's eyes appeared glassy and strange looking. Goran knew what kinds of drugs were passed around his club, and for the first time he began to believe him. "I think that you are being set up. The memory lapses, cottony feeling in your mouth, and your eyes all point to the use of some sort of hallucinogenic drug. Could someone have put something in your drink?"

Mikha was pensive, his memory coming back in bits and pieces. "All I remember is ordering a drink for Maria Manez and having one of the waitresses take it to her. I remember thinking I had said too much to her, but that I would deal with that later. Then I remember watching the girls dance some more. After that, I remember nothing until this morning."

"Maybe we can find something out from one of the other girls and from the security cameras. What are we going to do about this mess?" Ivan interjected. Goran nodded his head in agreement.

Mikha took a long sip of his drink before answering. "I can't have this right now. The Americans would never stop hounding me if they thought I was involved in a counterfeiting scheme. I didn't do this, and I'm not going to let this screw up everything that I've worked so hard to get. Not a word of this gets back to Nikola! This could ruin everything, " he repeated.

Goran looked around the apartment. There could be other incriminating evidence anywhere, he thought. He turned to the two men. "Ivan, get on the phone to order new furniture. Let's get this place cleaned out. I'll call over some of the boys. Mikha, we're going to have to tear this place apart."

Spates began the briefing without the usual pleasantries. He seemed particularly short with the staff this morning and they felt the tension. His deep bass voice had an edge when he addressed the team. "There's a lot going on in the Russian camp. Our fellow FBI agents have been busy following up on several leads over the past few days." Leaning back into his leather chair, he said, "Agent McCorkle will begin the brief."

McCorkle had been working in Goran's club as a waitress for several months now. She had been able to move around the club relatively unnoticed. Mikha seemed to have developed an interest in her, but not in the same way that he had with the dancers and other waitresses. He seemed to want to date her, and for that reason she had been playing a very effective game of cat and mouse, which she would continue until it was necessary to let him catch her.

"Mikha comes into the club most nights now. Sometimes he comes in for a drink, other times to watch the dancers, and others strictly for business. Two days ago he was seen leaving with an unidentified man. We believe this man may have drugged Mikha and coerced him into some other deal."

In a case beset with twists and turns, this new development was just one more thing his agents would have to deal with. Spates leaned forward in his chair, putting his elbows on the table. "This adds a new wrinkle to the case. A lot of the information from our sources on the street points to someone wanting Mikha out of the way. And if that's the case, we need to find out who and why. We're almost at the finish line, people, and we don't want some jerk messing up what we have worked so hard to put together. We are going to have to redouble our efforts to make sure the deal with Mikha and Nikola goes off without a hitch. There are several possible scenarios to explain what happened the other night.

"One of which might be that Nikola wants Mikha out of the way or taught a lesson. It may also have been something that Goran put together. We suspect that he wants to cut ties with Mikha, they have very different business philosophies.

"Right now we are just speculating and working up possible explanations. What we need is something more solid so that we can continue this operation." His frustration was evident as he tightened his grip on his pen. Spates turned to his senior agent on the case.

"Agent Thomas, what is your assessment of the situation? Do you have any ideas?"

Maria sat rigid in her seat. This was exactly the kind of thing that she had wanted to avoid. Any new wrinkle, any new circumstance could delay closing the case, and that would mean a delay in her ability to move on. To be with Alex, if he still wanted her. Had she lost him after their disagreement? Would they be able to work things out now that tempers were calm? *How long would he wait for this case to be over?*

She forced herself to concentrate and chose her words carefully. She said, "I don't think that this has to be a negative for the case. We might even have some bargaining room, especially if we let Mikha believe that there is overwhelming evidence to support that he had knowledge of the counterfeiting scheme. I agree that we need to find out who did this, but in the meantime let's see what his next moves are. Maybe we can even turn him if he feels cornered. With Mikha in our pocket . . ." Maria shrugged her shoulders.

She looked at her best friend, Helene, who had always understood how she thought. Maria hoped that she would catch on to help her explain where she was headed. She needed her analytical skills to work this one through.

Maria continued. "Let's think about this. Mikha has always been somewhat of a maverick. He is respected and known, but he isn't well liked, nor does he have clout like Nikola Mudiuranov. If we exploit that weakness, we just may be able to get Nikola and close down his operation with Mikha's help. Let's face it. Mikha was always the little fish in the big pond for us. We find out who could have set him up, we get Mikha and his saboteur out of the way, and then we get the big fish."

"That's true, but how do we find out who set Mikha up, and how do we prevent him from bolting? He's got to be concerned that people saw him with the printing presses and might be able to identify him, making him a suspect." Rod added.

Helene's eyes sparkled with excitement. "I think I have a way to get to the bottom of this and turn this situation to our advantage."

All eyes turned to her as they waited to hear her plan.

Chapter 28

Alexandro shut the computer down and looked at the clock. It was 2:35 A.M. He had to be up in four hours, and it looked like sleep would elude him again. He knew from Agent Max Wilson that the case Maria was working on was progressing well, but it didn't stop him from practically going crazy with worry. He didn't know which was worse, seeing her and knowing she was in danger, or not seeing her and not knowing what was going on. He willed himself not to call her every night. Their last conversation had set his nerves on edge. They had both said things they didn't mean.

She had set the terms of their relationship, and actually he didn't blame her. They couldn't go on as a couple with the case in the way. When it was all finished she would come back to him free and clear. Blind faith made him trust that they would work things out, that he could make it right between them.

At least that's what he prayed every night.

Alex saw Helene and Rod from time to time in the club, but not Maria. He guessed that seeing each other would be just as painful for her as it was for him. So tonight, like most nights, he tried to wear himself out until he was so exhausted that sleep would claim him in the early-morning hours.

Earlier in the evening he had practiced playing the saxophone pouring his heart and soul into the music. His fingers danced over the keys and produced a mournful soul-wrenching melody.

Alex had also tried swimming laps and playing basketball in the fitness center, but everything he did only served as a temporary fix. He wanted Maria, and no amount of exercise would take that longing away.

He stopped bringing alcohol into the house; he didn't want to drown his sorrows in a bottle. It was late fall now, and soon it would be Christmastime, which would bring with it a certain loneliness. He had hoped that with Maria he could recapture the sense of family that he'd lost while in the program. He tried to hold on to the memory of the special time they shared in Maryland, but knowing how good it could be only made it worse for him sometimes. Alex looked at the clock. It was 2:45 A.M. now. *Not another night like this.*

In contrast to his emotional upheaval, the club continued to do well. Memphis Nights was filled to capacity most evenings, especially on the weekends. He enjoyed the company of women whenever he wanted to make small talk and see a friendly smile. He set his own hours, which allowed him to explore the city with its rich culture. He had all the creature comforts that money could buy, a nice place to live, a great new car, and a secure future in a lucrative business. He got to meet new people and to help out local jazz talent by spotlighting them at the club.

And through it all he was absolutely miserable. There was only one person who could help him out. He knew that he should be very grateful for all the advantages that he had. Marisela would probably want to smack him on the head if she knew that he was brooding so much, but he had given Maria his heart. He would be unhappy until she was his wife.

It would be a long time before he would consider giving his heart to someone else if things didn't work out with their relationship. He kept a comfortable distance away from the opposite sex, leaving many young women unhappy. He could be counted on for a drink occasionally and a dance, but that was all he would commit to. Alex wondered how long it would be before his prayers were answered. How long was Maria willing to put her life on hold for the job? Would his presence ever take first place over the Bureau?

He couldn't be sure. When the case was over, it would be too fresh for her to make lifelong decisions. Maybe he should just back off. He didn't want to make things any harder on her than they had been on him. Maybe he should spare her the pain and discomfort that he felt. He was sure that she missed him, but maybe she didn't love him in the same way. Maybe he should just quit while he was ahead.

The alarm buzzed, signaling that it was time for him to get up. He looked at the clock again, as if staring at it would make the time change.

He showered and dressed, but not before making a few calls. He arrived at work an hour later in blue jeans and long-sleeved heather T-shirt. He found Max and Ramon already unloading the supply truck when he walked into the bar area.

"Great, you're both here. I want to thank you for coming in so early. It seems like we are always unloading supplies or taking inventory. I think I might have to hire some part-time help."

"Yeah, well my back would appreciate that," Ramon quipped.

Alex unpacked supplies while he spoke. "Things have been kind of crazy for me here lately so I've decided to do us all a favor and take a little trip. I booked myself on a seven-day cruise that leaves tomorrow morning. I know you guys can handle it, and when I come back, hopefully things will be better for me. I just need some time away to relax. I had a great time in Maryland, but it did nothing to help my objectivity and clarity concerning Maria."

Max and Ramon looked at him. They had been trying to convince him of that since his return. He hadn't been quite himself, and though he couldn't see it, they were concerned about how well he was keeping it together.

"So, where are you going to be while we are slaving away here?" Max asked.

Alex looked at him pointedly. "I'll be trying to get my head together in the Western Caribbean. I'm leaving from Miami tomorrow afternoon. The first stop will be in Labadee, Hispaniola, Haiti. The cruise winds its way along Jamaica, the Grand Cayman, and Cozumel. I know you are thinking lots of ladies, but I am not interested in a short shipboard romance. There's only one woman I am interested in, and she will be right here, where I hope she will be safe and sound."

Max assured him that she would be. "You just go and relax. Take advantage of the clean air and white beaches. We'll take care of everything here. Don't forget the Jamaican rum. For the bar, of course."

Alex grinned for the first time. "The sacrifices I make for my job. Don't worry, I won't forget about you. Let's get this done. I want to be out of here by 3:00 P.M. I have to run some errands. Max, do me a favor, cue up the Mike Phillips CD. I need some music to work by."

The three men worked through the rest of the morning and into the late afternoon. Alex ran a tight operation and didn't like surprises when it came to his inventory. It was bad for business to be unable to provide the customers with exactly what they wanted. When the trio completed the scheduled tasks to his satisfaction, he left the club to get ready for his trip.

He wanted desperately to call Maria. But he knew if he did he would beg her to come with him and that would defeat the purpose of going away in the first place. He vowed to himself that when he returned he would be stronger. He needed to get centered again, needed to get away from Maria while she completed her business. Playing the saxophone helped, but it also gave rise to his more sensitive side. These days, the last thing in the world he wanted was to be more in tune with his feelings. He needed to hold himself together, feel more in control. To do that, he needed to separate from the object of his desires.

Alex ran his errands, then returned home to pack quickly. He had learned how to prepare himself for a quick exit from his time with the Bureau. He gave himself plenty of time to catch his flight to Miami, where he'd be boarding the ship. He looked around the apartment for a final time while standing in the doorway. His heart tugged at the thought of leaving Maria. On impulse, he put his bag down to write her a note in case she stopped by. It had been several weeks since their wonderful time in Maryland and he hadn't seen her, but he never stopped feeling her presence or her spirit. Alex wrote quickly on a scrap piece of paper that he'd found in the kitchen, then walked out the door.

Thankfully, the trip from Memphis to Miami was uneventful, but Alex didn't relax until he was settled in his cabin. He received a few questioning looks from fellow female travelers. Some were even bold enough to ask if he was traveling alone. He smiled and told them it was by choice.

He was situated in an ocean-view stateroom with a balcony. He walked outside and let the warm air wash over him. The ship hadn't left the dock yet, but the view was still nice as he looked to the horizon, and he enjoyed the solitude. Minutes later the horns were blaring, announcing that the ship was on its way to the paradise of the Caribbean.

Alex felt the slight tug of movement under his feet and in no time, it seemed, they were out on the open sea. He watched the skyline of Miami disappear to give way to miles of ocean. He stood on the balcony thinking of Maria and how he would handle their impossible situation. He didn't want to keep going up and down the same road. He was tired of loving her, but not being able to truly have her in his life. He wanted it all of course, but what was he willing to sacrifice to be with her? Memphis was his home now, but the thought of having to move again plagued him. He decided if that's what it took to be with her, he would do it.

What would she sacrifice to be with him? He wasn't sure. She loved him, he was certain of that. Every time he looked into her soft brown eyes, he knew she did.

It was going to take a lot more than love though, he realized. He would go in soon. The breeze was turning cooler, coinciding with the chill his thoughts gave him. Darkness had started to descend on the ocean, which made the lights of the ship brighter, seemingly bringing the boat to life. He had to decide if he would eat in the cabin or in the dining room. His stomach started to grumble, making the need for a decision more immediate.

He unpacked his belongings and then left the room to explore the ship. He would pick up some snacks until he was really ready to eat. He left the cabin and wound his way to one of the ship's four lounges. He sat for a while to listen to the jazz the band was playing. At that moment he ached to have his saxophone in his hands. He would love to be on stage with them, feeling the power of the music as it released the burdens of his soul.

Maybe running away from Memphis wouldn't work. His thoughts returned to Maria no matter where he was. His only consolation was at least this way he wouldn't have to watch the door of the club every night, willing her to come in, or have to stare at the keys and parking pass he gave her still sitting on the kitchen counter. He didn't have the constant reminders that at any given moment she could be in his arms, but she wasn't. At least away he didn't have to stop himself every night from jumping in his car to find her, demand she come back with him, and beg her never to leave him again.

Aboard the ship, he got to keep his dignity for another seven days. He didn't know what would happen when he returned.

The band finished their set. A deejay was playing tunes while crooning to the small audience that had gathered in the lounge. There were a lot of couples, comfortable and snuggled together. Alex's mood was steadily going down. There was the occasional single man or woman or groups of both. Natalie Cole was playing now, belting out a tune of loss: "My only consolation is I've got nothing more to lose."

Alex decided to look for the dining room. He wasn't making things any easier on himself with his behavior.

* * *

Maria looked out the window of her Memphis hotel room. The clear black night sky shone bright with stars and lights from the many other buildings in the area. It seemed a perfect night: not a cloud in sight and comfortably cool. Thankfully, temperatures had remained mild for November. Thanksgiving and Christmas were around the corner. She usually enjoyed this time of year because she was able to spend more time with her family and good friends. Right now her heart ached and there was only one person she longed to unwrap gifts with: Alexandro.

Max had told her that he had decided on a weeklong getaway. She hadn't seen him in several weeks, and she had missed him every second that they had been apart. Knowing that he was on a trip without her gave her a moment for pause.

She longed to be with him, to leave Memphis and all the drama behind, to luxuriate in his arms, to be swept up in the passion of his kiss. The time they had spent in Maryland became all the more precious. Maria shook herself. *No need going down that road, girl.* She sighed and returned to her paperwork. The next few days would be crucial to the case.

Chapter 29

Mikha held his bag tightly as he got ready to board the plane. His outward calm was totally inconsistent with his inward nervousness. He wanted to get on the plane without mishap and get the heck out of Memphis. He was just about to hand the boarding pass to the ticket agent when he felt a strong hand clasp his shoulder. Mikha's heart sank.

He had been found despite his attempts to shield his departure. He'd purchased several tickets using aliases, to several different locations. Goran had made new identifications for him, and he was traveling under the name of Sasha Pavinov.

"Mr. Pavinov, don't turn around or try to make a scene. Stay calm and everything will be just fine. We were not sent to hurt you."

Mikha stiffened but did as he was instructed.

The man behind him told the ticket agent Mr. Pavinov was needed at the security office and wouldn't be taking this flight.

Mikha was told again not to turn around as he was led away. He knew putting up a fight was useless. New security measures would make it impossible for him to make it out of the airport. He resigned himself to finding out who wanted him and why.

He was ushered quickly into a car waiting just outside the baggage terminal. He soon realized that he must be in police custody because his abductors had too many privileges to be ordinary people. A black hood was placed over his face, and his hands were secured in front of him over his lap.

Mikha thought about his options. He was surprisingly calm given the potentially dire nature of his situation. His thoughts were on how to reason with the men who were holding him. Police would not have placed a hood over his face, but these people were obviously part of a legitimate authority; otherwise he would not have been escorted from the terminal the way he had been.

How could he get away without compromising all that he had worked for? Were his dreams of returning to Russia destroyed? His thoughts raced a mile a minute. He would have to find a way to get out of this situation intact.

They rode in the car for about thirty minutes, Mikha guessed. He'd had time to think of several scenarios, but no workable solution to his predicament.

Once the car stopped, one of the men checked the security of his hood, and he was not-so-gently ushered from the vehicle into a building. He was barely spoken to as he was guided through a series of rooms. He guessed there had to be at least two men, maybe three, with him, but he couldn't be sure how many were in the building.

He could hear the strains of classical music playing as he reached a room at the end of a long hallway. In the room, he was seated in a hard, high-backed, armless chair. His hands were unbound and then rebound behind the back of the seat. He was less than comfortable.

The room became very quiet, very still. Mikha knew he was being watched.

He was startled to hear a booming voice address him by his full name.

"Mikhail Stemenovich, you are accused of counterfeiting, illegal gundealing, tax evasion, fraud, and bribery. The sum total of these offenses will get you life without the possibility of parole."

Mikha tried to move in his seat, but the restrictions were too tight. He cursed violently in Russian. "Who's there? What do you want?" he asked angrily.

Agent Spates spoke clearly and loudly. "We are the people who are going to make your sorry life worth living. Somebody wants you out of the picture, Mikha. We know that you're not involved in counterfeiting. Besides, it would be pretty stupid of you to keep money and plates in your home. But what we know and what the Memphis Police Department are going to find out will be two very different things."

"Go to hell!" Mikha spat out.

"That's where you will be when you are given a one-way ticket to the Shelby County Jail. After they get through with you in there, you'll think your time as a prisoner of war in Afghanistan was a walk in the park," Spates said coolly. "Of course, counterfeiting is a federal offense, but we could make sure the transfer to federal prison could take a while."

Mikha shuddered; he had heard the stories about Shelby. It was a place where few survived unscathed. The facility had been declared unconstitutional by judges in the area; nonetheless, it continued to operate. "What do you want?" he asked in a less threatening tone.

Spates was silent for several minutes. He wanted

Mikha to squirm a little more, to imagine himself in jail before he let him off the hook.

Mikha was so tense he had trouble breathing. The hood was still over his face, which intensified the feeling. Fear crept through his body. His voice was a low whisper. "What do you want? Tell me."

Spates sensed all the bravado was gone. He was satisfied. His voice was low and deep when he addressed Mikha again. "We want Nikola Mudiuranov and his entire network. We want your lousy baby-killing guns off our streets, and we want you to go back to Odessa."

Mikha hung his head in defeat.

Spates motioned for one of the guards to remove Mikha's hood.

The two men stared at each for several minutes. Mikha nodded at Spates when he could see his face. "You are from the little initials, yes? Which one?" Mikha asked. He needed to know what kind of deal he could make.

To the Special Corruption Unit, Mikha would serve a purpose. He was a means to an end, nothing more, nothing less. Agent Spates was abrupt in his response, "Makes no difference. The initials are big enough to take you down; that's all you need to know. As of today *Gaspadin* Stemenovich, you are out of business. And how you spend the rest of your miserable little life is entirely up to you."

Mikha tried to quell the feeling of impending doom coursing through his gut. He looked around the room as he listened. Heavy mahogany wood paneling draped the walls. The room looked like a library or a study in an old Memphis plantation home. It smelled of furniture polish and old money. The wood, the books, everything about the room was authentic, but somehow he doubted it was such an innocent place. He wondered what sort of high-tech gadgets the walls were hiding.

His misery felt like a steel weight. Mikha knew it was over. "I'll tell you everything I know," he said finally.

Satisfied, Spates turned on a tape recorder before beginning the interview. "What do you remember about the other night?"

Mikha sighed resignedly. Stress made his Russian accent more pronounced as he spoke. "I remember meeting with some friends and drinking with them. I chitchatted with some of the girls, had more to drink. I met with my business partner and then went home." Mikha bit down on his lip nervously. "Yesterday morning my apartment was broken into and I found all this money. I swear to you, I am not into counterfeiting. I don't know how the money and other stuff got into the apartment."

When Spates spoke again, his tone was anything but genteel and kind. "You degrade and harass women and sell guns, but heaven forbid you should print your own money. You're despicable, Mikha, and I should have you spend one night in Shelby just for the heck of it. How does D Hall sound? The devil won't even take anyone from there; sounds like your kind of people."

Mikha shook involuntarily. "I've told you everything!"

Spates responded, "Good, and now you are going to listen. Your Russian friends Ievik, Viktor, and Gregor have sold you out. Nikola was going to let you do all the work, and then Ievik was going to take over. Your big empire was going to be snatched right out from under you. Even Goran can't help you out of this one. So you've got to ask yourself—how far are you willing to stick your neck out?" Agent Spates knew he'd hit home by Mikha's reaction. The FBI would be able to bring down the entire Russian gang with Mikha's co-operation. He continued applying the pressure.

If what this man was saying was true, Mikha had been betrayed by fools. He was livid.

"There's only way for you to help yourself," Spates continued. "Make the deal with Maria Manez. Involve Nikola as much as possible. We need to know more about the inner workings of his operation. You agree to do everything we tell you, and you might walk away from this with your life. Your alternative is Shelby."

Mikha shifted uncomfortably in his seat. He wondered how much bargaining room he had. If he gave them more than they expected, he might be able to negotiate going back to Texas. "How did you know so much about me?" Mikha asked.

"We've been watching you and Nikola for years." Spates leaned back and steepled his fingers. "Ivan has been very helpful with his detailed meeting and surveillance notes." Spates didn't bother to clarify his remarks. He wanted Mikha to think the worst, and believe he had been betrayed.

Mikha closed his eyes. His head ached, and he knew a migraine was not far behind. Not Ivan. They had sworn loyalty to each other after fighting side by side. Ivan would never betray him. He couldn't think, he couldn't speak, and he couldn't breathe.

Silence cloaked the library. There was no movement in the room until a guard untied Mikha's hands. "Read this document and sign it," Spates told him. "Your life depends on it."

Mikha quickly scanned the words on the paper. He realized that as soon as Nikola found out he had be-trayed him, and he knew he would, this document

would become his death warrant. His only consolation
was that if the Americans worked fast enough, Nikola
and those who betrayed him would go down, too.

Chapter 30

Alex sat on his balcony enjoying the beautiful calming water views. He wished he had brought his saxophone. He could just picture the notes that he wanted to play in his head. Some of the tension of the last few weeks had started to ease. He was starting to feel a little better, a little more like his true self. Striking the balance between thinking and keeping his body moving was tricky, but it was working. Thoughts of Maria had been reduced to twenty hours a day instead of twenty-four.

The trip had been all that the brochures promised. It was beautiful and peaceful. He spent time in open-air markets, ate traditional fare, and swam to his heart's content. He had even tried rock climbing and hang gliding.

Everywhere he went, he managed to pick up some trinket for Maria, and by the time he returned home Alex would have a suitcase full of gifts for her. He had used his time on the shores to explore the native shops and markets, often finding hidden restaurants and shops that most tourists missed. His travels through the markets had also given him the opportunity to use his Spanish all day. He loved conversing with Maria, but he always had sensual thoughts when talking with her. This trip afforded him a greater range of use of the language.

He found the people to be friendly and warm, especially when he used their native tongue.

Shopping was much more fulfilling when he could haggle with understanding. He'd had a little more difficulty in Haiti, but his basic French had helped enough to make it through. While there, he did more dining on the low-priced seafood than shopping, but he enjoyed his time visiting the different sections of the tiny country. He studied Haitian architecture and buildings and marveled at how the French influence was juxtaposed with the Caribbean flavor. He visited fantastic white pristine beaches on some parts of the island and ugly gray ones on others, but the people were accepting and hospitable no matter where he traveled. He found visiting Haiti a lesson in economics and social stratification. He found there were the haves and the have-nots, so he made it a point to spend, buying trinkets from almost every shopkeeper he ran into. Alex hoped that Maria would be pleased with his purchases; each gift had been handmade and was purchased from the heart.

In Cozumel, he found the Mexican culture to be fascinating. As far as shopping went, the city had not disappointed. He held the most precious gift in the palm of his hand. He smiled. The island would have very special memories for him.

Alex had run into a very quaint shop along a narrow alley road as he was headed back to the ship. He had spent several hours in the city, talking with the locals and exploring Mexican culture. He seemed drawn to the small shop, though it looked like little more than a dressed-up shack. After browsing for a couple of minutes, his eye was drawn to the perfect gift. He knew it was crazy and maybe it was too soon, but he made the purchase. He couldn't resist buying a delicate black coral and seven-diamond solitaire for Maria.

The elderly woman behind the makeshift counter was of indeterminate age; she could have been seventy or one hundred and seven. She smiled at Alex, her intelligent eyes seeming to look into his very soul after he selected the ring. She explained to him the story its origin and creation while he studied the treasure in great detail. She told him in a peculiar Spanish dialect that the ring had been made by a sailor for his intended bride many, many years ago. The sailor had come to the island on shore leave with the rest of his crewmates. He had fallen in love with one of the local girls who was a waitress at one of the inns. The relationship was fast and not well received by her father. The sailor wanted to find a ring to show her how much he loved her and to prove his worth to her father. The old man had been a town leader and forbade his daughter to have a relationship with a sailor, who would only break her heart.

The sailor and the waitress continued to see each other despite the warnings, and he proposed marriage to her. He had found the piece of black coral in the water and took it to a jeweler to have it made into a ring. The jeweler sold him the diamond to inset the stone, which the sailor promised to pay for on time. The story has it that the father was so angry that he had the fleet sent away from the island and the sailor was never heard from again. The young waitress never married because she believed that one day her sailor would return.

Milagros, the shopkeeper, told him that the ring would bring happiness to the couple who purchased the ring and peace to the souls of the unfortunate couple. She also told him that she would know when it was the right time to sell the ring. In her raspy voice she told him, "I can see by your eyes that you are in love. Your bride is very lucky, and you two will be very happy."

Alex smiled at the old woman. He didn't know how much of her story he believed, but he knew that he wanted the ring. He made the purchase without a second thought. When he looked back, Milagros had a twinkle in her eye that made her appear years younger. Alex decided the midday sun was playing tricks on his eyes.

Back on the ship, Alex held the ring in his hand. It would be their engagement ring, he hoped. It wasn't very traditional, but then again, neither was Maria. The ring was a symbol, a tribute to their rare and delicate love. It was smooth, strong, beautiful, and unbending. It was just like his bride to be.

Alex held the exquisite piece of jewelry in his hand, impressed with the craftsmanship. The softness of the black stone and sparkle of the diamonds reminded him of Maria, too. Milagros had not told him who the jeweler was, but somehow he knew that she was very close to the ring and probably knew more than she had indicated. He didn't know if he believed in legends, but he hoped that something good would come out of his purchase for Maria. There was no question about his love or devotion to her. He prayed she felt the same way and would say yes when he proposed.

When should he pop the question, that was the question. When would the case be over, and then would she be ready to marry him? Those thoughts plagued him and preyed on his confidence, but he refused to give in to doubt. He trusted that he would eventually get his way, and he and Maria would one day be able to build a life together.

Alex had to decide what to do for his last evening's entertainment. The trip had been everything that it was supposed to be. He felt more relaxed and had the opportunity to get away from the hustle and bustle. Being away had done nothing to cool his ardor for Maria, but at least this way he wasn't going crazy wondering when he would see her again. Running away from Memphis hadn't solved his problems, but at least now he had some distance, and with that distance, a little peace. Alex was glad he had been impulsive and taken the impromptu jaunt.

His forays into the ports of call had been satisfying in many ways, but when he returned to the ship, he wanted to do one thing, dance. He longed to visit one of the lounges where he'd heard Latin music, but he didn't know if he wanted to deal with the hassle of trying to extricate himself from his partner once the dance was over. He didn't want to appear available when he wasn't or lead someone into believing he was looking for a fling, which was the last thing on his mind.

After giving it some thought, he decided on using the ship's the full-service gym. He looked in the mirror after he had changed into a T-shirt and shorts. Seeing his reflection, he thought, not bad for an old man. Alex had no love handles, success paunch, or noticeable wrinkles. He was holding up pretty well. He would celebrate his thirty-ninth birthday in a few months, and felt no more worse for the wear.

He had tried to adhere to some sort of exercise during the entire seven days, especially since he had eaten many of the sinfully rich and exotic foods that the locals or the ship's staff had prepared. Without working out, he estimated that he would have gained about ten pounds easily. This evening, he would complete a total upper- and lower-body workout and then go to dinner. If the mood hit him after his meal, he would go to the lounge and hopefully find a willing partner or partners for some good old-fashioned clean fun. The mamba and tango were calling to him. He would save the dirty dancing for when he and Maria were together again.

Maria didn't know whether to laugh or cry. How could he? she thought. The cup of coffee in her hand was cold and bitter by this time. She had been sitting in her hotel room moping for most of the morning. She had gone by the club while Alex was away. She wanted to feel close to him even though she knew he was out of town. Watching Helene and Rod have a wonderful time on the dance floor, she longed to be held by Alexandro again. Much of her Sour Apple drink had been left untouched because that was her special drink with Alex.

Before leaving the club for the evening Maria stopped to chat with Ramon. However, she wasn't exactly prepared for his tidbit of information. She couldn't believe Alex had gone on a cruise without her! How could he do something so wonderfully romantic and exciting and leave her behind? What was he thinking? Did he go alone or plan to meet someone on board?

Max just told her he was out of town for a week, but Ramon had let slip that Alex was on a cruise. Jealousy fueled her emotional response to his going away. Was he with someone else?

It wasn't rational by any stretch of the imagination, especially since she had been staying away from him on purpose, but that didn't mean she didn't want to be with him. She missed him so much each day and night, sometimes she felt like she couldn't breathe. How could he be so unfeeling as to go on vacation? A cruise no less, like he didn't even miss her too. That hurt her much more than she wanted to admit.

She sat on her couch in her hotel room for the better part of two days. The case was in a holding pattern and she had plenty of time to let her imagination run rampant. She tried talking to Helene, but she found her friend to be of no use because she took Alexandro's side. As far as Maria was concerned Helene had broken one of the unwritten sister-friend rules: never side against your girl! She hung up with Helle feeling discontented and dissatisfied. Other than Helene, she didn't have too many other people to talk to. She didn't feel comfortable saying anything more to Rod; besides there wasn't much more to be said. Rod might sympathize, but she didn't need sympathy. She needed Alex!

Maria tried to deal with her feelings. She didn't want to allow herself to become a weak weepy woman—something that she despised—but it was taking all her strength. When she could stand it no longer, she drove to Alex's apartment. She didn't know what she was going to do. Although the Angela Bassett routine held some appeal, she wasn't that childish, plus she didn't have any proof he had messed around.

Maria arrived at his apartment after 1:00 AM. He wasn't due back until the next day. Before she had even thought out a plan, she found herself pulling into his parking lot. She didn't know what she wanted. Maybe she would feel better after smelling his aftershave. She knew she was acting like a real crazy woman. She entered the apartment by slightly less than legal means, since she had given up her keys when she walked out of his life weeks back. Still, he felt a constant part of it, no matter where she was or where he was.

She put her purse down on the couch and walked

straight back to the master bedroom. When she saw the bed, she almost cried. Hot tears were held at bay by sheer determination. She wanted to be in that bed curled into the spooning position with Alexandro by her side. She felt her chest tighten, causing her to have to force the air through her lungs. God, she loved that man.

Maria sat on the bed and then lay down, willing her breathing back to the normal rate. His scent in his sheets was intoxicating. A sense of calm flooded her body. *Just hang in there a little longer,* she told herself.

Wiping her eyes, she went back to the kitchen to retrieve her purse. Automatically, she went to the kitchen counter because that was where she usually put it. The purse was not there, but she noticed something else, something she missed when she first entered his home. On the kitchen countertop lay a note from Alex to her in his distinctive script.

Maria felt he heart lurch in her chest again. Was this it, the breakup? Was he tired of waiting for her? Her hands shook as she reached for the neatly folded piece of paper. How had he known she would show up?

Dear Maria,

If you are reading this then I can only say thank you. I have missed you these past several weeks. More than I thought humanly possible. I wake up in my empty bed and I can't stand the thought of you being in the same city and not waking up with you by my side every morning. I am taking a short trip to clear my head. I hope that you and your team can wrap up the case soon because we have a lot of unfinished business to attend to. Be safe and know you are in my thoughts and my heart forever.

Te quiero, Alexandro

Maria read the letter again. This man knew her so well, always knew the right to thing to say and the right thing to do. Her anger disappeared. Why be mad at him? She knew exactly what he was talking about. She understood how he felt because she was feeling it, too. She wanted to get this case over with and move on. She didn't even care what was next. Just something new, something less intense. These thoughts swirled around in her head, threatening to overwhelm her sense of peace.

The case and being team leader had taken much more out of her than she thought it ever would. No wonder Eric gave it up for Tangie, she thought ruefully. Agent Eric Duvernay, her former Special Corruption Unit team leader, had almost lost the woman he loved. He had waited two years to be with Tangie. It had taken a kidnapping disaster to bring them together. It was also during that same disaster that she'd met Alex for the first time, but not as Alexandro Milbon, instead as Kevin DePalma. So much had changed.

Could she do for Alexandro what Eric did for Tangie, and give it up? For the first time in her FBI/SCU career, she was beginning to think so.

Shaking her head, she folded up the note and placed it neatly in her purse. Then she looked around for a piece of paper to write one of her own.

She finished within a few minutes and left the apartment after making sure the door was locked. Maria drove back to the hotel in a much lighter mood. Alex loved her, and that was all that mattered. Rod met her in the lobby.

"Hey there, I was just beginning to wonder about you. We got a call while you were out. Spates needs to see us right now."

"Let me get decent, or at least change out of these sweats. I thought I was going to be turning in for the evening," she responded.

Roderick gave her the once over. "Come on, girl. We are going to a meeting, not on a date."

That comment brought a small smile to her lips. She looked at the gold watch on her wrist. It was 2:30 A.M. and her brief respite was over already. It was time to go to work again.

Chapter 31

The FBI returned Mikha to his former life after he had met with the SCU team. His full cooperation had been guaranteed and he made his next move according to plan.

Mikha called Nikola as soon as he heard that the old man was back in town. His suspicions were confirmed when he noted the surprise in the man's voice. Mikha knew then that Nikola had betrayed him and wanted him out of the way. *The game is up, old man, and now we both lose.* "Excuse my impatience, Nikola, when I heard that you were back in town, I felt it necessary to call. The *dealer* is becoming impatient, and I wanted to check with you before making further plans, as we agreed."

Mikha looked around his apartment. Goran and Ivan had worked wonders in it. The furnishings were new and modern, the walls freshly painted, and all traces of the ransacking eliminated. But he still felt spooked, knowing that he had been drugged and his apartment entered into by Nikola's henchmen. Mikha had never felt so vulnerable.

Nikola took a long drag of his cigarette before answering. Obviously his instructions had not been followed; otherwise he would not be having this conversation. "Mikha, how are you? I trust you were able to handle things while I was away, *da*? I have a few loose ends to tie up, but I would like to meet with you and your dealer at the end of the week. We meet Friday, at 10:30 P.M., but first you and I should meet at Goran's for a drink. We can talk about expanding the business then before we meet with the American woman."

So that's your new plan? "Sure, we'll be there. I'll make the call to Ms. Manez now to set it up. I trust you had a good trip?"

"Uneventful. The weather was cold and damp, too much like Russia. Your business went well?"

"As expected. I am looking forward to this deal. I'm thinking of taking a little vacation, maybe to the Middle East or to South America."

"Not running away, I hope—life has a way of catching up with you no matter where you go."

Mikha tried to sound nonchalant. The implied threat that Nikola posed was very real. He wouldn't be satisfied until he knew Mikha was dead.

"Not running, Nikola, just taking the time to enjoy life before I settle down. I will give Ms. Manez the good news and we will see you soon. *Paka*."

Nikola responded to him in his familiar raspy voice. "Yes Mikha, *da svidaniya*."

The conversation left Mikha warm, making him sweat in the most uncomfortable places. Maybe he had done the right thing by cooperating with the government. Bitterly, he thought about what Nikola had done to him. *You were such a fool, old man. There was much we could have done together if you had not been so greedy.* Maybe he should just run for it. Nikola could be the FBI's problem.

If Nikola wanted to eliminate him, there wasn't much to stop him. What would he do next? He wondered briefly if Maria were in any danger. Nikola was ruthless and had the soul of the devil himself.

While the idea of running had a lot of appeal, the truth was, his every move was monitored by the Bureau; he wouldn't be able to pull it off in the little time that he had left. Mikha closed his eyes against the pain and disappointment of his life. The acrid taste of bile welled up in his throat. Finally he spoke again, but not to Nikola.

"Did you get that, Agent Spates?"

He responded, "Every word. You did exactly as instructed; now let us do the rest. The two agents with you will bring you back to the safe house. Get ready for another hooded ride."

Mikha hesitated. "Ivan and Goran are going to wonder why they haven't heard from me. It is has been days. I need to call one of them before I just show up with Nikola. That's not the way we do business."

Spates considered that for a moment. "Fine, but you do it from here. I'll see you in thirty minutes, and remember my agent's orders. If you try anything they have been authorized to use deadly force."

Rod and Maria arrived shortly after Helene and the other members of the team. Chantal was still dressed in her skimpy waitress uniform from Goran's club. Maria didn't feel so bad about wearing her sweat suit now.

After everyone had fortified themselves with coffee or other caffeine, Spates began the meeting. He tapped his pen three times before he spoke. The agents took notice.

"As you know, we have been in a holding pattern while we wait for Nikola Mudiuranov to return to the United States. We just received word through our new acquisition that he has returned and is ready to meet. Nikola ordered Mikha to set up the meeting for Friday at 10:30

P.M. We need to get ready, people; this what it all comes down to. We move in three days."

Tension permeated the room. This is what they trained for, and now it was coming to a head. Each questioned their readiness, but knew no matter how tough the pressure, they would perform as necessary.

Spates looked down at his notes. He had made comments about each aspect of the operation, which had been analyzed and discussed with McCoy. He turned to his youngest agent, addressing her first.

"Agent McCorkle, how do you feel about staying in until the deal is done? I considered pulling you the day before so that you can go in with the rest of the team."

Chantal shook her head. "Sir, I'd like to remain on the inside. I can be much more effective as an extra pair of eyes for Helene. Besides, I don't want to do anything out of the ordinary. Nikola is so cagey that we could blow the deal with one little detail out of place. We already know that Nikola will have his men there; otherwise he wouldn't have insisted on a separate meet. I suspect he wants to poison Mikha or use some other technique. He wants him at the club for something other than a social call, for sure. If I stick around I might be able to find out what he has in mind."

Spates and Maria listened carefully. They admired her tenacity and knew she would be a great asset to the team. She was handling her first big assignment like the real professional she was.

Maria looked at her supervisor, simply shrugging her shoulders. "That's fine with me, but we should double the check-ins. Helene must know where you are at all times, and you never have a reason to go black, not even to go to the bathroom. These guys are ruthless. If we lose contact, Max, Rod, or I will come in and pull you out."

"Understood, ma'am."

Damn, make me feel old.

Rod and Helene looked at her across the conference room table and snickered for her eyes and ears only. Maria would deal with those two later.

Spates allowed for the moment of levity before regrouping. He was tickled too, especially since McCorkle had no idea how fresh and new she sounded. When she made senior agent she would look back at these days with fondness. He cleared his throat loudly when he was ready to proceed.

"Max, I want you to stay at the club with Alex for the next couple of days. On the day of the meet, leave there early and become one of Chantal's best customers. Alex Milbon should be fine. Ivan is no longer interested in him, and surveillance has been minimal. When we are done I will send a detail over to make sure he gets home safely."

The agents listened attentively, making sure that no one would be left uncovered. They would have to have each other's backs in this case—no one knew yet what kind of protection Nikola had for his shipment. Steven Caldwell, another agent, had been set up at the docks and loading warehouses for several months. As far as Mikha and Nikola were concerned, he was just another invisible worker.

"Caldwell, keep your ears open. No piece of information is too small to be recorded. Remember, we want to know as much about Nikola's operation as possible. We aren't satisfied just to shut down the gun dealing. We want it all, everything that we can get."

"Yes, sir," he responded.

Spates turned his attention to the rest of the group. "While you guys are the primary team, we are all in this together. No one, and I repeat no one, goes off like the Lone Ranger. If something goes wrong, you go to open channel and let us know.

"Now I know that it is getting late, but I need your attention for just a few more minutes. I want you to meet Mikha. He has agreed to be our asset in this operation, and his cooperation is critical. Use extreme prejudice once the takedown begins. We have one mission: take down the gun dealers. Keep focused and be careful. Mikha knows his responsibilities. He is to make the introductions and try to stay alive. And he does that on his own."

Mikha did not know that Maria was an agent. The team debated about letting him in on that particular piece of information, but in the end it was decided that it did not matter. If he tried to double-cross them, he would be killed on site.

While the team had begun their meeting, Mikha had contacted Ivan and Goran to let them know that he was safe. He told them that he had not taken the flight that Goran had arranged for him, but instead decided to lay low while things blew over.

"You and Ivan be careful," Mikha said. "I suspect it was Nikola who tried to set me up, and I don't know the lengths that he will go to. We meet with the Americans in three days."

Goran felt the familiar clinch in his gut whenever he disagreed with Mikha. However, he held his tongue. "What do you want me to do?" Goran asked weakly.

Mikha had grown impatient with Goran. Why was he always so reluctant? "Watch him. He wants to meet with me at the club before the Americans. He says he wants to toast. I think he wants to try to kill me."

"Goran, can I count on you? I need to know that right now."

"Yes, of course, Mikha. Are you in a sterile location? Maybe we should get off the phone."

"I am safe, but perhaps you are right. Contact Ivan and tell him what I've told you. I will call him tomorrow. *Da svidaniya*."

Goran gripped the phone with cold, damp fingers. Mikha was going to ruin him. The man's greed and impatience had angered Nikola; otherwise he wouldn't have wanted to kill him. He had to think. A few minutes after his phone call with Mikha, Goran called Viktor, Gregor, and Ivan, telling them to meet at the club right away. He didn't care that it was 5:00 AM.

He opened a fresh bottle of vodka as soon as the group had gathered. They were very vocal about being disturbed from their nights and mornings of pleasure.

Goran started without preamble. "Mikha is in trouble. Nikola no longer trusts him, and that means we all have a problem. Mikha wants reassurance that we will stand by his side. As for me, I will do what I can, but I am not going to die for him. We need to figure out how to help him and then get him the hell out of here. He can go back to Texas or Timbuktu. I want Mikhail Stemenovich out of my life for good."

Ivan spoke first, as Goran knew he would. "Where is Mikha? I will not betray him. Leave the arrangements to me, and I will see to his safety."

Goran nodded at Ivan. "Mikha says he will call you tomorrow. He plans to take over Nikola's operation. He wants to know who's in and who's out."

Viktor and Gregor were curiously quiet. Goran continued, "I want no part of guns. I am successful with my enterprises, and in my opinion, guns cause too much attention. Girls, drugs, and gambling are safer."

The men agreed all around that there were less risky and just as lucrative businesses to be involved in, and no one was convinced that running guns was the answer to their continued wealth. There was much discussion during the meeting about the best way to proceed. In the end, they yielded to Goran.

The silence in the room was deafening. The others had made their allegiance clear. Ivan alone remained committed to seeing Mikha out of this bit of trouble.

When Goran spoke again, he gave instructions. "I need you to watch Nikola when he arrives at the club. Make sure that he doesn't tamper with the alcohol that is served, or at least if he does, that we are informed. Also, when Ivan is ready to get Mikha out, be prepared to create a diversion or offer assistance. I'll do what I can and will ask one of the dancers to pay special attention to Nikola's group. I don't like surprises. Please make sure we don't have any. Are there any questions?"

The room remained quiet. "Good, now we drink."

Ivan was not very pleased with the way the meeting had gone. They had all known each other and worked together for years, but now it had come to this. He had three days until Nikola's arrival.

Mikha entered the room unaware that he would be coming face to face with his buyer. When he saw Maria dressed in a casual sweatsuit and her hair in a short ponytail, he almost stopped in his tracks. He stared open mouthed for several seconds.

Maria glared at him. "Surprise, Stemenovich. Sometimes what appears to be so, just ain't so."

Mikha looked around the room, recognizing more than one face in the crowd. A flicker of remorse coursed through him as he realized what his impatience had cost him. Maybe some of his anger at Nikola was misplaced. Ivan and Goran had advised caution, but he hadn't heeded their advice, and now he had to pay for that.

Mikha swallowed hard. He could feel his throat closing up. Finally, he nodded his head to the group. His gaze lingered a bit too long on Chantal, or Sunny as she was known to him while she worked at Goran's club. The total picture came into focus for him now. The FBI had been on to him for years. Defeat was defeat.

"Well done, Americans, well done," he said.

Chapter 32

Alex arrived at his apartment shortly after 5:00 P.M. He called Max from the airport to let him know that he was back in town. He had spent an extra few days enjoying the casual life in Miami before returning to Memphis. He spent his time checking out clubs and restaurants, getting fresh ideas for Memphis Nights. The cruise had also provided inspiration for making improvements there.

When he landed, he had wanted to call Maria. But when Max informed him that there had been significant movement in the case, he decided to let her be. She would come to him when she was ready—she had assured him of that before, and he trusted her.

He was nervous as he opened his door. *Had she come by?*

He dropped his three suitcases by the door and went immediately to the kitchen counter. He released the breath he had been holding when he saw the note.

Dear Alexandro,
  I have to admit that I was angry when I found out that you went on a romantic cruise without me, especially after our last conversation. But after I read your note I felt better. I know that this case hasn't been easy for either one of us, but you have to know how important you are

to me. When things settle down, we will work something out. I hope you had fun, and I'd better have some wonderful souvenirs. I love you too, Maria.

He dragged the bags into his bedroom, then went to take a long hot bath. He turned the water, then lit the candles that surrounded the tub. Alex had purchased several vanilla-scented candles to remind him of Maria while they were apart. The aroma and the steam served to soothe and rejuvenate him. He sent up a prayer for her safety and let the hot water take over.

He would be ready for her when she was ready for him. But for right now it would be business as usual at the club and with the Bureau. Max had assured him when he checked in that they would call him if they needed him, but it seemed that his participation in the case was all but over. Max didn't want to alarm him. "For right now you can turn in your gun and badge," he joked. "Alex, things are right where they need to be, but in this business always be prepared for surprises. I'll be in at the club behind your bar, so I can keep you posted. Maria is doing fine by the way. I think she missed you, though."

Alex breathed a sigh of relief. He trusted Max, and if he said she was safe, Alex would believe him. He planned go in to Memphis Nights about 10:00 P.M. The report was that business was steady and that they had developed a set of regulars who seemed to enjoy the club at least twice a week. A mountain of paperwork would be facing him when he went in, but his trip away had been well worth that minor inconvenience.

He felt better in his spirit and in his soul. Alex looked at the small box that contained Maria's new ring. Memories of its story and the old woman in Cozumel haunted him, but unlike that tale, he vowed, their story would have a happy ending.

That evening, he arrived at the club and went immediately to his office. There was a nice crowd at the bar and the dance floor was full. Alex smiled, pleased at the way things were going. He would mingle with the patrons and then chat with Ramon and Max when he finished reading his mail and taking care of the most pressing paperwork.

Alex breathed deeply. It was good to be back again. He had missed the atmosphere of the club, the people, and the music. The couple of days he spent in Miami showed him how much he was in the right business. Alex knew he had found home.

This was where he belonged, in Memphis with Maria. Somehow he would find a way to convince her to stay with him. He knew that she loved her job and life in Virginia. But he could make one promise to her and that was he would make her happy. If she let him.

Maria and Roderick had gone back to the hotel, where they'd had an uneventful night. Other than wanting to be in the arms of her lover, Maria was doing fine. She held the phone in her hand to call Alex, but she never dialed the number. She needed to leave him alone until this was done. Besides, she had left him a note. He would know soon how crazy she was about him. *Patience,* she admonished herself. Just a little bit longer and this would be done. She sat up for a little while, unable to sleep. After a cup of tension-tamer tea, she felt relaxed enough to sleep, falling into a deep, dream-filled slumber. Thoughts and images of Alex filled her dreams.

Helene spent the night in her surveillance trailer. She

was too keyed up to sleep after the briefing with Spates and the team. She had a pivotal role in making sure that everyone was safe, and her ability to track them and to respond was critical. She blew out a long, concerned breath.

Roderick hoped that everyone else was having a less tension-filled night than he was. The next couple of nights would be nerveracking, but this is what they did.

Alex picked up the phone and put it down a dozen times. Finally he picked up the phone and dialed. Maria answered on the third ring. Alex listened to her breathing for half a second before identifying himself. "Maria, I know I wasn't supposed to call. I just had to hear your voice."

"Alex! I'm so glad you did. I haven't stopped thinking about you, since the last time we were in the club. I'm sorry."

Relief peppered his tone. "Maria, I'm sorry. I don't know what got into me. I don't want to lose you. If anything happened to you, I—"

Maria stopped him before he could continue with any more negative thoughts. "Alex, I love you and there's no place I'd rather be than in your arms, listening to your heart beat, hearing the deep rumble of your laugh, and seeing you smile and the heat in your eyes when you look at me. But I can't. Yet. I just need a little more time."

Alex was cautious. He wouldn't push just yet. If he had his way, they would spend the rest of their lives together. "Time is all I have for you," he said gently. "Maria, I love you. More than I thought possible. I just called to let you know that I will always be here for you. I'm willing to take what you'll give me. For now. Be safe. I'll let you get your rest."

Maria hung up the phone and soon after again settled into a deep sleep.

Nikola sat behind his desk at the warehouse. His bones ached from his recent trip up north, and it was becoming apparent to him that is body preferred much warmer weather. He checked his machinery. The room had been swept for electronic devices just minutes before, but he always did his own visual check. He'd asked for a few minutes alone before he had to start his meetings for the day. He had much to consider.

The decision to eliminate Mikha had been difficult. On the one hand, he wanted the young man to succeed him, as he didn't have children to leave his business to; on the other hand, his disrespect could not be tolerated. If Mikha wanted Nikola to be his benefactor, there were certain rules to follow, a certain protocol. Mikha defied authority at every turn, and that made him too dangerous to keep alive. Few people could have managed to elude the authorities the way he had after being caught with the presses. Which meant only one thing—Mikha had been turned.

Nikola had to make a decision soon. He requested a meeting with several of the younger men who were looking to make their mark. He lit a cigar because it really didn't matter what his doctor thought now. The cough that rumbled through his chest foretold his future.

Nikola looked at the names of the men who could succeed him, reading over the information he had on each man. He flipped through the papers, making evaluations as he went along. Mikha, Ievik, Ivan, Goran, Viktor, and Gregor. When he reach the end of the list he gave a short, derisive laugh. *If the fate of Russia depended on this motley crew, we'd all go straight to hell.*

Agent Caldwell had discovered that the guns were mixed in with Nikola's regular monthly shipments from Russia. He exported various products from his homeland, including shipments of caviar, crystal, dishware, music boxes, wooden carved souvenirs, gold, and any other thing that would make him money. Russian craftsmanship was still very much in demand around the world. His network reached into many more enterprises than originally suspected. Chantal informed Spates that with all the things that Nikola had his hands in, there were other jurisdictions that would love to get a chance to bring down the Mudiuranov organization. Spates was pleased. This would be a good bust for the Special Corruption Unit.

They had decided on a two-part operation. The warehouse would be secured and the merchandise seized after Nikola and the rest of his group were apprehended for their one-way ticket back to the motherland.

Maria hated when Spates gave her that paternal, concerned look. It made her feel vulnerable and gnawed at her confidence. Today she needed to feel strong. She shrugged the tension out of her neck and shoulders.

Helene wired her for sound, using the very latest in covert technology to secure a listening device in the tight outfit she wore.

"Are you ready to do this? " Spates asked.

Maria avoided direct eye contact with her senior agent. "Sir, you cannot treat me like your daughter when

I'm getting ready to go out on a case. Did you give Agent Duvernay or Agent Radford this same treatment?" She inhaled deeply. A negative emotion like anger could interfere with her ability to work the case.

"Agent Thomas, I won't pretend that I don't think of you like my own child. I have known your family since before you came along, so yes, I care about you, but I know that you can do this. You were hand selected for this job because we have faith in you. My look of concern is just to let you know that I give a damn. This isn't just about whether you have backup, this is about being there for you no matter what. Save the attitude for Mikha and Nikola and bring me a good bust. I'll see you later tonight for the debrief," he told her.

Maria sighed. "Yes, sir. I'll make you proud, sir."

He looked at her, marveling at the tough young lady that she had become right before his eyes. *You already have,* he thought.

"Alex, man, you are making me jumpy. Calm down!" Max said. "Thomas knows what she is doing; she always has. She comes from a long line of folks who know mission, duty, and honor. It is in her blood. She can't fail."

Alex knew that Max was trying to make him feel better, but the tension he felt in his body threatened to unhinge him. Icy fear twisted around his heart. He wanted to trust that Maria would be all right, but fear for her safety wouldn't let him. He had been pacing in the office and bar area of Memphis Nights for about an hour. In some ways he wished he hadn't known this was it. Ignorance would have been bliss.

Alex made himself a drink at the bar, took one sip, then poured the rest out. When he continued to pace,

Max and Ramon left him alone. He would have to figure out a way to deal with this on his own. Max shook his head in sympathy for Alex. If he continued to deal with the case this way, he would give himself a heart attack.

Rod sat in his room for five minutes of meditative time. He checked his watch. It was 8:30 P.M. He had to admit that one part of him had been envious that Maria was the senior agent. However, he knew that at this very moment it was a burden that he was not prepared to carry. He could only hope that he held up his end of the bargain and did exactly what she needed him to do. There was one other person he especially did not want to let down, Helene. His feelings for her had become overwhelming. And he didn't know how long he could ignore them or her. He pushed aside those thoughts. They were demons to fight another time. Russians, guns, and other contraband were the order of the day.

Maria checked her appearance in the mirror. Tonight her Maria-wear was especially provocative. She looked very much like the *bad girl* she had come to Memphis to play. "Helene, are you there?" she said into the microphone hidden beneath her skimpy dress.

"I'm here, hon, what do you need?"

"About one minute to myself."

"You got it. Going black in two."

Maria covered the dark circles under her eyes with concealer. When she finished, she gripped the edge of the sink. She began slowly, whispering the words to herself, calmed by their meaning. "The Lord is my shepherd . . ."

* * *

She had just finished when she heard Rod's distinctive knock on the door.

"Ready, partner?" Roderick asked when he saw her.

"As I'll ever be. Mission first?" She released a long tense breath.

He looked at her and smiled. "Mission first, but I've got your back. Let's do this."

They walked out of the hotel, each holding a briefcase full of government money to make the gun payment. Rod loaded the trunk of the Bureau SUV and asked Maria if she wanted to drive.

"No, go ahead. I am fine."

Rod understood. She was too keyed up to get behind the wheel of a car.

Dressed in her waitress uniform, Agent McCorkle arrived at Goran's club at her usual time. The break room had been abuzz with gossip about a party later where the girls could make lots of tips. She'd heard Goran had offered quite a bonus to those who had come in earlier, too.

"Can I bring you anything else, sir?" Chantal turned on her best smile. She had taken care to pay special attention to Nikola's party. The men were sitting around a crescent-shaped table facing a small stage. This was Goran's VIP room, where the high rollers could play cards while watching the girls from front-row seats.

Goran seemed to ignore her. She was just another waitress to him.

Nikola wasn't so nonchalant. "What's your name, honey?"

The young agent blushed. "Chantal, but everyone calls me Sunny."

Nikola reached for her hand. She froze for half a beat. She felt moisture begin to pool under her arms. Helene whispered into her transmitter, "Stay cool honey. He just wants to know if you're new."

Nikola smiled, a gesture that makes most men look more appealing, but not in his case. "That's a very appropriate name. Are you from Tennessee? That's a lovely accent you have."

She flirted openly with him. She was so close she could smell the alcohol and cigarettes on his breath, and was glad she hadn't eaten recently. Batting her heavily lined and coated eyelashes, she responded, "I'm not from around here, but I am from the south. Do you prefer women from the south?"

His interest seemed to be piqued, based on his body's reaction to her. She subtly used her serving tray to put some distance between the two of them.

He grasped his drink with one hand and her bottom with the other. The ridiculously short outfit that pretended to be a waitress uniform left nothing for the imagination. She felt him caressing her. *Damn Viagra!* she thought. It had every old man thinking he was Don Juan. She pretended to enjoy the gesture and allowed her breast to brush up against him as she reached to clear an empty glass from the table.

Nikola tightened his grip around her waist. "I was just wondering why I'd never seen you before."

Goran began to take note of the conversation. "Sunny has been with me for about six months. She is quiet and makes good tips because she provides good service. I think that we have other matters to attend to right now. Maybe Sunny could come back for you later?"

She stood still, barely breathing, as she waited for his response.

Nikola gave her a sound pinch on the bottom before letting her go. Then he spoke as if she didn't have ears. "Yes. She'll do."

Goran spoke to her like she was produce on the market. "You'll come back when I send for the girls. You'll do as you are told and make good money for it. *Da?*"

"*Da*, I'll be back to bring more drinks." Chantal held her head down while she exited the room. She was nervous. These guys really scared her. She scooted from the room as fast as she could without arousing further suspicion.

Chaper 33

Helene breathed a sigh of relief in the surveillance truck. She checked her weapon and returned to her seat.

"It's okay, everyone, McCorkle is fine. Stand down."

Maria and Rod arrived at the club at the precise moment Helene gave the warning. The false alarm only served to heighten the anxiety each was already feeling. Roderick reached for Maria's hand before they exited the car and gave it a reassuring squeeze. She nodded at him and winked. "Let's go," she told him. "Helene, we are moving in, on three."

"I've got you, and I read you loud and clear. I love that outfit, by the way. Damn, I wish I had your figure."

Maria smiled, her nerves made a little less on edge by her friend's dry wit.

Rod smiled too; he wondered if she would miss her wardrobe.

Chantal came over the open channel again. They could hear the tension in her voice. "Something is going down or has gone down. Mikha arrived early like he was supposed to. He hasn't been drinking or eating anything. He looks pale, almost sickened. I didn't dare try to make eye contact with him while Nikola was talking to me. I'm going to see if any of the girls know anything. They have been in the back room for over an hour.

"Ievik, Gregor, and Viktor are here too. I don't think their allegiance is with Mikha anymore. I don't know where Ivan is right now. Goran seems too low key. My gut says we need to be very careful."

Helene responded first. "Chantal, keep your eyes open. We know Ivan is there somewhere, and we don't want any surprises from him."

Chantal met Maria and Rod at the door. She was the perfect hostess, asking if she could take their drink order. Then, Chantal approached the meeting room cautiously, knocking softly on the door.

Nikola indicated for her to enter. The club belonged to Goran, but Goran was simply another member of the rank and file with Nikola around.

She personified the naïve farm girl when she spoke to him. "I just wanted to let you know that there are some people out here that say they are here for your meeting. I am going to get their drink orders and show them in, if that's all right."

Nikola looked at Goran. Irritation was evident in his tone when he addressed him. "Is that the way you usually do things? Why aren't you outside greeting our new customers? Who is this girl?"

Goran looked stricken. She had told him that she was Cuban and her parents lived in Miami. She'd learned a little Russian since working in the club and was a hard worker. He wondered where the country girl came from. "She is my greeter and the head waitress. She's nobody."

"Go with her, check it out first." Nikola nodded for her to proceed. He had plans of his own.

Chantal disappeared for a couple of minutes, and she and Goran returned with Maria and Rod in tow. When she turned on her heel to walk out of the room, Nikola indicated for Ievik. who was closest to the door, to block her exit. She turned back to him, wide eyed and innocent. "Would you like for me to bring you another drink, sir?"

Nikola was gruff in his reply. "No, I want you to sit down next to my friend Mikha over here."

Chantal moved to do as she was told.

Goran moved toward the table where the group was sitting. Radford stayed a few paces behind, letting Maria lead the show.

The men in the room looked at her appreciatively. Her red leather dress stopped at midthigh and left no doubt about the natural curves of her body. She had piled her curly hair in a loose chignon, while several tendrils fell around her face. Her designer red shoes cost more than most of the strippers made in a couple of nights. In her heels, she stood as tall as Goran, who was at least six feet. His new business partner, Nikola, was shorter and seemed to be very intrigued with her exotic appearance. He seemed to be appreciate her smooth skin with almond coloring and glossy sable brown hair.

"So, Mikha, this is your American friend. I can see why she is your friend." His leer was distasteful and offensive.

Maria responded in perfect Russian. "I thought I was meeting with a man, Mikha, not a dog. You should have told me. I would have brought him some biscuits."

A chilling black silence enveloped the room. Nikola and Maria appeared to be the only two breathing.

He studied her very closely, not quite sure what to make of her. "Ah, the American is more than just a pretty face. I applaud your Russian. You speak like someone from Odessa." He replied finally.

"*Nyet*, St. Petersburg. That is where I learned."

Nikola approved, waving his hands for more drinks. He began pouring vodka into a shot glass for her. "Come, let us get properly introduced. I suppose you know everyone else in the room, however."

Rod remained standing not far from her. Maria moved closer to Nikola, where he immediately took out a funny-looking instrument and waved it over her body.

She stood still and acted nonplused, all the while praying Helene's gadgets would evade detection. She sat down next to him after he had finished his scan.

When Nikola appeared satisfied, she extended her hand and made a proper introduction. "Since my friend over there seems to be so quiet, let me introduce myself. Maria Manez from Baltimore, Maryland. It is a pleasure to finally meet the man that can get things done. And I hope that after tonight we can continue to do business. The demand for your product seems to greatly outweigh my supply."

She drank her shot of vodka only after she noticed others who had drinks from the same bottle consumed theirs with no ill effects.

"I'm glad that you see me as that man. We are having a little shake-up in our organization, so there will be some changes around here. After tonight, Mikha will no longer be your contact person."

Goran quickly poured himself another drink, and Rod noticed that it was a triple shot this time. He downed the liquid in the blink of an eye.

Tension and fear snaked through the room. Whatever it was that Nikola was up to wasn't much appreciated.

"Is that why you aren't talking to me, Mikha?" Maria asked, looking in his direction. He had barely moved the entire time she had been in the room. When he looked at her, he did so with dead eyes. She noticed for the first time how red and puffy they appeared.

Nikola watched the two intently. He was looking for any sign that the two were working together. He knew that Mikha had sold him out; he just didn't know to whom.

"I'm afraid today was Mikha and Ivan's last day with my organization. I don't tolerate traitors. Sunny, why don't you help Mikha with that box? Let's show everybody his present."

Chantal's hands shook as she reached for the box. When she opened it, she let out a scream that shook the walls of the room.

Nikola snickered. "Skittish, little one, aren't you.? I want you to be usable tonight. You can go now, but I want to see you in about another hour."

Chantal nodded, and practically ran from the room.

Nikola turned to Maria. "I'm sure a woman of your sensibilities and position can appreciate my stand. There was a traitor in my organization. Ivan came to a rather unseemly end. Is that the expression you Americans would use? Now, as for Mikha. I'm afraid Mikha will never speak again. We had a bit of an argument today. He lost." Nikola spoke with such nonchalance it was frightening.

Maria spoke quietly and confidently. Her time as a crime scene investigator had prepared her for the most gruesome discoveries. She suppressed her reaction to seeing Mikha's tongue in the box. Her voice was calm, though her stomach lurched. "You run a tight organization. I can appreciate that. I operate in the same manner. Will any of your reorganization efforts affect my ability to get the guns on time?"

Nikola raised his glass to her in salute. *Maria Manez is the real thing,* he thought.

She was growing impatient, and said so. They didn't have time for his theatrics.

"Business first," he agreed. He seemed more focused when he spoke again. "As long as you have the money, you will get the product. I am a businessman, above and beyond anything else."

Maria smoothed her hair, then spoke again. She wanted him to know that he was dealing with a true businesswoman. "What do you have for me? I trust that before you relieved Mikha of his tongue and Ivan of his life, you thought to discover the details of what I am looking for?"

Agent Radford watched her every move, looking for the signals that they had practiced and perfected as a team. Each gesture, each move told him something. His sense of anticipation heightened as he watched Maria and Nikola perform their dance. Nikola wanted to dominate, but Maria stood her ground. For each move he made, she had an equally subtle and assertive countermove.

Nikola chuckled. He admired her grit. "I understand you are in the market for fifty thousand guns. That is a lot for one person, and I have to admit I was a bit concerned until Mikha and Ivan shared your marketing plan with me. You plan to open up shop all along the Northeast. That is ambitious, but after meeting you tonight I suspect that you can handle it. I have arranged for a truckload to be delivered here so that you may inspect the merchandise. The remainder of the shipment is at my warehouse at the docks. Once the financial arrangements have been made, I will give you a code to use to pick up the rest of your order. I will accept a cash payment of $2 million, which is half of the order, with the rest to be deposited into an account number that I give to you. Once I receive confirmation, the codes are yours. Is that satisfactory?"

Maria nodded her head. "It is exactly as Mikha and I discussed prior to your arrival. I'd like to see the guns now." She stood to move out of her seat. Nikola wasn't too pleased with her action. Nikola then raised his hands to Ievik and Viktor, indicating that it was okay. "My apologies, my assistants aren't too comfortable with sudden movements. Perhaps you could have a seat and a demonstration will be arranged for you."

She felt an uncomfortable feeling course through her. Nikola was too oily and too unstable for her liking. She didn't like unpredictable people, and there was something about him, the way he carried himself, which indicated to her that he didn't feel like he had a whole lot to lose.

She looked over at Mikha, venturing to speculate about his injuries. His face was left relatively untouched, but she suspected his clothing hid significant injuries. She noticed his face was deathly pale.

Gregor had taken the seat Chantal vacated. Ievik, Viktor, and Rod remained standing close to the walls of the small room, while Nikola, Maria, Goran, Mikha, and now Gregor sat at the table discussing the transaction. Maria studied the room and all of its contents; she knew Rod would be doing the same thing. They would have to take down Nikola in the room as soon as the codes to the warehouse were furnished. They were outnumbered, but that's just the way they liked it. Surprise was their best weapon.

Nikola seemed satisfied with her pedigree. She doubted that Mikha would have given up any information, which was probably why he was still alive. Ivan would not have known that she was undercover and probably outlived his usefulness to Nikola because of his loyalty to Mikha.

Maria considered all these things as she watched and catalogued her surroundings. She turned to Nikola again, making a point to look at the gold watch on her wrist. "Have you ever heard the American expression, time is money?"

She appeared ready to leave the room again. Nikola was not amused. "You want to do business, we do business." He signaled for the curtains to be opened. Where the dancers would normally stand were boxes stacked upon each other. Nikola was quick to offer an explanation. "In those crates are some of the guns that you requested. As I mentioned before, this is a split shipment because of the large quantity."

"Very well. I'd like to open a crate and do an inspection."

Nikola smiled. "Of course you do. I wouldn't expect anything less. Right this way."

He led her to the stage and handed her a loaded gun to sample from the crate he'd just opened. Each crate contained one hundred guns. This would be one of the largest takedowns in Bureau history. Maria tried to quell her excitement.

Her inspection included looking for dirt and debris that would render the gun useless. When she was satisfied she put the gun down. "Very nice. I think we can do business after all." She motioned for Rod to bring the bags over. "My assistant will turn over the funds now. May I borrow your laptop?"

Nikola gave her another oily grin. "Of course. We wouldn't have it any other way. Let's proceed."

The machine was set up on top of the one of the crates. Nikola instructed her where to send the rest of the money, while he had Goran count the money from the bags that Rod had turned over.

In a matter of minutes, Maria appeared to transfer $2 million to Nikola's offshore account. When he was satisfied, he gave her the codes, which she repeated for Helene's benefit. Agent Caldwell and his team would secure the warehouse on the docks.

There was a flurry of activity in the room as everyone did their part. Max had arrived in the club area only moments before the warehouse operation began. It was time for act two.

Nikola left the stage area in order to reach for another bottle of vodka. A series of frantic knocks on the door stopped his motion.

Nikola motioned for Gregor to see what was happening. Gregor left his seat next to Mikha. Rod moved closer into the room so that he could be in a direct line with Maria.

Chantal appeared at the door in near hysterics. "I've got to see Mr. Goran right away. We have a very drunk customer out here, and I can't find any of the bouncers. This guy is trying to climb up on the stage and everything."

Goran was irritated at the disruption and went to find out what was going on. Max burst into the room and ordered everybody down. Guns were drawn, and bullets erupted from every corner. Gregor, who was closest to Chantal, was the first to fall. Maria took cover behind the crate where she'd been standing and grabbed the guns that she'd been checking out.

"On two," she yelled through all the commotion. Rod counted and then stood up to catch the weapon that she tossed at him. He caught the weapon in time to put two rounds into Viktor.

Max fired on Ievik, leaving Nikola without a bodyguard. Goran, who was close to the door, knocked Chantal to the ground and fled the scene. Mikha grabbed Rod's gun with one last burst of energy to fire on Nikola. Two bodies dropped when Maria also fired on Mikha. She couldn't risk Rod's life. She looked around the room. "Where's Goran?"

"He's on foot heading toward Beale Street," Helene said. "I lost him when all the commotion started because people were stampeding out of the club. He has a gun; he kept ordering people to get out of his way and waving it around."

Beale Street. "Check on Chantal and Max. I'm heading toward Memphis Nights."

Roderick opened his mouth to protest, but before he could close it she was on her way. Max looked at him and motioned for him to follow her. "I've got things under control here—go!"

Alex was sitting at his desk doing paperwork. He could barely concentrate, but he was making the effort. He heard a noise outside his door. Then Goran came into his office.

"What the hell are you doing?" Alex shouted.

"Shut up and sit down," Goran responded. "They will be here any minute and I need to think."

Alex noted the desperation in Goran's tone. Something had gone terribly wrong in the case. Cold fear snaked through him as he thought of Maria. Alex spoke to him again, hoping to help calm his own nerves. "What happened?"

Goran's response was distraught and disjointed. He aimed the gun at Alex's chest. "You are going to get me out of here. If Maria really cares about you, she will help me get out of this mess. Call her! Tell her to get down here and help me get away."

"Okay, okay, I will, but stop pointing that gun at me. You are making me nervous. I'll call her right now."

Maria heard voices in the back. She emptied the club of its patrons, but had the deejay leave the music on very loud. The only ones left in the club were Goran, Alex, and Maria. She crept along the wall, making sure that her approach to the office was silent.

Maria was worried that Goran would shoot Alex by mistake. She heard a noise behind her. Rod was creeping along the wall to her position. Using hand signals she told him that there were two people in the room. He shook his head in understanding.

Alex sensed Maria before he saw her. His heart began to beat at the normal pace. She was safe. Now he just had to get this maniac out of the way. There would be no repeat of New Mexico. Maria had to come to his rescue after his kidnapping. He wasn't going to let fear paralyze him. Goran would have no chance to hurt him, or Maria, if he could help it.

Goran was watching Alex behind the desk with his back to the wall. He didn't hear the movement behind him until it was too late.

"FBI. Put the gun down!"

Goran whirled around toward the voice, discharging his weapon as he did so. His movement created a momentary lapse, which Alex took advantage of. He grabbed the gun he'd hidden in his drawer for protection and unloaded the weapon at Goran.

Maria ordered Alex to drop the gun, knowing that he

was probably in shock. He numbly put it down and she rushed toward him. "Alex, are you okay?"

He looked at her, blinking several times. When the haze finally cleared from his eyes, he said, "I am now."

Rod shook his head in relief. "Good work, Milbon. Does this mean we need to add you to the team?"

Chapter 34

One by one, the team reported to the safe house. It had been a long night and was turning into an even longer morning. Helene hugged Maria when she entered the room. "You are the woman! Congratulations, your motley crew was successful."

Maria attempted to smile, but she was too exhausted. She flopped in the chair and closed her eyes. Was the case really over? She had more questions than answers, and her head was swimming. She was jolted back to reality with smelling salts. "What happened?" she asked. She noticed Helene's look of concern.

"You passed out." Helene told her. "You've been operating on little food and a whole lot of adrenaline. You've been out for five minutes. Here, drink this tea."

Helene shoved the cup in front of her. It smelled and looked like seaweed. Maria wrinkled her nose before gulping down the hot liquid. "Thank you, I'm okay now. What did I miss?"

"Oh, nothing," Helene quipped. "Just our recounting of how the SCU once again saved the world." She continued, all joking aside. "We're all exhausted. Spates wants us to write up what we can and then crash here. No one can leave the house until we are sure that we are secure. Steve was able to lock down the warehouse. Gunfire was exchanged there, but none of our people were hurt. Relax, we did it."

Maria's relief was evident. The tiny worry lines around her eyes softened. "Thank you, Helene. I am so glad we were able to work this one together."

Helene hugged her again.

Maria noticed that the room they were in was very quiet. "Where's everybody?"

Helene shrugged. "Trying to get the room with the Jacuzzi. Come on, let's get this done so we can go to bed! I think I have just one brain cell left. I heard about Alexandro. The man is definitely a keeper."

Maria's thoughts automatically turned to Alex. "I know. I just hope he knows that." *Just give me a little bit more time, darling,* she pleaded silently.

The caffeine-laden tea was beginning to work. Maria sat up straighter in her chair. "Okay, let's get down to business," she told Helene. Turning on her laptop, she began typing. She promised herself she wouldn't think about Alex again until the report was finished and the last "t" was crossed.

Agent Spates was on the phone talking with Agent McCoy. He relayed the details of the takedown. Her priority was not only the success of the case, but also the body count. She had to track the results of the SCU to protect the funding for the elite group. She listened attentively to his recount of the operation.

Spates sat up straight in his high-backed leather chair. "There were no fatalities on our side. The unit was involved in a shoot-out, but the injuries sustained were minor. We also had a civilian discharge. Alexandro Milbon was forced into a firing position. Goran tried to use him as a hostage, and when he was unsuccessful, threatened the life of our agents on the scene. They had things under control, but Milbon took the shot after he noticed the suspect's erratic behavior. It was a clean shooting."

Spates heard her tension-filled sigh. "Is there anything that the team did that I should be worried about? They have been breathing down our necks on Capitol Hill."

"No, ma'am, everything was by procedure. This was a good case. The agents will be arriving at Quantico this afternoon for the section meeting. They all deserve commendations for their excellent work."

McCoy was pleased. "Yes, I agree. Sometimes the politicians we have to fight are worse than the criminals are. I'll make sure the bonus checks and leave time are worth the team's efforts. Now, what do we do with our little protégé? She did good, didn't she?"

A thoughtful smile curved Spates's mouth. Pride was evident in his voice when he responded. "Yes, she did. It wasn't easy, and it certainly wasn't pretty, but she handled it. I was thinking maybe something long term in Memphis?"

"Agreed."

The team filed in to begin their briefing. After meeting with Spates, they would be flown by government plane to Quantico. It had been a tense couple of days, but it was over now and no one was any worse for the wear. A sense of relief flooded the conference room that served as their headquarters for the last several months. Now it was on to bigger and better things. Or at least the next case.

They would stay at Quantico for as long as it took to complete the search and seizure of all of the holdings of each of the Mafia members that had been involved in the undercover operation. A separate unit would come in to catalog the cars, planes, illegal merchandise, and, of course, the guns. The Special Corruption Unit had provided the means; now the rest of the FBI could do their part.

Chapter 35

Maria had been offered the opportunity of her career. She had been appointed unit chief of the Memphis office. She could be stationed in the city for years. They could finally think about a life together, if that's what he still wanted. A wave of nervousness swept through her as she got out of the car. So much was riding on the next few minutes. *What would Alex say?*

Alex knew she was on her way because he had called Agent Spates and Rod looking for her. He looked at the small box in his hand, sending up a small prayer.

He hoped she was hungry. Most of his day had been spent preparing grilled salmon, vegetables, and his special-recipe steamed white rice for her. The secret was spices and whole peppercorns for punch. Red and white roses formed the table's centerpiece. He wanted this evening to be perfect.

Taking a deep breath, Maria knocked on the door. Alex opened it instantly. She drank in the tall figure of man that presented himself before her. He was gorgeous. But all that mattered was the smile that greeted her as soon as he saw her. She practically flew into his arms.

He kissed her hair, her eyes, and her mouth. She returned his kiss with reckless abandon. Her body melded

into his like a snug-fitting glove. Both moaned in pleasure as desire rose, threatening to turn into a tidal wave
of passion. The week that they had spent apart had felt
like an eternity.

Finally, slowly, she broke off the kiss. She needed to
look at him, make sure he was real. "Alex, you don't
know how good it is to see you. I've missed you so
much."

His voice was low and husky when he responded. "I
am so glad to see you, baby. Come on in, you must be
tired."

Several minutes later she saw the table he had prepared. "Everything looks so beautiful, Alex. Does this
mean I'm washing the dishes?"

He paused, smiling at her question. "Not tonight.
Tonight, I'm taking care of you."

"Ohhh, Mr. Milbon, I do like the sound of that," she
teased. She went to the bathroom to wash her hands.
When she returned, they sat at the table together and
Alex blessed the food.

Maria marveled at him. He was so perfect for her.
"This tastes as fantastic as it looks. I was so hungry, but I
didn't want to stop to eat. All I could think about was getting back here to you."

Alex took a sip of wine. "I have to admit I was getting
worried about you. I am going to have to figure out a way
to relax when you aren't around."

She caressed his cheek. "I'm a big girl, Alexandro, and
I've been doing this for awhile. I'll always be careful."

He took her hand in his, sending delicious shivers up
her spine. "Thank you. I couldn't bear to lose you. Not
now. You mean everything to me."

"I feel the same way," she responded, as desire awak-
ened in her. "What would you say if I told that I was given

an offer to stay in Memphis? The job is a promotion and would require some travel, but not nearly the amount that I do now. I would be based here, and my job would be to make sure that we have truly crippled Russian organized crime in this corridor. They don't make a move unless we already know about it." She waited with bated breath for his response.

His eyes twinkled with happiness. "First, I would say that sounds like a lot of responsibility, which I know you can handle. Then I would say, that is very good news, especially if you told Spates that you would accept his offer."

Maria let out a small sigh of relief.

His eyes smoldered, desire lurking just under the surface. "I have wanted you since I first laid eyes on you at the club. I think you put some Memphis voodoo on me, woman."

She looked at him with gentle eyes. "Thank you, Alex," she said.

"For what?"

Her voice held a low, sultry quality when she spoke. "For always being there, for hanging with me in my moments of complete craziness, for being a fantastic cook, and for watching my back even when I didn't know I needed it. For everything."

Alex felt deep peace and satisfaction. "In that case, you are welcome. Thank you for making me feel alive again. I can't imagine how different and how utterly empty my life would be if you hadn't walked into the club all those months ago."

Her brown eyes were bright with amusement. "And if you hadn't been such a troublemaker almost ruining our case and kissing me, who knows how it would have turned out?"

Reclaiming her lips, he crushed her to his broad chest. His kiss was deep and slow. When he was finished, he said. "You mean like this?"

"Yes. I mean just like that," she responded.

"In my defense about almost ruining your case, if you hadn't been so irresistible in those tight designer clothes, I might've stood a chance against you."

They both laughed and moved away from the table to the living room to watch the water.

Maria repositioned herself on the couch to lay against his chest. She felt warm and loved.

Peace surrounded them. Neither spoke for several minutes, watching the light dance off of the water. The sky was a beautiful deep blue black, with virtually no stars. She moved to stretch her body along the curves of his chest. She wanted to feel as much of him as she could. When she was settled again, she let out a contented sigh.

Alex felt the sound reverberate through his body, sending an electric current throughout. He caressed her arms under her cashmere sweater. She felt so soft and so supple. Her skin was like almond silk. *I will never be able to get enough of you, lady.* "You always feel so good," he said huskily.

She loved to hear that quality in his voice. "You always sound so good. I love the way you say my name. It sounds so perfect coming from your lips."

"There's one thing that I would love to hear coming from your lips right about now."

Maria was intrigued. "Oh, yeah, and what would that be?"

"Yes." Alex moved her away gently to get down on one knee in front of her. Maria looked at him as if he'd lost his mind.

"Maria Marisela Thomas, also known as Maria Manez, will you marry me?" He took the black coral and diamond ring out of the box and slipped it on her finger. He heard the sharp intake of breath she took, but no other sound. She was speechless!

Before *he* could take another breath, she was in his arms kissing him with all that she possessed. He could feel her heartbeat as plainly as he felt his own. They were one.

His arousal became evident when he heard her moans. It took nothing for her to ignite the fire of desire in him. He pulled apart from her long enough to ask another question.

"Can I take that as a yes?"

"Yes, you can, *mi corazón*."

She captured his lips in another soul-stirring kiss. He wanted her so bad.

"Let's go to the room. Our room."

"I like the sound of that," she said, smiling.

Maria began to undress as Alex lit the vanilla-scented candles. Soon the light of several candles that had been strategically placed illuminated the room. The effect was stunning. Alex had also prepared champagne for their celebration; it chilled in a crystal ice bucket alongside a bowl of fruit, both atop a small table.

She took a sip of the fruity drink and munched on a juicy grape before saying, "Mr. Milbon, are you always going to be this romantic? A girl could kind of get used to this treatment."

He found himself jealous of the fruit. He wanted to be in her mouth.

"This man would love to give you whatever you want, every day of your life. I love you, Maria. Come to me. I want to finish undressing you."

Maria smiled at him. "Your wish . . ."

She crossed the short distance to where he was standing. He had taken his shirt off, revealing a chest rippling with muscles and a very light dusting of softly curling hair. Maria buried her face in it, inhaling the heady aroma that typified Alexandro Milbon.

She planted feather-light kisses along his chest, finally taking one nipple at a time in her mouth to tease it to a hard pebble. She loved to give him pleasure and his soft mewing was proof she was doing just that. She moved from his nipples to his neck, where she gently bit the skin along his jawbone, making a trail from his jaw to his clavicle.

Alex enjoyed her ministrations, giving her all the time and space she wanted. He unzipped her jeans, sliding his hands in position to move them down her long, shapely legs. Her hands sought to release him from his pants as well. She pulled urgently at his zipper while her mouth sought his. He helped her by pushing his pants down and out of the way. Their clothes lay in a heap on the floor. Alex kicked them away as they neared his bed, pushing things out of his way as they moved—the pillows, the comforter, whatever hindered their burgeoning passion.

He caressed the tops of her breasts through the silky fabric of her bra. He used his mouth to bring her taut nipples to full attention. Maria moaned her approval. Soon her bra joined the rest of her clothes. Alex licked her breasts one at time, gently sucking each turgid nipple until she thought she couldn't stand it anymore. Maria arched for him, her urgency getting his attention. She wanted him as much as he wanted her. He reached down inside her panties and felt her moisture wet his fingers. She was ready for him, ready to make love to him, but he wouldn't before he had a chance to taste her. He removed her underwear with his teeth. She giggled at his gesture. Soon her giggles turned to strangled moans as he took control of her body again.

Alex kissed down her abdomen, creating a trail of molten fire. His hands continued their assault on her nipples, keeping them rigid and ready for his mouth. Alex kissed the triangle of curly brown hair covering her sex. He found her nub and gently, then more firmly, loved it. Maria rocked with him as he stroked her. She felt herself melting under his power. He made her feel so good. He used his tongue and his fingers to bring her to her first release. She shuddered violently as the torrent of her orgasm ripped through her.

He moved up toward her mouth and engaged her in a powerful kiss. He could still feel her reeling from her orgasm. Maria could taste herself on his tongue. He deepened the kiss. She felt as if she would faint. He held her close, taking more and more. Maria gave all that she could. This man owned her soul. He broke the kiss long enough to remove his last piece of clothing. They lay on the bed completely naked now.

"Are you ready for me?"

"Always," she answered, still breathless.

Alex protected them before he slipped himself into her, sealing out the rest of the world. He stroked her, giving her more and more of him while he felt her body encase him. She was wet and hot. He took a nipple in his mouth, gently biting with his teeth. She moaned louder. He moaned too as he felt a powerful climax working its way through his body. Without warning he moved her on top of him. She was surprised but moved with his rhythm. His hands tangled in the mass of brown curls that framed her face.

"I love your hair like this. You are so beautiful."

Her breath came in short gasps. "You make me feel beautiful, Alexandro."

He dipped his head to tease one erect nipple. Maria called out his name.

"I'm right here, baby, give me all you've got," he responded.

She varied the tempo, feeling him fill up her space tighter and tighter. Maria put her hands behind his head as she rode him hard and fast. He pulled her closer to him so that they were breast to breast now, and their breathing was in perfect synchronization.

Alex was unable to hold back. He matched her pace as their tempo reached a frenetic beat. He kissed her long and hard. Their tongues dueled, then mated. Rising passion sent them both over the precipice. They arrived at that special place together. Their climax was white hot, blinding, and all encompassing. With sweat-dampened bodies, they lay on the bed. It was several minutes before either could speak or move. The sound of their labored breathing filled the silence. The scent of the warm vanilla sugar candles filled the air.

The church was filled with twenty of their closest family and friends, mostly other agents and those who knew them from the life they had created in Memphis.

Tía Marisela had surprised her with her mother's wedding gown. Before she died she had given it to Marisela for safekeeping. Maria splayed her fingers against the cream-colored satin and silk material her mother had once worn. She felt a strong connection to her the moment she touched the fabric. The gown was simple yet elegant. The fitted bodice had a wide rounded neckline completely encircled with beading. The gown's short sleeves were decorated with the same style beading as the neckline. Her parents had not been able to afford real beading but Maria had had the faux pearls and rhinestones replaced with genuine gemstones. Between the dress and the beautiful black coral and diamond ring, the wedding had almost a surreal quality.

All brides are supposed to be nervous, she tried telling herself. Maria's hands shook.

"This is it, kiddo," she told her reflection in the mirror. She took a deep breath, then opened the door where Helene was waiting for her.

"Come on, slowpoke. You've got one gorgeously handsome man waiting for you," Helene said.

She squealed in excitement like only best friends can when she saw Maria. "You look so beautiful! You two are lucky to have each other. I'm so happy for you, " she gushed.

Maria was so nervous she found it hard to speak. Her voice was barely above a whisper. "Thank you, Helene. For everything. You are the best buddy a girl could have. A meddling, wisecracking, best buddy, but still I owe you. So tell me again that I can do this."

Helene hugged her close, careful to watch out for the delicate beading of the gown. "Sweetie, you can do this and you will. Alexandro loves you. That's all you need to remember walking down the aisle. Nothing else matters."

Helene gathered the bouquet, wondering who would catch it. McCoy and Chantal made up the rest of the bridal party. Agent Spates had agreed to give her away.

Roderick, along with agents Caldwell and Wilson, made up the groomsmen. Alex wore a vintage black tuxedo made in the same era as Maria's dress. His cream-colored bow tie and vest were custom created to match Maria's gown.

Rod went to check on him before the organist began playing the processional. He needed to get Alex in position. "How are you doing in there?" Rod asked.

Alex smiled in nervous excitement. "This is it. Seems like I've waited a lifetime for this day, waited a lifetime for Maria. I think I'm as ready as I'll ever be."

The ceremony lasted just under an hour. After the vows, they were presented as Mr. and Mrs. Milbon. They lit the unity candle before descending down the aisle to receive the good wishes of their friends.

The kiss they shared to commemorate their coming together seemed to last just as long. Maria felt her knees buckle just as they did the first time he ever kissed her. He smiled down at her, pleased that he still had the same effect on her.

He whispered in her ear, "Te quiero."

"Te quiero," she whispered back before he captured her lips in another kiss.

Epilogue

Alex looked at the clock when he heard the front door opening. Although it was after 2:00 A.M., Maria was home from her trip earlier than he had expected. *She must have been able to get an earlier flight,* he thought. Lately she was full of surprises.

Maria looked at the sleeping figure of Alex before slipping off her shoes and walking quickly toward their bathroom. It had been a long day and she needed the hot water to relax her tired muscles.

Alex smiled as he waited quietly for her to come to him. Anticipation rose in him as he waited for her to come to their bedroom. Minutes after hearing her enter, he'd heard the shower water come on in the master bath. She had a particular routine whenever she returned from out of town.

Maria let the warm water soothe away the fatigue in her body. Alex had the Mike Phillips CD playing, which usually meant he had been having trouble sleeping in their bed without her. It was this way for both of them when she had to go away.

Her shower would be a quick one. She couldn't wait to wrap her tired body around him. After breakfast she would tell him that he was going to be a papa for the second time.

She was secretly hoping for a boy this time to continue the Milbon name. Maria was so proud of her husband and the life that they had waited so long to build.

Alex smiled, then settled deeper into the bed. He would have to take these few minutes of peace while he could. Their daughter, Marisela, had been fussy while her mom had been away for the past two days. Alex knew they had about two hours before she would wake up calling to her parents, seeking their reassurance.

Maria entered the bed quietly. She always did, afraid to wake him if he was sleeping. Alex inhaled deeply, then released a long sigh of happiness. He turned to take her in his arms. He kissed her long and deep. Desire ignited her soft damp flesh.

"Welcome home, Mrs. Milbon, we missed you," he said. "You're home early, aren't you? I didn't think we would see you until later on this evening. Is everything okay?"

Maria spoke quietly, pressing her body closer to his and inhaling his masculine woodsy scent. "Everything was fine. I didn't want to be away from my two favorite people any longer. I took the first thing smoking out of D.C."

She was closing one chapter and opening another in a totally new direction. "It's official. I am a freelancer. I'll only work on the cases that I want to. And that means you are going to be seeing a lot more of me, *querido.*"

"Love Is A Drug" played in the background. It sure it is, they both agreed silently, grateful that they had taken a chance on each other.

His kiss was long, deep, patient, and trusting. Alex was mindful their daughter would probably interrupt them. She had a knack for knowing just when to call out, but he pushed those thoughts away as he felt Maria's body arch for more contact.

She was on top of him now, her fatigue all but forgotten. Her long silky hair grazed his chest muscles as she kissed him, gently nipping at his neck and lips. She was such a tease. And he loved it.

Russian Glossary

English	Russian
Please	Pazhalusta
Thank you	Spasiba
Good morning	Dobraye utra
Good afternoon	Dobry dyen'
Good Eevening	Dobry vyechir
Hello	Zdrastvuytye
Goodbye	Da svidaniya
Yes	Da
No	Nyet
Mr/Sir	Gaspadin
Miss	Gaspazha
Mrs/Madam	Gaspazha
See you later	Paka
See you tomorrow	Da zaftra
Bottom's up.	Da dna
Hello, Ivan.	Zdrastvuytye Vanya
(Vanya is a nickname for Ivan)	
Thank you, where is Mikha?	Spasiba, Mikha gdye?
100	Sto
Nonsense	Yirunda

Source: www.babelfish.altavista.com

Dear Reader:

I hope that you enjoyed reading the story of Maria and Alex half as much as I enjoyed writing about them. It has been exciting for me to bring the stories of the Special Corruption Unit to life. This was a particularly interesting story to write because it gave me the opportunity to take a closer look into Russian culture. I find the language and customs of other countries fascinating and hope that you do too.

I hope to be able to continue to marry romance and suspense by bringing you more stories of the Unit.

Please let me know what you think of this story and my debut novel, *Love Worth Fighting For,* which was released in January 2004. You can check my Web site for updates and news on upcoming releases.

Until then, keep reading and take care,

Katherine D. Jones
PMB#36 8775 Cloudleap Ct, Suite P
Columbia, MD 21045
writeme@katherinedjones.com
www.katherinedjones.com

I hope you enjoyed the romance
and adventure of *Worth the Wait*.
Turn the page for a sneak preview of
Katherine Jones's next book,
Hidden Desire,
scheduled for release in February 2005.

Chapter 1

Helene looked at the clock. *Darn, three minutes late already.* She attempted to clear her things from her desk, haphazardly tossing pens, pencils, and papers into a drawer before she locked it. Her financial forensics class started at 6:00 PM and despite her best efforts, she was running late.

Grabbing her keys, she caught a glimpse of herself in the mirror. Her jeans wore the telltale evidence of her potato chip dinner, each thigh marked where she'd wiped her hands. Her shoulder-length light brown hair was carelessly pulled back into a ponytail giving her a college coed look. Okay, she smirked, so she would never win a fashion or etiquette contest, but her computer skills and her specialized FBI training more than made up for what she lacked in social grace.

Helene was Professor Reynolds's favorite student, and she knew he would forgive her for being late again. She had made it a point to become a star pupil, which fortunately was no problem for her. Helene had always found work and school to be the easiest parts of her life. It was the other parts, she thought regretfully, that gave her the most trouble.

Agent Helene Maupin was fascinated by her financial forensics night class. Tonight they were learning how to link financial transaction records with criminal behavior, a much-needed skill usually reserved for agents in the white-collar crime division. She was excited about the new training and hoped it would afford her more opportunities in the FBI's Special Corruption Unit.

During her last mission for the SCU, she had performed backup and surveillance duties. With the added skill set financial forensics would provide, Helene figured she should be able to be the lead agent on a case sometime soon. She didn't care what type of case it was, as long as she got to call the shots.

She poured over her course syllabus, glomming on to every complicated detail. With advanced degrees in computer science and mathematics, it was no secret that Helene loved figuring things out; nothing frustrated her more than not being able to complete a task. She had spent much of her adult life in school or on the job achieving difficult goals. She excelled in most subject areas, especially in the hard sciences, managing to ace all of her courses. Her personal life, however, was another story. She preferred things in black and white. Anything that was subjective, like interpersonal interaction and behavior, she had to study much harder for.

The instructor had given the class a thirty-minute dinner break and Helene was thankful for the quiet time that allowed for introspection. Helene popped the top on her energy drink and continued studying the class material. Absently, she drew hearts, flowers, and the letters R.R. in the corner of her paper while she consumed her beverage. She tried to ignore the initials and the person they represented as she reviewed the course material. But *he* was never far from her thoughts.

The doodles on her notepad were more purposeful now. She wrote the initials R.R. in every corner. No matter where she went or what she did, her mind invariably traveled back to Roderick Radford. Why had she chosen to pine over him instead of pursuing a real relationship? She considered that thought, along with the others, as one of the great mysteries in her life. She had considered herself in love with him for the better part of a decade. But she could never let him know her true feelings.

The SCU provided her with an escape from reality. Could she jeopardize that? Helene enjoyed her job with the SCU for several reasons, but her relationship with her coworkers was the biggest one. She loved casework and the feeling that she was contributing to the unit. For nearly ten years, she had been driven to prove she was just as good as any other agent, and it seemed her hard work and diligence was paying off. She was respected for her knowledge and achievements. Within the bureau, Helene found the acceptance and approval from her superior officers and other agents she never found growing up.

At work, she didn't have to deal with being the Maupin failure. Her closest friend was fellow agent Maria Milbon, whom she had met when the two were going through the Academy at Quantico. They had a bond that was closer than any she felt with her real sister. Maria knew her, knew all about Helene and her secrets, yet she didn't judge her. Helene didn't have to use her razor-sharp tongue to keep her at bay. Not that it would work anyway; Maria could give as good as she got.

During their time at the Academy, Helene had earned something of a reputation with the other agents in training. She used intimidation to keep her classmates away and her agents at bay, and most didn't bother talking to her for fear of being cut to shreds. Helene could ferret out any weakness, and she wasn't afraid to use that information against the person who posed a threat. She was five feet seven inches tall, a one-hundred-twenty-five-pound firecracker. She allowed those who lit her fuse to live only so that they could talk about the burns.

Training had been a true test for her. The Bureau had been very much a pro-male organization when she first joined. She had been the victim of several rumors during that time, and her sexual preference was often called into question because she wouldn't give most men the time of day. Helene decided to let the men think what they wanted—she was there to study to become a federal agent, not find a husband.

Somehow, she and Rod had become friends. Most likely because he never asked her out on dates or made inappropriate comments to her. Instead, they studied together and forged a friendship based on mutual respect. Back then, she often felt like he regarded her as the little sister he never had. When Maria learned of Helene's crush on Rod, she'd kept the secret, and the two had become fast friends with an unbreakable covenant. Between Maria and Rod, Helene knew that there was always someone she could count on to watch her back.

After graduating from the Academy and being accepted, along with her two good friends, into the SCU, Helene was happy to be a part of a real family, a clan of undercover agents who worked together to solve some of the most difficult cases in law enforcement. They traveled the world together to complete their missions, oftentimes putting themselves at extreme personal risk because their motto was *Mission First.* Personal feelings would take a back seat to accomplishing the goal, one of the many reasons she could never pursue her feelings for Rod.

Her classmates started to file into the room again. She finished the last of her drink and prepared herself to focus on her instructor. Tonight, they would be covering how to track and trace money trails. With a sigh, she pushed aside all thoughts of the green-eyed handsome devil with a café-au-lait complexion that intruded on her dreams nightly. It was time to focus on business.

Three hours later, with her class completed for the evening, Helene welcomed the sight of her home in northern Virginia. Visions of her whirlpool tub swirling with sheer freesia-scented bubbles hastened her pace. She wanted nothing more than to strip out of her jeans and sweater and flop on her bed after a long soak. But when Helene saw the red light blinking on the phone line she'd reserved for the Bureau, she knew it was not to be. She grabbed a cola from the refrigerator, kicked off her shoes, and then plopped down on her bed to listen to her messages.

She had one message of particular significance. Agent Spates had called asking her to call him as soon as she got the message—day or night. Helene knew it must be important. She let out a long, tired breath before she pressed one on the speed dial. It seemed she was instantly connected with him.

"Spates," he answered, sounding as chipper as if it were the top of the morning instead of fifteen hours after he'd started his workday.

"Hello, sir. I hope you don't mind me calling so late. I just got in from my forensics class. What can I do for you?"

"Maupin. I'm glad you called. How's that class going, by the way? It wasn't easy to enroll you in that type of training, but now more than ever I'm pleased it worked out." He paused, composing his presentation of the mission. "There have been some new developments in a case I've been monitoring. I'm calling because I'd like you to consider taking on the principal role in an assignment. Do you have time to come in first thing tomorrow to talk about it?"

While Helene considered his request, Spates checked his duty roster. He was pleased to see Roderick was also available for this assignment. He searched for the second number he needed to call.

Helene was eager for the opportunity. It was what she'd worked for since graduating from the Academy all those years ago. "I'll be there with bells on. It sounds intriguing. Who else is coming to the party? Were you able to get Maria?"

Helene could hear the sigh through the phone line and knew the answer. Spates would never give out that kind of information over the phone. "Okay, well, I'll see you in the morning. Have a good night."

Helene held her excitement at bay while she filled her tub. She was still tired, but this good news helped to buoy her spirits. Spates didn't take his cases lightly. For him to select her as primary agent was a huge confidence booster. Helene would sleep well tonight after pondering the possibilities. And maybe she could go to bed and not dream about being held in the arms of one Roderick Radford.

The music was loud and the words were spoken in a dialect of English he could easily understand. Rod sat back, leaning heavily into his couch. Beer and tortilla chips sat on a side table near to his recliner. It was good to be back in his own space again after a mission outside the country, he thought. He loved traveling to the islands, but it also made him appreciate home even more.

He'd spent the greater part of six months in the Caribbean working on a drug-smuggling case. Several government officials had been arrested by the time the mission had concluded, and a major drug operation had been destroyed.

Rod was off duty for the next three weeks, time he would spend acclimating to his stateside surroundings again. He enjoyed being back in his Alexandria, Virginia, home. It was the ultimate bachelor pad, a place where he could enjoy his books, his music, and most importantly, his couch. His favorite take-out restaurants were on speed dial, and whenever he wanted home cooking, his mom and dad were a phone call and short drive away.

Most times when he was back home and away from work, his life was normal. Well, as normal as could be for someone who spent most of his life pretending to be someone he wasn't. While he enjoyed undercover work, being at home was comforting, too. Just as long as a new assignment was on the horizon; Rod tended to get bored easily.

Rod got up to change his CD player, switching from Heather Headley to Ashanti. He took a long sip from his Heineken bottle. He was feeling very content. Working for the SCU was the best job in the world. It included travel both domestic and abroad, adventure, danger, and working with people that he would give his life for. What more could a man want?

His only problem right now was inactivity. It was hard

coming down after a hard case. Rod had always found it difficult to relax, preferring to stay busy. This was one of the reasons he had chosen to work for the Bureau. Graduating early from Rutgers University, he'd been courted by several agencies and corporations, but Rod was a government man. The FBI, and eventually the SCU, had offered him the best opportunity for personal growth and excitement in a job.

The men in his family had a history of devoting their lives to service, duty, and honor. For him, it was a no-brainer. He was a member of the Federal Bureau of Investigation for life. They would have to kick him out, and like a cowboy, he wanted to die with his boots on. He could think of no better way to go than in the line of duty.

Rod was temporarily rousted from his musings. He turned down the blaring music before checking the ID box on the ringing phone. He instantly recognized the number.

"Agent Radford," he said into the receiver. He wasn't much for exchanging pleasantries—it was always business first with the boss.

"Radford, it's Spates. I know you haven't been back for long, but I need to run something by you. Do you have time for a little chat?"

His body went on alert. He doubted Spates had ever just chatted with anyone. "Yes, sir. I've been back long enough. Besides, I'm starting to get a little antsy."

Spates continued. "You did great work in the Caribbean, but it's great to have you back." He was trying to butter Rod up. Spates suspected he probably wouldn't be crazy about the details of the case, but he knew his agent's skills were appropriate for it. He wanted Rod to team up with Helene to investigate a large identity-theft operation. The two had worked on assignments together many times before, but they'd never been asked to work as closely as they would now.

Finally, Spates responded. "Maybe we can do something about your being antsy. I need you to be in my office first thing tomorrow morning. I have an opportunity for you to be lead on a local case. It won't be like any other assignment you've worked before. I promise you that. Are you up to the challenge?"

"I'll be there, sir. I'm ready to get moving again," Rod said, intrigue reflected in his voice. It would be nice to work on something a little out of the box for a change. No drugs, no strippers, no Mafia like the other cases.

To date, the most intricately involved mission he had worked on was with his buddies from the academy, Agents Maria Thomas and Helene Maupin. It was an organized-crime case in Memphis a couple of years back. The assignment had been long and difficult, but they had been successful in the end. When it was over, Rod had promised himself he wouldn't work with either agent for a long time.

His mettle had been tested in more ways than he cared to remember. By the time the case was finished, he was so turned around and upside down emotionally that he'd refused to accept major SCU cases for months, choosing to work behind a desk in the intelligence analysis division instead.

There were several reasons why he felt compelled to make that choice. First and foremost was Helene Maupin. He thought about an embarrassing incident with her. The memories of the case they worked together still burned bright. His self-control around her was tenuous at best, yet she seemed to delight in making a bad situation for him even worse. His discomfiture over the incident in their Memphis hotel still caused his cheeks to color. He gritted his teeth just thinking about when she'd walked into his room unexpectedly, catching him in the act of pleasuring himself. His neck muscles tensed as he recalled the incident and he shrugged against the memory.

Ashanti's lyrics spilled over him. Still , he could not get Helene out of his head. Even beneath the nondescript jeans and baggy sweatshirts she usually wore, he could envision her long legs and tight athletic body. He'd only been privileged to see a few glimpses of her firm, lithe figure, but he knew she was hiding something he'd like.

Time helped to heal old wounds, he reminded himself. With a few more cases under his belt, he was starting to feel like the old Rod again. And Spates offering him a team-leader job was indication his boss had faith in him, too. Rod had more to offer now. His assignment in the Caribbean had marked a fresh start for him, a change in attitude. He'd lost some of his edge in Memphis, but maybe this new case Spates had in mind could give him full redemption.

Rod turned off the stereo. Crossing the room, he looked at his reflection in the mirror. Finding an open barbershop was a definite must. His sun-lightened sandy brown hair was just a bit too long to return to SCU head-quarters. He was also going to have to trade in his wardrobe, he thought. Looking down at his casual Caribbean attire he'd become so fond of—tan Bermuda shorts and a white T-shirt—he knew it would not be ac-ceptable around Spates. A former military man, Spates did not appreciate a careless wardrobe, and preferred business attire.

Rod knew he was sure to look like a real beach bum at the meeting tomorrow morning. His fair complexion was just now starting to lose some of its tropical tan, but after a few more weeks of Washington D.C. weather his appearance would be back to normal.

Rod thought about his beautiful island experience. High in the mountains, he had thoroughly enjoyed the view of the warm, clear blue water. He missed the sand and the seashore already. But for a new assignment where he was the lead, he could put those memories aside. He smiled to himself. *This could be good.*

"You know I trust your judgment, but are you sure you know what you're doing?" SCU Executive Director Bee McCoy asked.

Spates, the only name he was known by to his colleagues and subordinates, listened to the gentle lilt of her voice, momentarily distracted. It was late and he was tired. "I know that they are the two best agents for the job. They may not appreciate my small omission of information, but last time I checked, I still called the shots."

Agent McCoy was unnaturally quiet at his brusque response.

"Bee, I'm sorry. I know it's your head on the line." Spates shifted the phone from one ear to the other. "Yes, I know what I'm doing. Maupin and Radford have both done outstanding work over the last couple of years, and I think it's time we reward their diligence."

Spates hesitated, allowing Bee time to interject. Satisfied he hadn't shoved his foot too far down his throat, he continued when she didn't speak. "You know I don't usually have my agents share lead status, but in this case I think it's warranted. Having a couple undercover is the best way to catch these guys."

He'd just avoided telling Bee that he'd noticed an undercurrent of attraction between Helene and Rod during their last mission. They tried to hide it well, but Spates's instincts about agents were usually right on target. Was he making a mistake by putting them together on this case? Rod and Helene would have to live together under the same roof for several weeks, maybe even months.

Bee took a deep breath. "I can agree, but keep me posted. If they become too emotionally involved in this relationship or start to act like they can't complete this mission, let me know immediately. I want nothing but the best for each agent, but just as important to me is success. If they can't do it, we'll put in another undercover team. Let me know whom you would use as backup." Her voice softened then. "And get some sleep for goodness' sake. If I know you, you've been going nonstop for days now."

"Yes, ma'am. Is that an order?" he said quietly.

"No, just a plea from my heart. I need you to be around and healthy. The stakes are becoming higher as we go along." Bee chuckled softly. "Besides, we both need all of our strength to deal with these two. Tomorrow's meeting should be very interesting. Call me."

ABOUT THE AUTHOR

Katherine D. Jones sold her first contemporary romance to BET books in January 2003. Her writing is reflective of her travels, experience with government agencies and desire to help women become more aware of their personal power and strength. Jones believes in strong characters that are firmly grounded in real-world issues and problems. She had been married for seventeen years to a fellow Hampton University graduate; they have two sons.

In the writing industry, she has served as a coordinator and moderator for the Multicultural Program for the 2001 Romantic Times Convention, workshop moderator and presenter and judge for the Emma Awards at the 2003 Romance Slam Jam, and a moderator at the 2003 Romance Writers of America convention in New York.

**BOOK YOUR PLACE ON OUR WEBSITE
AND MAKE THE ARABESQUE
ROMANCE CONNECTION!**

We've created a customized website just for our very special
Arabesque readers, where you can get the inside scoop on
everything that's going on with Arabesque romance novels.

When you come online, you'll have the exciting opportunity
to:

- View covers of upcoming books

- Learn about our future publishing schedule (listed by
  publication month and author)

- Find out when your favorite authors will be visiting a
  city near you

- Search for and order backlist books

- Check out author bios and background information

- Send e-mail to your favorite authors

- Join us in weekly chats with authors, readers and other
  guests

- Get writing guidelines

- AND MUCH MORE!

Visit our website at
http://www.arabesquebooks.com